Michael and Leesie's Saga:

Taken by Storm
Unbroken Connection (Taken by Storm Book #2)
Cayman Summer (Taken by Storm Book #3)

Meet Beth, Scott and Derek—they'll break your heart next!

Sing me to Sleep

# Cayman Summer

*Taken by Storm* Book #3

# Cayman Summer

by Angela Morrison

Published by Angela Morrison
Mesa, Arizona, USA

Cayman Summer

Published by Angela Morrison
Mesa, Arizona, USA

Copyright 2011 Angela Morrison

ISBN: 978-1461090793

Printed in the United States of America

To all my readers at http://caymansummer.
blogspot.com!

# Chapter 1

## JOURNEY

### LEESIE'S MOST PRIVATE CHAPBOOK
### POEM #74, FLIGHT

Michael pushes the wheelchair
down the chilly jet-way.
SEA-TAC pre-dawn,
no midnight escape flights
from the Spokane airport.
He drove all night to make this
6:00 AM AA flight to Chicago,
while I rode wrapped
in a hospital blanket,
a gift from my nurses—
who all had a crush on him—
my seat tipped back,
my broken hand elevated
on a pile of pillows
to reduce swelling,
more pillows to keep my feet up,
my right arm in a sling

with a complex web of bandages
doing figure eights around my body—
collarbone stabilization.

Pumped full of morphine,
I slept. First time
without dreams.

He greeted me with a yawn stifled
into a smile, when I
opened my eyes to discover
we'd roamed to the other side of the state—
bays and islands, seashells and tides,
gulls in the distance like the ones we fed
at Grand Coulee dam
the first time we talked
back when I was lonely but not alone.

"You okay?" He touched my arm.
"I'm fine," I lied despite the
undrugged reality of pain,
 as desolation lapped like waves
against my heart.
Alone. Lost. Forever fallen.
My eyes sought his.
At least, I won't be lonely—
not with his ring glowing
on my finger. My glance
slid down his face and arms,
dropped to my hand, searching
for that reassuring gemstone.
My fingers purple, puffy,
empty.

He patted the pocket

of his saddle-brown leather
jacket that matches the coat
draped over me. "It fell
off. I've got it safe."

He pulled over for gas,
slipped the ring on the chain
he used to wear,
fastened it around my neck,
and gave me a double
dose of pills.
"The nurses said not
to let the pain get out of hand."
I wanted to protest.
I needed the hurt,
something real to suffer,
not like the ache in my spirit,
the divine hole that will never heal.
But I swallowed for him—
for his fingers touching my lips
as he placed capsules on my tongue,
for his hands holding up my water bottle,
for the kiss I demanded as reward.

Now, he lifts me from the wheelchair,
settles me in cushy first class,
front row, window seat.
He sinks beside me, lightly
touches my garish fingers sticking
out of my cast, closes
his eyes. "Just give me a minute."
I stroke his hand with my fingertips.
"I love you."
His mouth corners turn up
as he drifts away.

I analyze the minute contractions
of his nose when he inhales.
His chest lifts, fills, falls
as the air silently escapes.
I close my eyes and trace the vision—
jeans, jacket, his hair getting long again,
curling along his neck like it was that day
on the bus when he rescued me from Troy—
cementing it in my mind,
in case he evaporates
again.

I catch my reflection
in the pre-dawn dark window
beside me, ignore the black eyes,
the scarf that doesn't camouflage
my shaved, wounded scalp,
focus on the ugly white
gauze holding my nose in place,
wince when I try to use it,
force air in through my mouth,
slow and steady,
like Michael taught me.
"Max the 02," I imagine he says.
"It's good for your head."
The surgeon said I'll snore.
Poor, Michael. I'm such a freak.
The doc also told me to breathe deep.
Pneumonia attacks in hurt rib
territory. A sharp twinge, dulled
but perceptible, accompanies
every breath. In. Out.
Deeper. Deeper.

Michael sleeps the whole flight.
An attendant reaches across him
to hand me a soda that I can't hold.
"Wish I could snooze like that."
I direct her to set the cup on my armrest
table thing that blocks my knee from
touching his. "Shhh. He deserves it."
Every minute.
Three hours I watch.
It isn't enough.

He wakes when we land.
"You surviving?"
I nod. "You?"
"I'm great." He smiles,
but it's thin.

How can I say I love him?
I high-jacked his life.
Kidnapped his destiny.
He says all he wants is me.
What if he's lying?
What if I'm not enough?
What if he gets sick of being
my hero?

What if he can't love me
this ugly?

I force a smile. "Where to next?"
"Miami."
"Your condo?"
He shakes his head. "Too easy.
That's the first place they'll look."
"Didn't know you were that into

this evil mastermind gig."
He doesn't laugh. "We can go
there if you want.
Gram would fly out—
stay with us awhile."

My heart pounds.
"She'd tell my dad."
"Yeah. He could come, too."
He combs his fingers through what's
left of my hair. "Just like old times."

I close my eyes—thankful
that my face is masked—so
he can't see what I
desperately desire.
He sees anyway. "I can
take you home, babe"—
his whisper holds hope—
"just say the word."

I inhale again and the pain
from my ribs
knifes to my heart.
"I can't
ever
go home
again."

He shakes his head.
"When you're ready,
I'll take you." His lips
imprint the promise
on my mouth.

"I'm ready for you."
My kiss says it better.
"Only you."

O'Hare is packed. He says
it's always like this. But—
he's got a shiny white cart
waiting that whisks us like
magic through the masses.
I get to board our plane first.
We don't bother with a wheelchair.
I start to hobble through the gate,
but Michael sweeps me in his arms
again.

"The doctor said I should walk."
"Walk tomorrow."
His breathe tickles my ear.
"Aren't you tired of this?"
I let him into my eyes
where all my fears hide.
He cradles me close. "I'll
never get tired
of *this*."

## MICHAEL'S DIVE LOG—VOLUME #10

**Dive Buddy:** Leesie
**Date:** 04/27
**Dive #:** first night
**Location:** Grand Cayman
**Dive Site:** Summer Breeze Resort
**Weather Condition:** clear skies, full moon
**Water Condition:** choppy
**Depth:** way, way, way over my head

**Visibility:** I can't see anything but her
**Water Temp:** steamy out
**Bottom Time:** all night long
**Comments:**

The hotel doesn't have wheelchairs like the airport. I follow
the porter to Leesie's room carrying her in my arms. It's steamy
in Cayman so we stripped off our matching Bonnie and Clyde
get-away jackets waiting in line at emigration. Leather and the
tropics don't mix. I stuffed them in one of Leesie's duffel bags
when we claimed them. All I've got is my backpack.

As I walk down the hall, my feet sinking into the plush
carpet, I'm hyper-aware of Leesie's wounded head pressed
against my shoulder, her breath on my neck. Holding her turns
me on, and there's nothing I can do to stop that. Half her head
is shaved, and there's forty-two stitches running down into her
forehead. The bruising around her eyes is less purple tonight.
Her lip is gashed and swollen. She's banged up, swollen, bruised,
wrapped up and plastered, but she's still Leesie. I still love her.
Touching her still makes me want her. "Hang in there, babe," I
whisper into her ear. "We're almost there."

"Hurry." She wouldn't use the john at the airport. "I'm
going to explode."

Me, too, babe. Me, too.

The porter opens the door, and I follow him inside the hotel
room. I take Leesie right into the bathroom and set her down. I
whisper so the guy can't hear us. "Can you manage?"

"Not the snap." Her eyes find mine, and we step further
into the new reality we find ourselves in.

I shake my head and drop my eyes. Careful not to touch
anything but her pants, I unfasten her jeans and shut the door.

I get the porter to unlock the connecting door to my room,
dump my backpack in there, press ten bucks in the guy's hand,
and usher him out. I pull Leesie's pain pills from my pocket,
shake four out and place them beside a bottle of water on the
nightstand next to the bed closest to the bathroom.

Leesie hobbles out of the bathroom. "I've never had to go that bad in my life." Her jeans are pulled up but undone.

I force myself not to stare at the white underwear triangle between the open zipper teeth. "Let me help." I steer clear of her zipper, but scoop her up for the thousandth time since we signed her out of that hospital room in Kellogg, Idaho. I push the pillows off so she can lie flat and lay her down on the bed—have to stop myself from kissing her neck.

I haven't slept for more than an hour or two at a time for the past five days. We're alone in a hotel room for the first time. I've got zero self-control left. I move to the bottom of the bed and go to work relieving her of the ugly blue Velcroed boots that cover her wrapped up sprained ankles.

Leesie yawns and stretches her legs. "Are you sure we want this bed? You can't see the TV very well from here."

I pull off the first boot. "I'll move you. Just let me finish."

"It doesn't matter." She swallows. The bottom half of her cheeks and her pale, lovely neck turn pink. "If this is where you want to sleep—"

"Leese." It kills me to say this. "My bed is in the room next door."

The heightened color drains out of her face. "I need you here." Her eyes fill with terror. "You're not going to leave me?"

I slip off the other boot. "This isn't the hospital with nurses and aids coming in and out all night. That door is locked. We're alone." I stare down at her bandaged ankles and can't stop myself touching both her feet, caressing them. "I don't trust myself." I bend down and kiss her big toe.

"I'm yours now, Michael." Her broken left hand reaches for me. "Whatever you want."

I take her hand and kneel down by the bed. "I'm not going to hurt you more."

"I'll be okay." Her grip on my hand gets tight. I know she's lying. Scared. Of me. "Just," her voice drops so low I barely hear, "don't put any pressure on my upper body."

My mind instinctively flies to solving that problem. Freak. What a creep. It takes all the self-control I thought I didn't have to let go of her hand, stand up, and back away from her bed. "I promised your dad—"

"You called my dad?" She scowls, but I hear longing in her voice.

My eyes shift to the phone on the nightstand. "Let me, Leesie. Please."

"No—that's over." She sets her jaw and struggles to keep the tears at bay. "They don't exist. Anything you said to him doesn't matter." She takes a deep breath. Her eyes lift to mine. "You're all I am now."

I'm hearing what I thought I always wanted her to say, and it's torture. "Don't be crazy like this." Her whole life has been about being a Mormon. There's no way I can replace that—ruin it. "It does matter."

No sex unless we're married, Leese. Those are *your* rules. I remember my conversation at Thanksgiving with her dad. *Almost* isn't good enough for him. Isn't good enough for my Leesie. "I'm keeping that promise."

Tears flow down her face. She says God won't forgive her for what happened to Phil. Thinks she should suffer—die. If there is a God, I don't think he'd want that. I don't know if she's screwed things up or Mormonism is really that crazed. She hasn't told me what went on in the cab of that pickup truck. It's destroying her, though. Whatever it was. When she's ready, she'll tell me, and I can help her process the pain of it like she did for me when I felt so guilty about my mom.

Her tears weaken me. I soften my voice. "You lost Phil. That's awful, but everything else is still there."

She wipes her face with her broken left hand. "I disgust you now." Her hand comes to rest on her chest where her engagement ring hangs from my old chain.

"I want you so badly, babe, that I got to get out of here." I take another step back. "Take your pills. Sleep."

"You can't go." She needs help getting undressed, help taking her pills, help getting under the covers.

"I wish I could stay and take care of you." My eyes sting, and I have to swallow hard. "But I'm a guy, and I love you." A sob chokes me a moment. "If I touch you one more time tonight—"

I bolt through the door, slam it shut, lock it. Press my ear to the wood.

"Michael." She calls me. "Michael, Michael, Michael."

# Chapter 2

## PILLS

### LEESIE'S MOST PRIVATE CHAPBOOK
### POEM # 75, REBELLION

I wear out my voice calling
him to come back, wear out
my heart, wear out
my desolation.
"Take your pills, Leese."
His voice through the door triggers
rebellion. Those stupid pills—
his solution for everything.
Drug her up so I won't
have to deal with her,
hear her, touch her, kiss her,
love her.

"Take your pills, babe. The nurses
said."

I sweep them off the nightstand.
The capsules mock me
from the carpet, glowing
in the light he left on

in my room.
I pick up the bottle of water,
grind it open with my teeth,
spit out the lid, drink,
it runs down my neck, slam
the bottle down, close
my eyes against the light.

I invite pain to be my comfort,
seek solace in suffering. If Michael
won't fill my nights, guide me
into another realm, I'll linger here
just as he left me, encourage my wounds
to be my companion. My head, hand, ribs,
clavicle, ankles, and heart
seethe, stew,
seer.

I breathe deep, deep, deep.
Pain mounts and rolls as the clock
on the nightstand flicks past number
after number, until hurt is all I know.
I'm lost in its waves, oblivious
to anything but it's pulsing embrace.

I don't need you, Michael,
I want to scream.
You and your pills just
get in the way of what's
most important.
My pain.
I manage to get his chain
with the ring over my head
and fling it at the door
to his stupid connecting room.

All is silent on the other
side of the door.
I hush my moans, writhe
in silence. I don't want
him in here forcing
those pills down my throat.
I clutch this exquisite ache,
discover a white hot ball
of anger festering deep
in my gut, coax it to bloom
and engulf my guilt,
my sorrow, my shame.
I point it at
my dad, for being too kind, too good,
my mom, for her funeral schemes,
Phil for attacking me over Michael,
and dying, the jerk, how could he do that?
Michael for refusing to take
what he use to beg for.

And God for letting it all happen.
I thought you loved me?
I thought I was your daughter?
How could you?
A familiar comfort tries to slip
into my heart.
I block it—wall it away—
revel in pain and rage.
I don't deserve that touch.
Can bear the comfort
I know is lost.

I killed my brother.
And that is the biggest

pain of all.

## MICHAEL'S DIVE LOG—VOLUME #10

**Dive Buddy:** Leesie
**Date:** 04/28
**Dive #:** FREE DIVE
**Location:** Grand Cayman
**Dive Site:** Summer Breeze Resort
**Weather Condition:** sunny
**Water Condition:** flat calm
**Depth:** 20'
**Visibility:** can't tell, no mask
**Water Temp:** 82
**Bottom Time:** 5 minutes total
**Comments:**

I wake up to Leesie moaning. I'm lying on the floor in front
of the connecting door, drooling on the carpet. Gross. I get to my
feet and press my ear to the door. She should still be knocked out.
Could she make that noise in her sleep? It's the saddest sound
I've ever heard.

"Leese," I call quietly in case she's asleep. "Did you take
your pills?"

The moans cease.

"Leese. Babe."

No answer.

The nurses told me to give her a "sedating dose" to get her
through the night. These pills won't kill the pain like the hospital
strength stuff they pumped into her through her IV, but they're
supposed to help. Better than nothing. "The pills are right there,
babe—on the nightstand."

Still no answer. I wait and wait. Maybe she went back to
sleep. Or she's stifling her suffering, gritting her teeth so I can't
hear, fighting back the agony.

"Leese. Answer me."

Nothing.

Nothing.

Then a muffled moan meets my ears.

I grab the door handle, turn it, start to push it open, but something stops me cold.

I'm just going to give her the pills.

*No.*

I won't stay. I won't touch her.

*No.*

I can do this. Trust me.

*You can't.*

So I have to leave her like that all night?

*Yes.*

In pain?

*Yes.*

I want to move, but I'm frozen. I stand glued to the door listening to her moans mount louder and louder until Isadore sweeps down on me, and I'm lost to wind and waves. My mom's screams mingle with Leesie's cries—freak—it seems like hours.

Gray dawn light fills my hotel room when Isadore releases me. Whatever stopped me earlier is gone. The door opens easily. I walk through, try not to look at Leesie writhing on the bed, try not to hear her moan. I find her pills on the floor. Freak, she chucked them. Get four fresh ones out of the brown prescription bottle. Sit on her bed and slip my arm behind her back to raise her up. Put the drugs in her mouth. Pour water into the mix. She tips her head back and swallows. Falls against me.

I settle her down on the bed, grab pillows to prop up her hand and feet, slide onto my knees beside her, cradle her hot, sweaty, broken hand in both of mine. "Freak, Leesie, I'm sorry. I had to get out of here last night. I couldn't live with myself if the first thing I did when I got you alone was like rape you."

She closes her eyes and considers my confession. "It wouldn't," she manages to whisper, "have been rape." Her eyelids lift, and she drills me. She's angry.

I bow my head over her hand. "You're hurt—not thinking straight. It would have felt like rape."

"That's what"—she pauses to gather each word out of the pain haze that quakes her body—"I need"—her hand breaks away from mine—"now."

I raise my head and try to find a way in through her eyes. "No, it's not. You need that good old Leesie magic you poured all over me. Remember?"

Her eyes retreat. "That's over." She inhales and exhales, gathers another phrase. "It's—gone."

"No, it's not, Leese." I take back her hand, clasp it in mine. "It's here. Protecting you—from me. It kept me on the other side of the door."

"You wanted to come in?"

"All night babe." My voice drops to a whisper. "I wanted to be with you. Really with you." I let go her hand and hide my face in the bedding.

With an obvious effort, she strokes my head. "That's what I want." Her voice catches. "Love me your way."

I raise my head, sit back on my heels. "This isn't about love." I don't want to continue, but I can't stop. "You want to sleep with me to prove that you're lost, a sinner—mound up the guilt. Add to the pain. I'm not helping you with that."

She clenches her fist and pounds the bed. "You don't understand."

"Yes. I do. More than you know." I sit on the bed, clasp her face between my hands so she can't look away. "I refuse to be that guy."

"You won't love me?" She reaches to kiss me, but I pull back.

"I won't destroy you. If that's what you want, find some-body else." I let go of her face, but I don't move away.

She closes her eyes. Won't look at me. Won't open them. Won't talk. I watch her face go slack as the drugs get into her system. Listen to her breath steady.

Freak, where's her ring? Not around her neck like when I left her. I search her covers, check the nightstand, the floor by the bed, under it. Nothing. Widen the grid. Find it in front of my door smashed into the plush carpet. I must have stepped on it coming in here. How did it get from her neck to here? I put it safe around my own neck.

My stomach rumbles. I don't know when I last ate.

I check my pocket to be sure I have a room key, tiptoe to the door that leads out into the hall, ease it open, and close it safe behind me. I double check to make sure it's locked.

I notice myself in the elevator mirror, rub the drool off my chin, and finger comb my hair. It's greasy. I stink. My mouth tastes sour. A shower sounds so good. A long hot one. Leesie needs to get cleaned up, too. How the freak am I going to manage that one?

I stop at the front desk. "Is there somewhere close I can get food?"

"Room service?"

I shake my head.

"We've got two restaurants. They open in"—she checks her watch—"about two hours."

My watch reads 5:15 AM. Great. "What about a drug store or 7-11?"

"Two blocks down. Turn right when you leave the hotel. Go out the front entrance."

"Great, thanks." I muster up a smile.

She seems to appreciate it.

"I need a nurse. Do you know where I can get a nurse?"

She gives me a weird look. "I'm not sure what you mean, sir."

"A nurse." I frown. "Like from a hospital."

She glances over at her computer monitor. "We've got a doctor on call. Would you like us to page him?"

"No. We don't need a doctor." A doctor wouldn't take Leese to the bathroom or get her cleaned up and dressed. "I need a nurse."

A second girl at the desk butts in. "You can check with the rehab center across the street. It's a couple blocks past the convenience store."

"Rehab center?" My brows scrunch together. "You mean like for drug addicts?"

"No." She shakes her head, leaves her stool, and walks over to her colleague. "My uncle went there after he had back surgery. He was ready to leave the hospital but not to go home. They make them do physical therapy. A bunch of doctors and therapists work there. And nurses. I'm sure there are nurses. They taught him to get dressed and made him exercise. Stuff like that."

The confused knot in my guts begins to unravel. "And the nurses are nice?"

She nods her head. "My uncle liked them. My aunt not so much. My mom got an earful every time she called."

"Why?"

She giggles. "Something about sponge baths."

"She got jealous?"

"Acted like that." She shrugs. "My mom said she was scared out of her mind."

I can relate. "Thanks. I'll check it out." I turn to leave. "Which way again?"

They both motion with their thumbs sticking out. "Right."

I grin. "Thanks."


It's fresh dawn cool outside. Not muggy hot like last night when the cab dropped us off. The air smells like ocean. Two blocks and I'd be there. The edge of the water. There's got to be a beach. If I run, I could be there in minutes—seconds. Saltwater, soothing, cool. I won't stay in for long.

I do run.

Stalk through a beach front condo resort like I own it. Strip down to my boxers on the sand. Leave my jeans and shirt crumpled on the sand. Race into the foam of a retreating wave.

Slide onto my belly when it gets knee deep. Stretch my arms
forward and pull them back. Kick. Submerge. Freak, it feels so
good.

I swim out until I find a clump of coral in this sandy desert,
take a deep breath, another and another—swim down to the
coral, wishing for a mask. Two tiny fish dart in and out of the
holes in the stony coral. Ignore me. I surface, lie on my back as
the sun rises.

I love Cayman. I haven't been here since my parents died.
I can't wait to dive. I never thought I'd be tough enough to come
back here without them. But it feels right to be here now. Leesie
can do her open water dives. Finish her cert with me training her.

Leesie.

Freak.

I wonder how long until she can dive. Broken collar bone.
Cracked ribs. The cast on her hand. I hope they say it'd be good
therapy. We'll get snorkels and fins—wrap her cast in plastic. I'll
bring her down here every day as soon as they take that thing off
her nose.

They. Who is they? I got to get back to figuring that out.

I swim twenty feet down to the ocean floor again, wave
good-bye to the fish, drag myself free of the water, let it swirl
around my feet while I put my dry clothes on my wet body.

I retreat to the hotel and turn left since I'm coming from the
opposite direction, find the snack place, slam three power bars,
and a quart of juice. Grab some for Leesie and head up the street
searching for that rehab place.

It's right where they said it was. A low sturdy building
between two high-rise hotels.

I try the door. It's open. How long have I been gone? Oh,
crap. It's past 7 AM. I don't want Leese to wake up alone writhing in pain.

A woman at a huge mahogany desk sitting in the middle of
the entry way stands up. "Can I help you?"

"I hope so." I make such a mess of describing Leesie and

me and what we're doing here that any sane person would have called the cops.

She doesn't bat an eye—launches into fees and services and expectations.

"Can I bring her in this morning? Right away?"

"Of course."

# Chapter 3

## REINFORCEMENTS

### LEESIE'S MOST PRIVATE CHAPBOOK
### POEM #76, MR. SUNSHINE

Michael steers a wheelchair
into my room, waking me.
He pours pills down my throat.
"Come on, babe. We're going
for a walk."
I'm not talking to him
ever again. He's wrong.
I'm right. And he's going be sorry.

He picks me up, plops me
in the chair. "Ow, watch it."
I scowl, licking wounds.
"Sorry, babe, does it hurt?"
He squats beside me and kisses
my cheek. "How do you like your chariot?"
He puts the chain with my ring
back around my neck,
ties my headscarf do-rag style,
straps on my stupid footgear.

I raise my eyebrows.
"In case you want to wade."
He pulls a bottle of OJ out
of a grocery bag swinging from
his wrist and hands it to me,
kisses me when he bends to twist
the top off. "Forgive me?"

I can't hate him when
he's like this. The Ice Queen
relents. "Do I have a choice?"
"No." He kisses me again.
"You're stuck."
My eyes swim. "No, Michael.
You're stuck. I'm sorry I did this to you."
He gets down on his knees and
lays his head in my lap.
"I don't ever, ever, ever
want to hear you say that again."

I can't answer or I'll cry.
I stroke the top of his tangled head.
It's damp. "What've you been up to?"
"I just got out of the ocean."
"Saltwater therapy?"
"Yeah. It's the best."
"Earth to Michael—I can't
go in the water."
"But you can get close."
His smile—so big and beautiful—
coaxes the corners of my mouth to
ease up for a moment.

His head tilts toward the bathroom.
"Do you need to go?"

I shake my head and sip my juice.
"You got up by yourself?"
"Twice."
"That must have hurt."
I look away from his pity.
"Freak, I got to use the john."
He dumps granola bars
in my lap. "I'll be right back."

He disappears into his room.
I sip juice, nibble at a bar,
my stomach in knots that
won't admit food,
listen to the sink, then the shower.
He returns scrubbed, shaved,
and glowing, garbed in garish
purple and lime green swim-shorts
and an "I love Cayman" T.
My jeans feel cemented
to my body. "No fair."
"Jealous of my snazzy outfit?"
"Your clean hair."
"We'll take care of yours after
the walk—I promise."
"You're going to undress me?"
"Shh. It's a surprise."

The beach is glorious.
Caribbean blue water,
even brighter than I remember
from the Keys. The wheelchair
gets bogged down in the deep,
dry sand. Michael powers
through it to firm damp beach,
pushes me right up to the surf's

edge—a tiny wavelet swirls
around the wheels,
the sun catches the diamond
hanging from my neck.

He tips back the chair
on its two big wheels,
ignores my squeals
and pushes me into the water.
The turquoise sea rushing in and out
uncovers a childish delight—simple,
pure, a bit tarnished and battered—but
I can feel. He keeps me out there
until his arms can't hold the chair
up anymore.

Then those arms, moist with sweat
and ocean spray, free me from
confinement. We lie
on the damp sand, me
on my back gazing up at the flawless
blue sky. Michael on his side
staring at my face.
He leans over and sucks ever
so gently on my unblemished
lower lip. He stops too soon.
"Is my breath gross?"
"Yeah. You're a mess. Sandy
now, too."
"What are you going to do
about that? Dunk me in the ocean?"
"If that's what you want." He scoops me
up and runs towards the water.
"Stop it, Michael." I pound on
him with my cast—yelp at how

much that hurts.
He pulls up short.
"How about nurses?"
"What?"
"I found you nurses."
"You're sticking me back
in a hospital? No way."
"No hospital—I promise."

He takes me to a short cement building
set down in a tropical garden—hot pink
bougainvillea spill from pots,
palms, high and low, fan out in all
directions, orange and yellow
flowers carpet the ground.
Inside—cool, clean elegance,
marble floors, wood-paneled walls,
paintings of ocean sunrises.

My room's a plush prison—
white bed draped with gauzy netting
like a room in a swank resort.
"You're leaving me here?"
"Nurses, babe. They can take
care of you. I can't."
"You didn't even try."
"You need therapy and wound care,
pain management. I can't do that."
"How long?"
"At least stay long enough
to get cleaned up."
He picks me up from my chair,
sniffs in my direction. "You stink."
"Now that's romantic."

He lays me on the bed.
I sink into a world of soft
feather luxury.
He leans over me with
encouragement leaking
from the corners of his grin.
"They've got a therapeutic
whirlpool you can soak in
all morning. Wouldn't that feel nice?"
He's starting to convince me.
"What are you going to do?"
He blushes under his tan.
"Oh, my gosh—
you're going
diving?"
He bends low to give
me an enormous kiss.
"Please?"
"As if I could stop you."
"Are you sure?"
"Get out of here."

The smile that slips onto my face
as I watch him leave me
knows only him, only here,
only this moment.
Today, it's enough.

## MICHAEL'S DIVE LOG – VOLUME #10

**Dive Buddy:** guiding
**Date:** 04/28
**Dive #:** lost count
**Location:** Grand Cayman
**Dive Site:** Fish Eye Fantasy

**Weather Condition:** sunny
**Water Condition:** slight chop
**Depth:** 87 ft.
**Visibility:** 80 ft.
**Water Temp:** 82
**Bottom Time:** 42 min.
**Comments:**

I wish I could go out to the East End—best diving on
the island. North is good, too. Lots of eagle rays up there. But
those guys will be long gone by now. I'm close to Seven Mile
Beach. Lame dives by Cayman standards. Excellent compared to
Thailand.

I borrow the rehab center's phone and call a guy we used to
charter. Great. He's got a boat going out at 10 AM.

"It's a private charter, though." He sounds like he's trying
to get rid of me. "Tough luck."

"Wait." I offer something no dive captain can resist. "Look,
I'll haul tanks, guide, set up all the gear. Whatever it takes. It'll
be the easiest day you ever spent on the water."

"I don't know, dude."

I pull out my secret weapon. "Are there females in the
party?"

He pauses—checking the list most likely. "Four."

"Bring me along, and they'll be back."

He laughs. "You can guarantee that?"

I'm so glad Leesie can't hear this. "Just stating the facts."

"This is Michael Walden—Mike's son?"

"Uh-huh."

"Okay. You're in. Remember the dock we pick up at?"

"Yup."

"I'd do anything for your dad. He was the best."

My eyes smart, but I manage to thank the guy without
blubbering. "I'll need gear, too."

"Figures."

The dive isn't spectacular. The women are annoying, but still it feels awesome to be breathing through a reg, finning over coral beds, relaxing in my native element where I don't have to talk or think. Just be.

After the trip, I swing by the hotel and pick up my laptop on my way to see Leesie. She's not in her room when I get there, so I lounge on her bed, email Claude to ship me my junk— especially the stuff I bought for Leesie, silk skirts and there's a necklace I hope she likes. It'll have to come by air or we'll never get it. If Claude wasn't such a jerk, I'd send him a ticket and have him bring it out here. But Claude is—Claude. No thanks.

I sign into ChatSpot, notice Kimbo69 is online, and decide it's time to bring in reinforcements.

# MICHAEL WALDEN / CHATSPOT LOG / 2:35 PM 04/28

**liv2div says:** hey, Kim…it's Michael.

**Kimbo69 says:** Leesie's Michael? Didn't know we were friends. I'm so not talking to you.

**liv2div says:** I need your help.

**Kimbo69 says:** No way. Leesie's my best friend…you broke her heart, ground it into minced meat, and fed it to the sharks. Go back to your pretty prostitute—or buy a new one. Stay away from Leesie…you messed up her life enough. I know the whole no-sex thing must be tough on you, but that's no excuse—you promised, her. She hasn't been online. What have you done to her?

**liv2div says:** you haven't heard?

**Kimbo69 says:** Don't tell me you're back together.

**liv2div says:** Leesie crashed her pickup driving home from BYU

**Kimbo69 says:** Crashed??? Leesie????

**liv2div says:** yeah, last Thursday

**Kimbo69 says:** I don't believe you!

**liv2div says:** why would I make this up?

**Kimbo69 says:** Why don't I know about it?

**liv2div says:** her parents haven't called you?

**Kimbo69 says:** I don't think they have my number. You're serious?

**liv2div says:** I don't joke much anymore, Kim…haven't had much to laugh about for a long time

**Kimbo69 says:** I used to feel sorry for you but not after what you pulled in Thailand. If this is some kind of trick to get me to help you get back with her, it's not going to work.

**liv2div says:** freak, Kim…don't you care what happened to Leesie?

**Kimbo69 says:** She banged up her truck. Big deal…craa-aap!! She must have been hurt or she would have been online. We were supposed to chat. Oh, crap. She's dead. Crap!!!! Why didn't you say that?

**liv2div says:** calm down…she's not dead…lots of broken stuff… it's rough

**Kimbo69 says:** Don't you dare tell me to calm down!!!! How bad is it?!? What's broken? Is she like paralyzed? Oh my gosh!!!!!!

**liv2div says:** the pickup's totaled

**Kimbo69 says:** I don't care about the damn pickup! She's dying, isn't she? What hospital is she in? I need to come see her. Don't let her die!!!

**liv2div says:** listen a minute…stop jumping in before I can type out what's happening…she'll be okay

**Kimbo69 says:** Okay? Like paralyzed in a wheelchair the rest of her life or totally fine?

**liv2div says:** physically she should recover…totally…she's got a stitched up head…they shaved off half her hair…her hand flew into her nose when the air bag blew so they are both busted… her collarbone snapped, ribs cracked, sprained ankles…she's in a ton of pain

**Kimbo69 says:** Tell me the hospital she's in. I'm coming right now. To hell with my classes!! When did this happen? Crap, why didn't you tell me before? You suck, you know!!! You really, really suck!!!!

**liv2div says:** hang on a minute...you can't visit her

**Kimbo69 says:** Like hell, I can't. Leesie and I are soul-mates. You don't have a clue what that means. I'm coming!

**liv2div says:** hang on, Kim...I need to tell you the worst part

**Kimbo69 says:** It gets worse? You suck at breaking it gently. What are you hiding? What's really happened to her?

**liv2div says:** I've been trying to tell you...Phil was with her...you know, her brother...he didn't make it

**Kimbo69 says:** Phil's dead? Dead? That's horrible. Awful. Oh, my poor girl. She's taking it bad?

**liv2div says:** really bad...I thought if anyone could deal with something like this it was her, but she blames herself...won't tell anyone what happened...not even me

**Kimbo69 says:** I'll come visit today. Where is she?

**liv2div says:** she's so messed up...she thinks God won't forgive her...she's turned her back on her family and all her Mormon stuff

**Kimbo69 says:** Leave it to me. I'll talk to her.

**liv2div says:** Leesie's broken up more inside than out...her wounds will heal...I don't know about the soul part

**Kimbo69 says:** I told her once I wanted her down here groveling in the dirt with the rest of us mortals...but no, not her...you can't let her go under, Michael! DO YOU HEAR ME?

**liv2div says:** I need some help, Kim...I think she'll listen to you

**Kimbo69 says:** Of course she will. Get her right now!!! Tell her it's me.

**liv2div says:** she's not here

**Kimbo69 says:** when will she be back?

**liv2div says:** the nurses have her...I don't know

**Kimbo69 says:** I have to go to a stupid class that I've blown off too many times. I'll head out after that. We'll have a long, long girl talk.

**liv2div says:** she can't really type

**Kimbo69 says:** Face to face, numbskull. What hospital is she in?

**liv2div says:** they released her Sunday night…she couldn't bear going home…so we ran away together

**Kimbo69 says:** You kidnapped her?

**liv2div says:** rescued her…she's nineteen…we can do what we want

**Kimbo69 says:** You total creep! How could you be so selfish at a time like this?

**liv2div says:** she was desperate, begged me…freak, it broke my heart to see her so pathetic

**Kimbo69 says:** That's no excuse for doing something so stupid.

**liv2div says:** I tried to talk her out of it…still trying…she won't even let me call her parents

**Kimbo69 says:** You stole her from the hospital with all those injuries?

**liv2div says:** her mom wanted to take her home…look after her there…Leesie's so eaten up with guilt…she can't stand to be near her mom…it's sad, wrong…but I'm here…I'm taking care of her…better than her parents could

**Kimbo69 says:** I'm sure you are. You disgust me—taking advantage of my best friend when she's like this!!!

**liv2div says:** Leesie never told me you were vicious…and for the record I'm NOT taking advantage of her

**Kimbo69 says:** How did you even get back in the picture? What happened to your concubine?

**liv2div says:** don't call her that…I helped Suki get out of a bad scene…that's it…I never touched her

**Kimbo69 says:** Right. You got Leesie to believe that?

**liv2div says:** she believed it enough to send that missionary dude packing

**Kimbo69 says:** Jaron? Crap. I was rooting for him. Not you. Not you. Not you.

**liv2div says:** whatever, Kim…hate me all you want…will you talk to Leesie?

**Kimbo69 says:** where are you guys…can I phone her?

**liv2div says:** Leesie won't let me tell anyone

**Kimbo69 says:** Thailand?

**liv2div says:** of course not...I'll let her tell you...I think chatting would be safest...she'll go for that...I'll have to do the typing until they take the cast of her left hand and let her use her right arm again

**Kimbo69 says:** What happened to her arm?

**liv2div says:** It's in a sling and strapped down because of her collarbone. The arm's okay.

**Kimbo69 says:** It'll be weird knowing you're eavesdropping.

**liv2div says:** you'll never know I'm there...then you'll do it?

**Kimbo69 says:** Of course, I'll do it. Don't be stupid.

**liv2div says:** just don't get too gross, okay?

**Kimbo69 says:** Me? Never.

# Chapter 4

## HAIR-RAISING

### LEESIE'S MOST PRIVATE CHAPBOOK
### POEM # 77, WHO AM I?

Nurses dressed in sunshine yellow
pour into my breezy room.
Soft island hands,
some black, some white,
undress, unwrap, unwind,
expertly draping and
robing so I'm never
exposed, so gentle I only
cry out once.

That cry earns me
an IV bag and a morphine
pump until I'm sufficiently
numbed.

The clinical whirlpool bath

isn't like a hotel hot tub—
metal, deep, sterile.
I'm in it up to my neck,
arm sling, diamond and all,
my straggled hair bundled
in a clear shower cap,
left hand encased in plastic.
"Don't get your face wet," they tell me.
"When can I get this off?"
I point to my nose wrappings.
"We'll check with your doctor."
"I don't have a doctor."
One glances at my chart.
"You do now."

The enormity of the burden Michael
shouldered for me makes
my eyes glisten.
"Don't cry, sugar. It'll make your
cast soggy."

I stay in so long I'm dizzy.
"You need to eat."
"Not hungry."
The "sugar" nurse brings new
cotton underclothes and a large
frothy fruit drink rich
with banana and mango.
I sip and remember.
"I think I used to
use this on my hair."

Sugar and company hook me
back up to my morphine,
hit the pump a bunch before

they clean my wounds and soothe them
with aloe and ointment.
They wrap my ribs fresh,
change my wet sling for a dry one,
admire my ring, and
wind new figure eights.
"Keep that immobile," Sugar orders.
I nod meekly, dozy from the drugs.

My blue bruised ankles
are less swollen now.
They snug on fancy post-op
cast boots lined with support—
nothing like the floppy foot gear
I've been wearing. Sugar gets
me to walk, dragging my IV along.

My walk ends at a black and gold salon
with too many mirrors.
Bruised eyes, fat lip, bandaged up nose,
ugly, ugly stitches and so much of my hair
shaved away—nearly half my head.
A stylist washes what's left clean.
"This is going to be a challenge."
She holds up the ugly, wet mop
that seems foreign.
That's not *my* hair.
Not my long, full mane. Not the silky
locks Michael tangled into knots
whenever we made out.

The stylist frowns at it.
"You'll have limited mobility. Looking
after this will be tough. Will
you have help?"

I think of Mom at home
who would wash and blow dry
my hair every day if I asked her.
"Cut it, then. I don't care."
She chops it to my shoulders,
parts it on the side,
experiments with a comb over,
but there isn't enough hair
in the world to cover my stitches.

I stare in the mirror and hate it,
detest the silliness of the pathetic
subterfuge, loathe who I am,
what I've become, revile
against any effort to cover
up my damnation
with a transparent attempt at normal.

The stylist shrugs her shoulders,
agreeing with my silent assessment.
Yes. It's awful. Yes, you are hideous.
Yes, it's no use. She combs a bit of hair
down over my forehead. "Bangs
will help when this shaved part
grows back."

Shaved? Good idea.
I challenge the freak in the mirror.
She caves. I squeeze my eyes tight.
"Shave it then. All of it."
Deaf to dissuasion. I insist—
"Shave it. Shave it. Shave it."
Clippers buzz, tickle my scalp,
barely touch me.
It'll grow back better, longer, stronger.

Who am I kidding? I don't deserve
hair. A few skillful
passes free me of my broken beauty.
Buzzing stops. Silence. I touch
but can't look—won't open my eyes
until they spin me around.


Michael, sun-kissed and saltwater fresh,
sleeps on my bed when I hobble
back to my room. I dismiss
my guides with a promise to rest,
touch his hand to wake him.
"Michael. Hey."

His eyes open,
focus,
explode.

"Freak, Leese. What the hell
did they do to you?"
He's on his feet, wrapping
me in his arms, getting tangled
in my IV's tubes.
"I'm sorry, babe." He trembles with emotion.
"I thought they'd look after you."
He chokes back a sob.
"Come on, let's get out of here.
I'll find someplace else."
He touches my stark white
new-shaved scalp like it's lethal.
"What did they do with it?"
"My hair?"
"Did they save it?"

Tears fill his eyes.
"I don't think so."
"It's gone?" His finger withdraws.
"It'll grow back even this way."
He swallows hard. "But your hair, Leese."
"I couldn't look after it."
His head shakes denial.
"That's why I got nurses."
I close my eyes to block out his pain.
"I can't stay here forever."
"I would have washed it for you,
babe, every day." His voice throbs.

I open my eyes and watch tears,
one by one, roll down his cheeks.
I wipe at his tears with my robe's sleeve.
I never thought of that—
thought of him—thought of
what he might need to hold
on to.
I thought only me.
And what I'd lost.

I try to kiss away his tears
and feel like a coward.
A cruel, selfish coward
who crushes,
maims,
and kills.

## MICHAEL'S DIVE LOG – VOLUME #10

**Dive Buddy:**Leesie
**Date:** 04/28
**Dive #:** --

**Location:** Grand Cayman
**Dive Site:** Rehab Center
**Weather Condition:** Stormy
**Water Condition:** pouring down my face
**Depth:** can't tell
**Visibility:** 0
**Water Temp:** hot
**Bottom Time:** the rest of my life
**Comments:**

I don't know how we go from me sobbing like a wimped-out baby over Leesie's lost hair to us making out on her cushy white bed, but that's what happens. She starts it. I don't resist.

I have to be careful not to lie on her IV's hose, careful not to jar her injuries, careful not to lose control. Leesie offers no barriers but makes no demands. She just lies flat on her back, my ring balancing on her stomach. The chain's too long for her. I'm on my side so I can reach her.

We kiss soft and slow. Her lip doesn't bleed this time. She's pumped full of drugs so I don't think it hurts her to kiss me. She kisses me over and over. The movement of her mouth on mine is tender—like I'm the patient. And she the comforter.

I move my mouth to her unhurt lower lip, suck softly a moment, slip my lips to her chin, her neck, her ear. I hesitate a moment then move my mouth to the soft skin of her new shaved head, exploring every inch, trying to fall in love again.

"I'm sorry," she whispers.

I pause and murmur, "More safe skin," and go back to kissing it, absorbing every contour of her skull into my soul. I avoid the jagged gash and purple stitches holding it together. Her scalp is warm, vibrant, alive against my lips. That's what counts, I try to convince myself. She's here, alive—not on that mountainside dead.

"I love you, Michael, forgive me for making it harder for you."

"Will you marry me, Leese, at the end of the summer?"

"I'll marry you tomorrow."

"Sorry, babe. No can do. I want you in shape for 24/7."

We both laugh at that, and I cradle her head, afraid to let it go again.

# HEARTLESS

## LEESIE HUNT / CHATSPOT LOG / 04/28 9:37 PM

**Kimbo69 says**: Where've you guys been? I signed on three hours ago.

**Leesie327 says:** Hooray, Kim!!! Michael just told me he found you. This is a cool surprise. He says he filled you in.

**Kimbo69 says:** With everything except where you are and why you're hours late for our chat.

**Leesie327 says:** We were busy.

**Kimbo69 says:** Busy? He told me he wasn't taking advantage of you. You big dirty liar. Busy? How busy?

**Leesie327 says:** Be nice to him or I'm signing off.

**Kimbo69 says:** Was that from him or you?

**Leesie327 says:** Me. I fell asleep because I'm pumped full of morphine. Before that, we were truly busy. I shaved my head, and Michael asked me to marry him.

**Kimbo69 says:** Cause and effect? Odd strategy for getting him to commit.

**Leesie327 says:** He's always been committed.

**Kimbo69 says:** You believe that?

**Leesie327 says:** He's very convincing in person.

**Kimbo69 says:** I'll give him that much. So he proposed for the hundred millionth time. What did you say?

**Leesie327 says:** Yes, of course. He didn't really need to ask. I've been wearing his ring since I woke up from the accident.

**Kimbo69 says:** Get you when you're down, huh. When's the big day?

**Leesie327 says:** He says end of the summer. I say tomorrow.

**Kimbo69 says:** Don't you have a cast on your hand and other broken stuff?

**Leesie327 says:** Michael is creative. I'm sure he can work around my shortcomings.

**Kimbo69 says:** Did that come from you or the scribe?

**Leesie327 says:** Me. The scribe is blushing.

**Kimbo69 says:** I'd like to see that.

**Leesie327 says:** It's totally irresistible. (Change the subject, girls, or the scribe is out of here.)

**Kimbo69 says:** Touchy, touchy. Listen up, Leese. Take it from your friend with years of experience. If you're going to finally do it, wait until you can use your hands.

**Leesie327 says:** (Come off it, Kim. Don't go there.)

**Kimbo69 says:** Butt out, Mr. Secretary. This actually has nothing to do with you. She needs to hear this. I bled for like a week after my first time. You need to be able to deal with the mess.

**Kimbo69 says:** Hello? Where are you? Don't get mad at me. I'm just telling you what you need to know.

**Kimbo69 says:** Hey guys, this is getting rude.

**Leesie327 says:** sorry slow

**Kimbo69 says:** He bailed?

**Leesie327 says:** yup

**Kimbo69 says:** Figures. Such a wimp.

**Leesie327 says:** be nice

**Kimbo69 says:** I don't trust him, Leesie. What the hell are you thinking?

**Leesie327 says:** he saved me

**Kimbo69 says:** Don't go making him a hero.

**Leesie327 says:** i wanted to die
**Kimbo69 says:** He told me you blame yourself for the accident. Don't be crazy.
**Leesie327 says:** all my fault
**Kimbo69 says:** Even if you made a mistake driving, accidents are accidents. Your parents won't blame you.
**Leesie327 says:** not that easy
**Kimbo69 says:** What happened in that pickup? It must have been bad for you to react like this.
**Leesie327 says:** promise not to tell anybody?
**Kimbo69 says:** I'll help you sort it out...it can't be that bad.
**Leesie327 says:** i haven't told anyone...trying to hide
**Kimbo69 says:** It must be rough, girl. But you'll get through this.
**Leesie327 says:** can i trust you?
**Kimbo69 says:** Do you even need to ask?
**Leesie327 says:** we had this huge fight
**Kimbo69 says:** You and Phil?
**Leesie327 says:** that's why i crashed
**Kimbo69 says:** I don't think so—you always fought with him.
**Leesie327 says:** the last thing my brother heard was me screaming at him and squealing tires
**Kimbo69 says:** I know he's dead and he's your brother and all, but if he was being a snot and distracted you, it's his fault, too.
**Leesie327 says:** he said the worst things about Michael
**Kimbo69 says:** Michael? When I talked to you last, it was all about Jaron. What happened?
**Leesie327 says:** i drove through mountains and realized i couldn't love jaron because i still love michael...so excited... knew i'd see him soon somehow...i told phil
**Kimbo69 says:** He didn't agree?
**Leesie327 says:** i've never been so angry...i wanted to kill him
**Kimbo69 says:** no you didn't
**Leesie327 says:** but i did...i murdered my brother
**Kimbo69 says:** No, you didn't.
**Leesie327 says:** shoot, kim...you can't say anything about this

to michael...he'll think it's his fault...and that's so wrong
**Kimbo69 says:** Take it easy with Michael.
**Leesie327 says:** im living now for him...doing a crap job so far but trying
**Kimbo69 says:** How'd you convince him to get baptized?
**Leesie327 says:** hes not
**Kimbo69 says:** But that was your thing. You wouldn't say, "yes," until he joined your church.
**Leesie327 says:** doesnt matter now
**Kimbo69 says:** excuse me?
**Leesie327 says:** i dont even care if we get married first
**Kimbo69 says:** What's got into you? You told me it was huge earth-shattering sin to do it without being married.
**Leesie327 says:** nothing compared to what I did to Phil...God won't forgive me that
**Kimbo69 says:** He forgives everybody—even girls like me. That's what I'm counting on.
**Leesie327 says:** not me...i murdered my brother
**Kimbo69 says:** It's twisted to call it's murder. It was an accident. God won't blame you. I don't think your parents blame you, either.
**Leesie327 says:** they will if you ever tell them about that fight
**Kimbo69 says:** So you're hiding with Michael? He says the Mermaid Thai Queen was a friend. How can you buy that?
**Leesie327 says:** his eyes dont lie
**Kimbo69 says:** When are you going to come clean about the accident?
**Leesie327 says:** never...keep your mouth shut, too...you promised
**Kimbo69 says:** Go home, Leesie. It's not too late. Tell your parents everything. They'll understand.
**Leesie327 says:** no...what if they tell michael? or blame him?
**Kimbo69 says:** They won't. At least call them so they know you're okay.
**Leesie327 says:** no

**Kimbo69 says:** They just lost their son. Running away like this is too cruel. How can you do that to your dad?

**Leesie327 says:** had to…cant go home

**Kimbo69 says:** Can I tell them where you are?

**Leesie327 says:** did Michael tell you

**Kimbo69 says:** No. Can I at least call and tell them you're safe?

**Leesie327 says:** dont

**Kimbo69 says:** Come on. Give them something.

**Leesie327 says:** ok call

**Kimbo69 says:** Good girl. You owe me huge for this, by the way. Gigantically huge.

**Leesie327 says:** don't tell them about my hair

**Kimbo69 says:** What should I tell them?

**Leesie327 says:** best medical care

**Kimbo69 says:** That's good. What about you're wedding plans?

**Leesie327 says:** no

**Kimbo69 says:** You want them to think you're shacking up with him?

**Leesie327 says:** no

**Kimbo69 says:** Okay. I'll try to explain that. What if they ask me why you left?

**Leesie327 says:** dont tell them…i trusted you…please…i'll die if my mom ever finds out i was screaming at her boy when i lost control of the truck

**Kimbo69 says:** She'll understand. They love you. You call them. Tell them everything. Michael will take you home. He told me so.

**Leesie327 says:** no…im fine…tell them that…nothing else or i'll hate you forever

**Kimbo69 says:** Okay.

**Leesie327 says:** crap

**Kimbo69 says:** Is he back? You better delete this chat.

**Leesie327 says:** jarons online got to get off

## LEESIE HUNT / CHATSPOT LOG / 04/28 10:27 PM

**jRun says:** Leesie? You're online? What happened to you?
You're parents are going crazy. They called me. Your dad's voice.
I've never heard so much pain.
**Leesie327 says:** please tell him im sorry
**jRun says:** I blame myself for trusting that creep, Michael. He
came off so sincere. And you wanted him not me. That much was
clear. I couldn't stand to see you with him like that, so I walked.
**Leesie327 says:** not your fault
**jRun says:** But he stole you. Where are you? I'll come get you.
I'll call your Dad. We'll both come. The whole branch will come.
Anything to get you home. I love you. You got to believe that.
I'm kicking myself for leaving you alone with him. Whatever's
happened with him—I don't care. Let me make it up to you,
Leesie. Please. Where are you?
**Leesie327 says:** my idea to run
**jRun says:** You must have felt so desperate. I didn't realize. I
should have stayed.
**Leesie327 says:** forget me
**jRun says:** No way. You'll get through the grief. I saw it on my
mission. I can help you.
**Leesie327 says:** im a murderer
**jRun says:** No. You're not. Talk to my dad. He'll help. That's not
what those scriptures mean.
**Leesie327 says:** im dead
**jRun says:** That's stupid. Think about what you're doing. Who
you're hurting.
**Leesie327 says:** you?
**jRun says:** Your mom and dad, Stephie—all of us back at the
branch. And, yes, me.
**Leesie327 says:** sorry
**jRun says:** I still love you. Doesn't that matter?
**Leesie327 says:** it did in high school but you ignored me
**jRun says:** Ancient history—don't throw that in my face at a time

like this.
**Leesie327 says:** when would be a better time
**jRun says:** I didn't know you were like this.
**Leesie327 says:** honest
**jRun says:** Heartless.
**Leesie327 says:** taken
**jRun says:** Tell Michael to remember what I said in the hospital. I meant it. Every word.
**Leesie327 says:** my idea…not his…leave him alone…leave me alone
**jRun says:** Don't say that. A week ago you kissed me and said you loved me.
**Leesie327 says:** no, i didnt…i couldnt say it…remember? i love him…thats never going to change

## LEESIE'S MOST PRIVATE CHAPBOOK
## POEM # 78, HOME?

Run home,
run home,
run home.

Heartless.
Heartless.
Heartless.

Run home,
run home,
run home.

Heartless.
Heartless.
Heartless.

Michael discovers me,
laptop slammed closed
on my stretched out thighs,
propped straight up in my
bed that sits for me,
beating my broken hand
against my glossy head.

"Whoa, babe. Stop."
His hand closes around mine.
"Kim's an idiot. It won't be
that bad. I promise."
I slit open one eye
like a cornered creature,
realize he's talking about
our first time. My face
squinches up. "Do you think
I'm heartless?" emerges beyond
my control.

He doesn't answer right away,
doesn't pat my head and kiss it better.
"Michael?"
He won't meet my eyes. "Please,
let me call your dad. That's what
I feel worst about."
My eyes drop, too. "Phil's funeral
is tomorrow."
"Can I call in the morning?"
Our hands meet in the covers.
"Kim's going to call and—"
"Then I should, too. Please."
He kisses my head, and I melt.
"Okay."
His next kiss finds my mouth,

speaks relief. "You're not heartless."
His lips press against my beating,
bandaged sternum.

I should warn him about Jaron
who is probably calling right now,
screaming into the phone,
cursing me—cursing Michael.
Maybe Kim called first.
"What time is it there?"
He glances at the silver globe
iPod dock alarm clock by my bed.
"About 8:15."
"Call him tonight then. Back
at your hotel."
He nods, frowns. "You're
okay? I can leave?"
I force a smile and hold up
my white nurse buzzer.
"Yup. I've got nurses."

I hold his lips too long
when he puts them on mine
to say good-night. "I'll
stay 'til you sleep."
I kiss him once more, push
him away. "No. Call him."

# UNSAID

## MICHAEL'S DIVE LOG – VOLUME #10

**Dive Buddy:** Leesie
**Date:** 04/29
**Dive #:** not in the water
**Location:** Grand Cayman
**Dive Site:** Rehab Center
**Weather Condition:** mild
**Water Condition:** dry
**Depth:** wading today
**Visibility:** better
**Water Temp:** thermocline—cool to hot
**Bottom Time:** 24 hours
**Comments:**

It's past midnight when I get back to the hotel. New day. Yesterday seemed like a lifetime. Leesie's home phone is busy when I try to call. If her dad has a cell, I don't know the number. Leesie never had one back home. Too broke. Crap reception in a wheat field.

I try again in ten minutes. Busy. Fall asleep before the next ten minutes are up.

I wake up a couple hours later. Don't know where I am.
Freak. Figure it out. Pick up the phone. Try again. It's still not
too late back there. Eleven. Big deal. He'll be up.

"Hello?" It's him.

I should have planned this better, written it out or something. I'm at a total loss what to say. "Please, sir. Don't hang up."

"No. No. Of course not." His warm voice sounds like
rescue. "Don't be afraid, Michael. Just bring her home. That's all
we care about. She's hurt."

I want to tell him we're getting on a plane tomorrow.
"She's getting the best care on earth." Plus Cayman sunshine.
Nothing can beat that.

"Where are you?"

"She won't let me tell anyone yet."

"That's okay." His voice breaks. It takes him a moment to
regain control. "Bring her back to us. We don't blame you."

"I beg her to let me every day." Now emotion gets to me. I
swallow hard and whisper, "She won't listen. She's—ashamed."

He breathes a moment and whispers back, "Tell her we
love her. Is she close? Can I talk to her?"

"No." I should have called from her room, put her on. She
knew she'd have to talk to him. That's why she made me call
from here. "She thinks you'll be angry with her."

"Never." His voice is stronger, solid again.

I stand and walk to my window. "I know." The parking lot
is dark except for one light. "I'll tell her, though."

"Has she"—he pauses so long I think he's gone, but finally
gets the words out—"said anything more about the accident?"

I wish I could give him something, but I've got nothing.
"No. Just that it's all her fault." I hesitate, hating the words that
rise to my lips. "She thinks her mom hates her. And your God,
too."

"Tell her that's a wicked lie." Wicked? Yeah. Evil and
wicked. He says in a voice that sounds like a prophet. "No matter
what. We love her."

"And, sir. I want you to know." I swallow, switch the phone to my other ear. "I'm keeping that promise I made at Thanksgiving." My hand grows slick with sweat. The phone slips. "I won't touch her—not until we're married."

"You're getting married?" Does that scare him worse than anything else? "When?"

End of summer? Tomorrow? What do I tell him? "Someday."

"Bring her home first."

"If I can, I will."

"Take care of her, son." His voice fills with infinite sadness. "We miss our girl."

Him calling me "son" chokes me up like it always did. "She's sorry. Tell her mom, too. She's sorry."

I sleep past nine in the morning. Feel half-way human again. Talking to Leesie's dad grounded me. We're going to be okay. It's all going to be okay. I got to tell Leesie—get her grounded, too. I book it down to the rehab place, but when I get there, Leesie's room is full of nurses and a tall, black man wearing a white doctor's coat.

"What were you thinking," he speaks with a Caymanian accent, "traveling all this way injured as you are?" His island voice fills the room like a preacher's.

Leesie holds up her ring with purple swollen fingers. "We're supposed to be on our honeymoon. I crashed two days before our wedding. The hospital said I was good to travel." Leesie lying? Weird.

"Well, they were crazy to let you leave." He flips through the release papers I turned over yesterday when I checked Leesie in here. "How long is this honeymoon supposed to last? You'll get no beach time for weeks."

"All summer." I walk in and shake the guy's hand. "I'm a dive instructor. Looking for work."

"Have you got Cayman papers?"

"Working on it."

He knows I'm lying. "Have you been here before?"

I nod. "It's my favorite place in the world to dive." At least Little Cayman is. Got to get Leesie over there.

The doctor turns back to Leesie. "Let's see what we have here." He casually pushes the button on her morphine pump before he starts with her head, examines her cut. "Nicely done." He glances back at the clipboard. "Concussion?" He flashes a penlight in Leesie's eyes. "Good dilation. Does your head pound?"

"Not right now."

"When you're not on morphine?"

"Yeah."

He raps under her knee with the side of his hand. It jumps like it's supposed to. "Good. The headaches should subside in a few more days. No permanent nerve damage."

"That's good?" Leesie looks over at me and smiles slightly.

"Yes." He snips off the bandages to examine her nose. Black, blue, purple, green. The colors twist together and scream pain. He touches her nose. "The packs your surgeon placed in the nostrils are well-positioned." He runs his finger over the bump high up on her nose. "You'll end up with a bit of a bump here. But we'll keep the nose straight. You can opt for cosmetic surgery once all this is healed up."

"I can have any nose I want?"

No way. She's going to stick with the nose I fell in love with. He keeps touching it, and Leesie gets paler and paler. The garish colors seems to ooze and twist, moving, crawling, spreading all over her face. The room grows hotter. My heads turns fuzzy, and I can't breathe. I think I sway.

The nurse Leesie named, Sugar, takes my elbow. "Let's get us some fresh air why don't we."

I jerk my elbow away. "No, I'm fine." I sway again.

"Do you want to faint in front of her?" She grabs my arm, guides me out Leesie's sliding door, and deposits me on a bench

in the garden. "A few deep breaths, sugar, and you'll feel better."
She disappears.

I cycle through my free dive breathing, inhale the flowers around me. Smile when I detect my mom's favorite scent. Gardenias. I'm glad she's close. I could use her help about now. I wander around, find the bush and break off branch after branch of dark green leaves and small white fragrant flowers.

When I make it back to Leesie's room, she's got a new pink bandage on her nose, and the medical team is gone.

"You are a wimp."

I inhale gardenias for strength. "If you saw your nose, you'd faint, too."

"Pretty gory?"

"The goriest." I stick my bouquet in her half-empty water cup.

She motions towards her hospital gowned torso. "Do you want to see my ribs? He left them undone."

"Are they gory, too?"

She nods. "The bruising is ugly, but the doctor is most worried I'll get pneumonia." She's supposed to breath deep so the air sacks in her lungs don't stick together. "I told them I learned everything I know about heavy breathing from you."

I crack a smile. "You didn't."

"No." She manages a crooked smile back. "But it's true."

I bite my lip. "I was just out there doing free dive cycles."

"That's what I told them." She punches a button so the bed sits her up more. "You're now my coach."

I sit beside her. "Cool." I smooth my hand over her head.

She closes her eyes and leans into my caress. "He thinks it's a good idea to keep me trussed up like this for another week so the collarbone can set. After that I'll just need the sling." Her eyes open.

"What about your hand?" I pick it up, inspect the fingers, wonder when my ring will fit on them again. "Did we keep it elevated enough?"

"He said that's just for the swelling." She wiggles her fingers. "We're past that crisis now. I don't have to worry about it anymore."

Her fingers still look puffy to me.

She pulls the sheet up to show off her footwear. "I have to wear these new boots night and day for the next three weeks so my ankles heal strong." Her new boots, lined with support, snugged tight with Velcro, are nothing like the floppy footgear she had before. She looks tired, worn out, strained.

I try to read her eyes. "Did he hurt you—poking and prodding?"

She holds up her morphine pump and pushes the button. "This stuff is great, but it makes me dozy." She yawns. "He said I'll need it around the clock for at least another week. Then we can taper off."

"No more skipping your pills?"

She nods—so obedient today.

I balance her hand on my outstretched palm. "When do you get your cast off your hand?" And your nose, but I don't want to bring that up again.

She pulls her hand away, lays it on her own chest. "Another five weeks—maybe longer. They're going to X-ray it tomorrow and put on a new waterproof one to match my nose."

"Pink?"

"Yes." She scowls at my tone and sticks out her tongue. "And then we can go to the beach."

I smile. "Cool." The smile fades as I remember what I came to tell her. "I got a hold of your dad."

She closes her eyes and turns her face to the wall.

I bend down, hover over her. "They aren't mad. Don't blame you." I stroke her silky scalp. "You can go home." I lean closer so I can whisper in her ear. "You rest here another couple weeks, get really strong, and then let's fly home."

She speaks in a small tight voice. "I can't. He doesn't know."

"He does, Leese." I kiss her temple. "He says God doesn't think you're guilty. He says they love you."

"They'll hate me."

I nuzzle my lips against the side of her bare head. "Let me call him and tell him I'm bringing you home." I slide my arms around her so I can embrace her. "They need some hope right now, babe. You got to go home." I squeeze her close, .

She doesn't answer.

I kiss the back of her neck.

"No."

My arms relax defeat. "What happened, Leese? This isn't you. Why—"

She turns terror-filled eyes towards me. "Don't ask me. Ever again. If you love me—"

I wish I could press this. What could be so ominous? She looks so pathetic. I back off. "Look." I slide off the bed and pick up the flowers. "I brought you something to inhale deeply."

She bends her head toward the branches and tries to smell the gardenias. "Sorry. I can't smell anything. I've got stuff shoved up my nose holding the bones in place."

"No problem. Let's get to work on those free dive cycles."

She looks at me through her eyelashes. "I can inhale you."

Sugar comes in, unhooks Leesie's IV, and tapes the needle sticking out of her hand down. I help Leesie to her post-op surgically booted feet, guide her out to my bench, hold her on my lap and coach her through cycles one to three. She's not ready to pack yet. Then we make out in the sunshine.

She whispers, "Kissing you is the only thing that feels right."

My lips moves against her mouth. "That's just the morphine talking."

"Then let's enjoy it." She sucks my tongue into her mouth and keeps it.

I do enjoy that. Way too much. I finally break loose, sit up straight. "Freak, Leese. That so not allowed."

"But we're officially engaged." She picks up the ring, dangling on its chain, and twists it so the diamond flashes in the sunlight.

"No—on our honeymoon." I nuzzle her neck. "You little liar."

"You backed me up." She tries to get my lips again but can't reach.

"What else could I do?"

"Let me have your tongue back."

I move my mouth to her ear and whisper, "Not until you can follow it up with more action."

"Party pooper."

"Torturer."

A lopsided grin breaks out on her face. "That totally frustrates you?"

"Totally."

"I'll have to remember that."

I peck her lips one last time. "I won't let you forget."

## LEESIE'S MOST PRIVATE CHAPBOOK
## POEM #79, PHIL

They buried my brother
today. It hangs in the air
between me and Michael
unsaid,
untouched,
unwept.

If we don't speak it,
is it real?
Could it happen
without my words?
My consent?

He's there in the locker
room, driving the tractor,
dancing with Krystal
wrapped tight in his arms.
Not cold in a coffin
too gruesome to open.
Not slid into a hearse
filled with flowers.
Not lowered into a deep hole
in a place he didn't want
to rest. Not whispering
at the edges of my soul.
"I'm here, Leesie.
Let me in. I'm here."

Michael doesn't bring it up.
Keeps the silence—even
when he tells me about dad.
He sticks by me all day—drinks
half my smoothie, shares his
French fries and does his best
to make this ugly bruised cue ball
so hideous to look at he nearly fainted
feel sexy,
adored,
beloved.

He sits by my bed
while I nap—worn
out by doctors'
ministrations, Michael's
attentive encouragement,
and holding Phil back.

I dream I'm there.

Dream fingers point.
Dream angry faces
screaming condemnation
surround me.
Dream rocks, big ones,
clutched in their hands.
Dream they raise them high
over their heads and no
gentle Savior intercedes,
no quiet voice says,
"He who is without sin."
The stones fly but I feel
nothing—they form a cairn
around me. I'm entombed,
untouched—imprisoned
forever.

Hands knock on the outside,
voices call my name—
Michael, my dad—mom—grandma,
even Phil,
and a sweet, strong voice
I know so well.
I block my ears
scream and scream and scream.
Michael wakes me, holds me.

Haunted by his own alternate
reality, he doesn't leave me alone
with mine. The morphine dulls my pain
but doesn't make me sane.
He does.

We watch movies all night—
stupid ones, funny ones

and one that makes me cry.
Those tears are the best
medicine yet.
And Michael kissing my
fingertips, lotioning
my itching bare scalp,
sitting on my bed beside me,
dozing on the sofa
when I wake late the next
morning from a sleep touched
only by dreams
of him.

# FOR NOW

## MICHAEL'S DIVE LOG – VOLUME #10

**Dive Buddy:** Alex
**Date:** 05/05
**Dive #:** 6
**Location:** East End, Grand Cayman
**Dive Site:** Cinderella's Castle
**Weather Condition:** perfect
**Water Condition:** perfect
**Depth:** perfect
**Visibility:** perfect
**Water Temp:** perfect
**Bottom Time:** perfect
**Comments:**

"Hey, babe." I close the door to her room and take up my station standing beside her bed. "Ba-abe. I'm back." She made me go diving. Saturday, too. She knows I'm dying to get out there in the sun and saltwater—knows I wouldn't leave her for a second unless she insisted. I feel guilty about that first trip I took. Guilty for diving the North Coast on Saturday. But, today, I don't feel guilty at all.

Leesie sleeps a lot in the day. Nights are hell. But in the day she makes me go to my hotel to get some decent sleep. Then Saturday she started in on diving. "You need to get out of here. I don't want you to get sick of me."

At first I was hurt she thought I could *ever* get sick of her. But I didn't resist long. I mean—it's diving. Sorry. Hate me. I deserve it.

She seemed happier Saturday when I got back. Slept better that night. Sunday I freaked her out by asking if she'd like me to try to find her a Mormon church to go to. Sugar said she could leave for a couple hours—no problem. Leesie wouldn't talk to me the whole rest of the day. Had nightmares again that night. At least that's what Sugar told me. Leesie wouldn't let me stay.

So when she was calm and sweet again on Monday, I wasn't going to argue when she brought up me going diving.

"I'll take you over to the beach when I get back." I plastered a grin on my face.

She didn't flash me that smile that makes her so beautiful. Even a tight-lipped smile rarely happens. Her face just looked less sad for a moment. "I'd love that."

I left her sleeping soundly, and when I phoned from my hotel early this morning, Sugar said she stayed that way all night. I didn't feel too bad hopping into the burnt orange RAV4 I rented last Friday and practicing driving on the left-hand side of the road like they do here in Cayman all the way around to the East End.

And now, zero guilt.

I'm glad I went.


"Leese." I press my lips on her forehead. Her scalp is stubbly—like kissing sandpaper, so I don't do that.

Her eyes open. "Hey." She purses her lips together until I kiss them. "Scratch my head, okay?" She closes her eyes.

I don't know if it really itches—she's numbed up. If she's drugged enough not to feel her broken collarbone or her ribs smart when she inhales deeply, would she be able to feel an itchy head? I think she likes me touching it. I scratch her head, lightly. She presses into my fingers.

I avoid the gash. She's supposed to get the stitches out tomorrow. "I have news."

Here eyes tighten—ready for a blow. "Did you talk to Stan? Are they going to charge me with vehicular manslaughter? Reckless endangerment?"

I move from scratching to rubbing her head. It feels freaky, but I keep stroking it. "Bad guess. Relax. It's good news. Us news."

Her eyes open wide. "We're going to get married this afternoon instead of going to the beach?"

"Better guess." I laugh. She never gives up. "But not that good."

She doesn't respond.

I draw my hand away from her head. "I found a job, and it comes with a place to stay." The grin I've been holding back breaks out on my face.

Her face falls. "How far away will you be?"

I put my hand on her arm. "The room next door."

"Here?" Her eyebrows squinch up.

"No, babe." I lean over and stroke her cheek. "I got a job with our—my—favorite dive guys out at the East End. Two of their dive masters took off. They are way shorthanded and can get an emergency work VISA pushed through for me." She's not smiling, not excited. I try again. "They are a great bunch of divers. You're going to love them."

"How far away from here is it?" She presses her lips together to still the trembling.

"Don't worry." I kiss her forehead. "I'll drive you back down for physical therapy and check-ups."

She clutches at my arm. "Where am I going?"

I pat her hand—notice her fingers are no longer swollen. "They are going to take you off the morphine on Thursday. Try you on regular pain pills. If that goes well, you don't have to stay here anymore."

She inhales, holds it and blows it out. "It will go well. It has to."

Am I pushing this too soon? "How do you feel about leaving?"

She musters a smile. "You've got a condo for the two of us?"

"Yeah. Well—not just us."

The smile slips off her face.

I cradle her hand in both of mine. "There's not a lot of decent apartments near the resort, and their units aren't exactly booked up these days, so they rent out one of their condos to all the foreign dive masters and instructors. There's like eight of them crammed into one two-bedroom condo. Or there was. And there will be again when we move in."

Her eyebrows shoot up. "I'm moving in with seven guys?"

I don't like how that sounds. "No. Alex needs a roommate."

"Who is Alex?"

"The girl running things on the boat today."

Incredulous. That's the only way to describe the face she turns away from me. "Not *another* old girlfriend."

I nudge Leesie's chin back in my direction. "Nope." I kiss her. "Relax, babe. It's all good. Alex is new here. She's cool. She told me about the job—set the whole thing up for *us*."

I try to kiss Leesie again, but she tilts her head to the side to avoid me. "I bet she did."

I thought we were beyond jealousy. I nuzzle the side of her face and whisper in her ear. "I talked about you—my fiancé—the whole freaking time."

She relents and lets me kiss her.

"You, my coddled princess"—I kiss her again—"get to share the master ensuite with Alex, and I'm stuck on a cot in the living room with three other guys."

She kisses me back and goes for the jugular. "So I'm only

moving in with *six* hot dive instructors?"

I tickle her for that.

"Don't, it hurts to laugh." She bats at my hand and pumps her morphine a couple shots.

I sit on the bed's edge and gather her up in my arms. "Just remember who you're with, babe." I suck on her lower lip to remind her.

We make out for awhile, and then she rests her cheek on my chest.

I rub her back. "So we're good?"

"It's seems weird to move in with a bunch of strangers."

"They aren't strangers. They're divers. I met them today."

"My mom would—" She stops, struggles a moment. "Okay." Her voice wavers. "If that's what you want to do."

I hold her closer. "I know it's not ideal—kind of a zoo."

Leesie shifts so she can see my face.

I smile encouragement. "Alex is great. She's got advanced rescue and some EMT training. She said she'd be happy to help you if you need it."

Leesie manages to smile back. "I should be able to take care of myself."

"Cool." I seal the deal with a kiss on her forehead.

She pulls her eyebrows down, accusing. "Aren't we going for a walk on the beach?"

"Have you got enough of that stuff in you?" I motion to her IV paraphernalia.

She pushes the morphine button three more times. "Give it ten minutes." Her eyes close.

"Good. We can talk. I think it's time, babe. You can tell me. It'll help."

Her eyes fly open. Her face squeezes into a knot. "What about 'never' don't you understand?" She turns her face to the wall.

I sit back, my head in my hands, defeated again. It's me, babe. You can tell me. It hurts that she doesn't want to share the accident with me. I know this is dumb and selfish, but I'm doing everything I can for her—spending a chunk of change to make this work, and she still won't talk about what happened in that pickup cab before the accident. That's what eats her. I know. She knows. All the nurses and morphine pumps and casts and stitches won't heal that. I'm here. I can listen. I can help her. And she won't try.

I'm a fool. I admit it. It's way too soon. I go find Sugar, so she can unhook Leesie and help her get dressed. Smile and play like nothing happened. She'll tell me someday. When she's ready. I'll be the one.

## LEESIE HUNT / CHATSPOT LOG / 05/06 2:58 AM

**Kimbo69 says:** Leesie living with six guys? That's a picture I can't process.

**Leesie327 says:** Ick. You make it sound like they'll be passing me around.

**Kimbo69 says:** You don't have a "Thou shalt not share an apartment with guys" commandment?

**Leesie327 says:** That's an old Leesie rule. It doesn't matter now.

**Kimbo69 says:** And Michael doesn't have a problem with it?

**Leesie327 says:** I'm sharing a room with Alex.

**Kimbo69 says:** Right. She sounds fishy to me.

**Leesie327 says:** Michael says she's like one of the guys.

**Kimbo69 says:** But she jumped to get him hired.

**Leesie327 says:** When they are down two dive masters it puts all of them at risk—too much diving. They could get bent. It's dangerous.

**Kimbo69 says:** She went after him for her health?

**Leesie327 says:** She didn't go after him.

**Kimbo69 says:** She convinced him to move in with her.

**Leesie327 says:** I'm moving in with her.

**Kimbo69 says:** Yeah. That's a nice touch.

**Leesie327 says:** Michael and I are way beyond that petty stuff.

**Kimbo69 says:** And I'm not? Mark and I aren't? We've been together way longer than you have.
**Leesie327 says:** Our situation is different. No one else exists for either of us.
**Kimbo69 says:** Liar. You are insanely jealous.
**Leesie327 says:** Shut up.
**Kimbo69 says:** Be honest.
**Leesie327 says:** Okay. I'm scared. I'm scared to leave here. I'm scared to unplug my morphine pump. I'm scared she's pretty.
**Kimbo69 says:** You're pretty.
**Leesie327 says:** I'm hideous.
**Kimbo69 says:** Michael doesn't think so.
**Leesie327 says:** He has eyes.
**Kimbo69 says:** That are glued on you 24/7.
**Leesie327 says:** But what if she has long hair?

## LEESIE'S MOST PRIVATE CHAPBOOK
## POEM #80, I'VE GOT YOU

First day off morphine starts
sore—even after I swallow
their pills. "You're job, young lady"—
the doctor hands me a full bottle
of pain-a-cide—"is to take these pills
only for pain—not comfort, not anxiety."
His golden Cayman tones echo off the
sunny walls. "Don't skimp at first.
Taper off as soon as you can."

I hurt too bad to eat breakfast—or even drink
my smoothie. I manage not to puke
my guts up but just barely.
The sore gets worse and worse,
when I breathe, when I move, when I think,

but no way I'm telling because
he's moving in tomorrow, and I'm
going with him.
Period.

Michael gets excited when they
unwind the figure eight bandage
that's trussed my collarbone in place.
"Keep your right arm in the sling."
Sugar moves it gently back in place.
"But you can move it to dress and bathe."
Michael rushes over to the tourist trap
across the street, comes back with
a bulging, plastic bag. "Let's REALLY go
to the beach." The dressing on my nose
now is more of a brace than a cast.
He tosses the bag on my lap.
I pull out a hottest pink, tropical print
bikini. "You've got to be kidding?"
My ribs are unwrapped, but still
black and blue.

Doesn't he remember my rules?
Bikinis are contraband.
Is this a hint? Does he recognize
I'm lost? Or is he as clueless
over bikinis as he was me
moving into an apartment full of guys?

He digs in the bag and pulls out a t-shirt.
"I got this to keep you decent—
matches mine." He bought himself less loud
swim shorts and another Cayman T-shirt.

My day's been too long already. If only

I could lie in bed with the shades pulled down
counting the waves of pain. But
I'm fine. Remember. Nothing wrong
today or tomorrow.
Sugar helps me change, wraps my hand cast
in a bread bag. "Don't get your face wet
or sand in your boots." She just washed them.
They stunk. She sprays my head with
sunscreen and ties a scarf around the stubble.

I limp half way, Michael gets impatient,
carries me the rest of the way.
He sets me on the sand, spreads
out a straw beach mat, trimmed
in hot pink to match my t-shirt
draped bikini. (Feels like sin to wear
it—even hidden away like this.)

We lie together in the sun.
His thigh touches mine. I squint
my eyes against the bright light.
"I forgot." His hand goes
into his pocket. "One more present."
He puts sunglasses over my eyes that
have faded from purple to greenish black.

We laze in the sunshine.
"Do you want to talk about it?"
"Moving?"
"No." He raises up on his elbow.
"You'll feel better, babe.
It's me—I'm not going to judge you."

I ignore him, lie there until sweat coats me.
"This t-shirt's too hot." He took

his off—why can't I?
His hand reaches down and unvelcroes
the straps on my boots.
"What are you doing?"
He pushes off my scarf. "We're going
swimming."
"No we're not."
"No waves today. Come on, babe.
I've got you."

He picks me up, still wearing the shirt,
carries me into cool, silky
water deep as his chest.
His arms loosen. I clutch him.
"Take it easy. This will feel good."
He makes me lie flat on my back
one arm in my sling, my good hand
holding my broken one on top of
my stomach.
"Fill your chest with air."
I inhale.
"Hold it."
I'm beautifully buoyant in the
salt and sun and Michael's arms.
"Relax. Put your head back."
I obey—cool ocean blueness
laps around my body, easing
away heat and a measure of ache,
calming me as I lie embraced
by it's subtle rhythm.
"Saltwater therapy." His lips
find a patch of my stubbly head.
"You need more of this."

"I could lie like this forever."

"That can be arranged."

If he knew what a beast I am,
would he say that? Would
he float me in the waves?
Or swim away—farther
than Thailand, farther than
forever.

# FORWARD STEPS

## MICHAEL'S DIVE LOG – VOLUME #10

**Dive Buddy:** Leesie
**Date:** 05/09
**Dive #:** last one at this site
**Location:** Grand Cayman
**Dive Site:** Rehab Center
**Weather Condition:** stormier than I knew
**Water Condition:** choppy
**Depth:** I can't tell exactly
**Visibility:** clearing
**Water Temp:** chilly
**Bottom Time:** 20 minutes
**Comments:**

I drop by the rehab center on my way to pick up my bags from the airport. Claude finally sent them. I got his email last night. He's been busy. Shorthanded. I'm not easy to replace. French bull.

The air freight plane landed at 6 AM. The airport's on our route to our new digs in East End, but I don't want Leesie to have to tough it out waiting if there's problems at customs.

Sugar's serving Leesie breakfast. Tea and toast. Guess her stomach's not up to her usual fruity smoothie. Shoot. She usually lets me finish it off.

Tea? Gross. And she can't drink it. One of her rules. You can't get a decent can of Coke on the entire BYU campus. She said caffeinated pop is a gray area. It's not officially part of the rule—commandment. Lots of Mormons drink it, but my Leesie was a purist.

She starts to say something to Sugar. Stops herself. Picks up the spoon and stirs the cup.

"Leese." I nod to Sugar as she leaves. "Don't drink that."

She takes a spoonful, sips. "Damn." She drops the spoon onto the table that swings over her bed and touches her lips. "It's hot." Great, now she's swearing.

I point at the cup in her hands. "What are you doing?"

"Sugar said it would settle my stomach." Her tongue makes "bleck" motions. "How do you drink this stuff? Even with honey it's nasty."

I cross the room. "What's wrong with your stomach?"

"Just a bit queasy." She focuses her eyes on the teacup. "I'm fine."

I fill her in on the morning's agenda. "I'll be back soon. Are you excited?"

She plasters a fake smile on her face. "Of course." She picks ice out of her water pitcher and plunks it into her tea.

"What's wrong?" I need her to be pumped about this. She's still holding the accident in. I don't know if she'll ever be pumped about anything again if she refuses to deal with it.

She concentrates on stirring the cup. "Can you hold this up for me? I'm afraid I'm going to spill it."

"No. I told you." I take the teacup. "You're not breaking the rules with me around."

She scowls. "Who made you my judge?"

"You did." I take the tea into her bathroom and dump it down the sink.

"I was supposed to drink that," she yells, shrill and tense.

"Don't be like this, Leesie," I call and turn the water on to rinse out the sink. "It freaks me out."

"Do you even care what freaks me out?"

I shut the water off and stare into the mirror. "Of course I do. That's *all* I care about." What is it, babe? What's made you like this? I miss the old Leesie more and more every day.

"You and Alex," she shouts, "that freaks me out."

"What?" I stand in the doorway of the bathroom, shocked. That came out of nowhere. "Alex?"

Leesie has her knees pulled up to her chest. She huddles there hanging onto them like a broken butterfly. I walk towards her.

"Don't send me home." She blinks fast. Her eyes have gone pink. "I'll be good. I won't drink tea."

I stop halfway to her bed. "Why would I send you home?"

She drops her face to her knees and mumbles.

I take another step closer. "What?"

She lifts her face, squeezes her eyes shut. "You've got her now."

"Who?" I take another step closer.

"Alex."

"That hurts." I pound on my chest like some kind of stupid ape. "Really hurts."

Leesie raises her head. Tears stream down her face. For the first time since the accident, I see the girl she sees in the mirror. Shaved head. Ugly scar. Bruised eyes hiding a secret that rips her to pieces. Two long strides close the distance that separates us. I sit on her bed and surround the Leesie bundle perched on it with my arms and whisper, "How can you even begin to think that?"

"Is she pretty?"

"No." I hand her a tissue and kiss her temple.

Leesie blows her nose. "Is she stacked?"

"She's all muscle. You're stacked compared to her."

"Doe she have long hair?"

I shrug my shoulders. "I couldn't tell you. I think it's short. I didn't notice."

"Really?" She sits straighter and looks pleased.

"Really." I kiss her moist cheek. "Are you going to be okay now? No more crazy ideas about Alex?"

"Why are we moving in there?"

"Because I got a job and"—I hug her—"I think you could use a friend."

She relaxes against me. "I'm sorry. I'm stupid."

"Idiotic." My lips find hers. "Better?"

She nods her head and kisses me again.

"Trust me."

"I'm trying."

If I keep telling her that, maybe she finally will.

## LEESIE'S MOST PRIVATE CHAPBOOK POEM #81, MOVING WITH MICHAEL

The clothes I wore here are clean,
folded on a chair. Sugar coaches
me getting the bra on by
myself. I wince, and she sees it.
"You missing the morphine?"
I grit my teeth and pick up my jeans.
She puts her hand on mine, hands me
a package from her and the girls.
"Too hot here for denim."
I unwrap the gift. I'm getting
dang good with my broken hand.
Can do almost anything if I enlist
my teeth. I shimmy into a short,
soft T-shirt dress that hits me
mid-thigh. Yellow as the sunshine.
The top is striped with turquoise

to match the jeweled water.
No zippers, no buttons, no snaps.
I hug her and cry.
"Hush now, we'll see you on
Wednesday. Don't forget your
exercises." She watches me
get my sling back on by myself,
hands me a cute yellow baseball hat
to match the dress. She winks.
"Make him take you shopping."
I lift my eyebrows. "Good idea."

I wait in the garden, breathing
in gardenias, wondering if
his mom knows my brother yet.

Michael arrives, red-faced and muttering
about customs tearing his bags apart
hunting for drugs. "You should have
shaved." I'm jealous that the hair
on his face is already longer than
the itchy growth
that shadows my head.
"I like your hat." He helps me to my
feet. "And the dress is way hot."
He strokes the few inches of bare
thigh exposed between cast and hem.
His fingers send pulses up my legs.
I inch the skirt higher and will
his hand to follow. The fingers retreat.
He shakes one at me like I'm three
and naughty. "Let's go."

We drive along Seven-Mile Beach,
through the honking, packed

downtown core onto a wild
highway that hugs the coast.
All the way the water's too turquoise
to be real. Looks painted, fake—until
a wave rolls up and crashes
into the coral coast, spurting
white spray high in the air
through funnels in the cliffs that amplify
the power. I want to stop and watch,
but Michael's late. Working
the PM boat.

We pull into the resort parking lot.
Rectangular buildings built
to deflect storms. Three stories.
Colored a dark echo of the water.
Not much after Seven-Mile swank.
He grabs my bags. "Most of my
stuff is gear. I've got a locker down
by the dock." He totes my duffel bags
up all three flights of stairs
and bursts in through a door at the top.
I'm dizzy and hurting by the time
I catch up.

"Hey, Leese. This is Alex."
He disappears into a room.
An over-tanned girl
with uber-short hair
gives me a hug.
"Welcome to the hovel."
I feel the muscles in her
arms. She wears a rash
guard over a bikini.
Her legs are solid muscle—

like a skinny weight lifter.
She lets me go.
"You're late," she yells
at Michael like a boss.
"Our boat leaves in fifteen minutes."

I find Michael in my new room.
It's dominated by a giant
king-sized bed.
Alex hollers on her way
out the door, "They're bringing
our new beds in an hour.
Can you let the guys in?"

Alex and her last roomie shared?
That makes me nervous.
What did Michael leave out?
"Is she gay?" I need to know.
What if I say the wrong thing?
Michael shakes his head. "Broken-
hearted. Her boyfriend took off."
"One of the defectors?"
He nods. "Gabriel says she sleeps
on the floor. Can't stand
to get back in that bed."
"The other woman was here, too?"
"She was with Seth."
"Poor Alex."
"Yeah. You'll be good for her."
He kisses me good-bye.
"Unpack. You get half
the closet and these drawers."

I wave with the last
tidbit of endurance I possess

as he evaporates from the room,
collapse on the forbidden bed,
close my eyes, drift
on the pain that radiates
out from my collarbone,
dwarfing every other malady.
I dream I'm in the pickup
screaming at Phil, defending
my Michael. Tires screech.
Glass explodes into pellets.
Metal shrieks.
Again.

The buzzer ringing and a loud
hammering knock shaking the door
startle me awake.
I hobble fast as I can to open it.
Two guys. Two mattresses.
"Where do you want these?"
I lead them to the room.
They shift bedding off the big
mattress and pick it up.
I retreat into the kitchen
to get out of their way.

A major ripped guy bursts from
the other bedroom, clothed
only in boxers—glares at me.
"What the eff's going on?"
I manage to squeak,
"Just moving in," around
the nervous shock that clogs
my thought process with,
*Flight, flight, flight.*
He looks at me like I'm

circus freak meat.
"Who the hell are you?"
"Leesie." More squeaking.
He heads into the bathroom—
doesn't close the door.
I decide it's time to enjoy
the view from the balcony.

The moving guys finished fast,
wave good-bye.
I'm chicken to go
back inside. I'm alone
in this dump apartment
with a total stranger.
But Michael knows him.
Maybe? Trusts him.
Who knows?

It would serve Michael right
if this boxer jerk attacks me.
He stuck me here with the creep.
I hobble back in the apartment
prepared for the worst.
No sign of the guy.
His door's closed again.
I trip over cots, towels, blankets,
and a pulled out hide-a-bed
hurrying to make it back to my room.
Pull the door tight. Lock it.
Go in the ensuite bathroom.
Lock that door, too.
Slip my right hand free
of it's sling, splash water on my
burning neck and cheeks,
pull the chain with my ring

over my head, fumble to get
it unlocked, slide the ring off
and jam it onto my left hand,
third finger so I can wave
it in that guy's face if he
comes near me, wishing
Michael was here
to take me floating again.

I sit on the toilet and gather
strength to face my afternoon's labors.
I move at last—unlock the door,
unzip my first duffel bag
scared of what I'll find inside—
muddy damp refuse from
the side of the mountain?
No. The clothes are fresh laundered,
folded sloppy-sweet like a guy did it.
Jeans and sweatshirts. Useless here.
Two pairs of capris, my old one-piece
swimsuit, ugly work-out shorts, socks, panties,
a couple of embarrassing worn out
double A bras that have always been
too big. Lots of T-shirts.

As I put the T's in the second drawer down,
I pick up a shirt that's not mine.
Navy. Guy cut. BYU logo across the front.
I see it on Phil the day before we left.

Drop it.
Panic.
Breathe fast.
Sweat.

I kneel down,
stare at it,
willing it to move.

It doesn't
so
I
do.

# MATES

## MICHAEL'S DIVE LOG – VOLUME #10

**Dive Buddy:** Guiding
**Date:** 05/09
**Dive #:** 7
**Location:** East End, Grand Cayman
**Dive Site:** Barrel Sponge Wall
**Weather Condition:** sunny
**Water Condition:** 3' surge
**Depth:** 107'
**Visibility:** 100+
**Water Temp:** 82
**Bottom Time:** 49 minutes
**Comments:**
    Felt bad dumping Leesie in that trashed apartment and bolting, but boats don't wait. Maybe this isn't going to work. She didn't look happy when I left. Not that I expect her to look happy. Lost. Scared. Wiped out. Hurts to look at her.

    I thought about buying us our own condo down here or even a house, but we can't stay there alone if we're not married. We could get married, but I'm convinced she's so eager to tie the knot because I'm off limits. Marrying me is as taboo as shacking up with me. It wouldn't be "major sin," but when I asked her before Christmas, she insisted I believe all her Mormon stuff and join up before she'd even consider putting on my ring. She's so screwed up now. She's got to be thinking a lot straighter before we get married. What if she comes out of it in a year and hates me forever because I took advantage of her when she was desperate?

I don't think she'll ever be a hundred percent like she was before. I'll take fifty—twenty-five. Heck, I'd be pumped if she just came clean about the accident. I'm crazy to think she'll be close to that by the end of summer. Whenever I think of getting married "tomorrow" like she wants, I get this dark feeling. I'm not going to be the evil infidel who carries off the virgin. I'm not going to let her do drugs or smoke. Freak. I won't even let her drink a stupid cup of tea. So what do we do? No clue.

And then all of a sudden these guys need me and Alex needs a roommate. Perfect answer. Almost. Me dumping her there and running off to dive—even if it's work—is so not perfect. I beg her to trust me and then do this to her.

I grab my bag of gear out of the back of the RAV, tote it down to the dock, and hand it into the boat to Alex.

"Have you got everything you need?" She shades her eyes with her hand and squints.

"No idea." I step down into the dive boat, take my bag, check it to make sure Claude actually sent all my gear. It looks good. I give Brock, an Aussie dude who's captain today, a thumbs up, and Ethan and Gabriel, who will leave later on the other boat with Cooper, cast off the ropes. I catch one. Alex gets the other. Brock motors towards the break in the reef and the wild three foot swells beyond it.

He guns the boat through the cut and we're into the pulsing ocean. Our divers hang on tight. "This is calm for East End," Brock yells down to them.

Alex and I get the clientele geared up and thrown overboard. She gave me all the jocks. Nice. We go deep first dive.

I push my group to the edge to get down to my favorite swim-through at this site. We wind through the coral cave that narrows into a tube. One of the divers gets hung up. I send the others ahead—fin back and help his useless buddy untangle the dude's hoses. The group misses the turn that takes them up to the top of the reef. I get their attention banging on my tank with a heavy metal d-ring I keep hanging on my B.C. I motion them to return and follow me. They maneuver around in the tight space. Eventually, we're, one by one, carefully rising through a chute forty feet to the top of the reef.

We finish off the dive, toss around in the boat until we motor back inside the reef where it's calm enough to wait out the interval without all the divers puking their guts up. So far no one's blown chunks. Good day in East End.

I change over all the gear while Alex cuts up fresh fruit and passes out bottles of water. I figure I owe her. I don't mind doing the heavy work.

Second dive is shallow, strong surge, and too short. A couple of my divers suck through their tanks too fast. I let the rest explore this easy site on their own, get the goons topside and safe on the rocking boat, and when I go back the rest are surfacing, too.

As the boat makes the dash through the break in the reef, I notice somebody lying on the beach. Nobody much uses this beach. It's kind of there for show. Everybody who comes to this resort dives all day long. We get closer, and I recognize Leesie.

I hustle, heaving up gear bins and empty tanks. The other boat got in before us, so there are lots of hands to help. Alex is strong as a guy. She hands up tanks and gear almost as fast as I do.

I climb out of the boat, pick up my gear bag, and dump it in the soak tank. I'll deal with it after I check in with Leese. She hasn't moved since I first saw her.

"Hey, mate." Brock calls after me. "When do we get to meet your fiancé?"

I stop, turn back. "Now's good. She's down on the beach."

"I'll gather the mates, and we'll present ourselves to your

lady. See you in ten."

"Cool." I hustle down to the beach to warn her.

She's sleeping in the sand wearing only that ugly T-shirt I bought her and the bikini bottoms. She looks way too sexy like that to meet her new apartment-mates.

"Hey, babe." I nudge her with my toe.

She doesn't stir.

I drop onto the sand on all fours hanging over her. "Babe." She opens one eye. "Hey."

I sit next to her and speak low. "What's with the wet T-shirt contest?"

She yawns and opens both eyes. "I couldn't tie those stupid strings."

"You could have left your bra on."

"My sling covers everything."

"Not everything. Here." I hold out my towel. "Use this. The guys will be here in a few minutes. They want to meet you."

"You don't want them"—she glances down at what's showing through her damp T-shirt—"to see that?"

"No."

"You're jealous?" She sits up and takes the towel.

"Protective. These guys seem nice—divers and all—but did you see the bathroom? Animals."

"I can clean it up for you."

"Don't go near it. It's toxic. You'll end up back in the hospital."

"I've cleaned up after guys back—" She closes her eyes tight and puts her hand over her mouth to hide her trembling lips.

I sit next to her, wrap my towel around both of us, loop my arms around her shoulders and pull her in tight. "It's okay, babe. You can tell me."

She shivers and puts her head on my shoulder. "I found his T-shirt mixed in with my stuff." Her whisper is so quiet I can barely hear her.

I chafe her shoulders. "That's why you're down here

half-naked?"

"I guess." Her voice quivers. "I dropped it. Couldn't pick it up. Isn't that stupid? It's still on the floor."

I squeeze her. "Not stupid at all. I'll go up and take care of it."

A shudder runs through her body.

"Do you want to meet these guys later?"

"I already met one. Why didn't you tell me there was a guy asleep in the other bedroom?"

"I had no idea. Was he nice?"

"Hardly."

"Must be Seth. I guess he has a right to be grumpy. I heard Ethan and Cooper had to pull him out of some bar late last night. He must've been sleeping it off." I start to get up. "I'll go tell the others you'll meet them later."

She holds me next to her. "Too late. They're here."

I stand up, leave Leesie the towel. "Hey guys—this is Leesie."

She stays sitting in the sand, waves and even manages a smile. "Sorry I can't get up. Both ankles are sprained." She tips her head towards her blue post-op boots cast off beside her.

Brock squats down in front of her. "I'm Brock. These goons are Gabriel, and my Commonwealth brothers, Ethan and Cooper."

Gabriel acknowledges her with a nod and a flashy smile and trudges through the sand toward the condo building, but Ethan and Cooper sit down beside her. I take up a proprietary station behind her, slip a possessive arm around her waist.

She glances from side to side at Ethan and Cooper. "Where are you guys from?"

Cooper, who has bleached blonde hair and a perpetual burn, smiles and says, "Guess."

Leesie squints her eyes. "You don't have an accent."

Ethan tips his head close to hers. "Aye, he does lass. Get him to say 'eh.'"

"Canadian?"

Cooper's face gets a little pinker. "Guilty. And Ethan's a loud mouth Scot."

He leans forward so he can glare at Cooper. "She was supposed to guess."

Brock settles cross-legged in the wet sand in front of her. "That leaves me. I'll give you a hint. I'm not here to get out of the gloom and cold like these other two blokes are."

"Braggart." Ethan flicks sand at him.

I lean forward and whisper in Leesie's ear. "He called me 'mate' like a thousand times today on the boat."

"That could be English? No. Australian."

Brock laughs. "No fair, mate. You gave it away."

"Sorry, dude." My arms tighten around Leesie's waist. "I don't like to see my damsel in distress."

Brock takes the hint. "Well," he stands, "we'll leave you two to it." He drags Ethan and Cooper off their butts. "Let's give the lovers some peace.

"See you upstairs, eh?" Cooper exaggerates his accent.

"Glad to have you aboard." Ethan puts out his hand, and Leesie takes it. "Alex is that pleased to have another lass in the place."

Leesie smiles and let's go of his hand. "Thanks. We'll be up soon."

She watches them out of sight. I watch her. She plays with my fingers clasped around her waist.

I notice she put my ring on her finger. Cool, babe. That's where it belongs. "What do you think?"

"I like the Commonwealth Brothers."

I nod. "Divers."

"What's with Gabriel?"

"He's a Latin playboy who will inherit half the known universe."

"He is gorgeous."

"I heard that." I kiss the soft spot where her neck and

shoulder meet.

She relaxes against me. "They are all a lot nicer than that guy upstairs."

"Seth."

"He's gross."

"All guys are gross after they've drunk themselves numb."

She cranes her neck so she can see my face. "You'll never do that will you?"

"I can only think of one thing that would make me do that." I tip my forehead so it touches her head.

"What?"

"What do you think?" I release her waist and rub her shoulders.

"Me?" She shifts so she lying in my arms across my lap. "In Thailand"—she touches my face and her voice drops low—"when I accused you"—she turns her head and stares at the ocean like she's trying to see me on the other side of the world—"what happened?"

I follow her gaze. "I became a work-a-holic."

"I'm glad you had that job."

"I should have blown it off—come right home and set you straight."

She turns her face back to mine. "I should have believed you. Trusted you."

I should never have stormed off in the first place. But freak, girl, you should have taken my ring. I feel echoes of how angry I was even now.

She kisses my neck. "I'm sorry." She finds my lips. "Things would be so different if I'd believed you."

"What do you mean?" I murmur against her mouth.

"Nothing." Her lips are on mine for a long time. "Why didn't I trust you?"

"I don't know, babe." I scoop her closer so I can kiss her better. "It doesn't matter now."

I'm starving, and I've got all those tanks to fill, but I can't let go of her. I forget about why we're here, her secrets about the accident, needing to take her back to her parents. All that matters are her lips. We make out with the ocean lapping at our feet and the sun setting behind us.

Alex interrupts us. "Sorry." She holds out a paper plate with two sandwiches on it. "I'm not much of a cook."

I grab a sandwich and take a big bite. "Leesie is."

"Bonus." Alex sits down by Leesie. "I knew I liked you."

They start to jabber about clothes and stuff. I slip away, leaving the girls to get to know each other. I've got a date with forty empty scuba tanks and a big fat compressor.

As I walk down to the dock, I'm engulfed by a wave of intense emotion. It takes me a moment to figure out what it is. Freak, I'm happy. It's tinged with ache for Leesie and her grief and pain. But we're together. She's mine.

And nothing can change that.

Ever again.

# Chapter 10

## HOME

### LEESIE HUNT / CHATSPOT LOG / 05/10 10 AM

**Kimbo69 says:** Report. Report. How did the big move in go?

**Leesie327 says:** I'm like Frankenstein living in The Bachelorette Mansion.

**Kimbo69 says:** You mean his monster.

**Leesie327 says:** Everybody's a critic.

**Kimbo69 says:** Your roomies are that hot?

**Leesie327 says:** Alex isn't hot—just like Michael said. But the guys? Droolworthy in the extreme.

**Kimbo69 says:** Stuck up?

**Leesie327 says:** Not really. Gabriel is a bit too good for the rest of the world, but when he walks by with no shirt on you don't care.

**Kimbo69 says:** You're typing way faster than last time we chatted.

**Leesie327 says:** Using two hands. Don't tell my doctor.

**Kimbo69 says:** Is Michael regretting moving you in with all those hunks?

**Leesie327 says:** Did you actually use the world "hunk"? I thought we banned that word when we were Juniors.

**Kimbo69 says:** If you'd give me more details, maybe I'd be more inspired.

**Leesie327 says:** The guys didn't look twice at me. Well, they took in the mess and looked away fast. Michael did seem kind of jealous. It's cute. He got all romantic.

**Kimbo69 says:** Mark would be dragging me out of there by my ponytail.

**Leesie327 says:** Ouch. Don't talk to me about ponytails.

**Kimbo69 says:** Sorry. Lame one. How's your head?

**Leesie327 says:** Itchy. Prickly. I guess that's a good sign. I've got five o'clock shadow all over it.

**Kimbo69 says:** Back to the men folk . . .

**Leesie327 says:** Alex is cool.

**Kimbo69 says:** I don't care about Alex.

**Leesie327 says:** She helped me unpack then we stayed up until two in the morning talking.

**Kimbo69 says:** You haven't described in breathtaking detail the rest of the guys.

**Leesie327 says:** You'll never believe what I found on the bottom of my second suitcase.

**Kimbo69 says:** A digital camera so you can send me pictures?

**Leesie327 says:** Rough drafts of all the poems I wrote last year.

**Kimbo69 says:** I don't get it.

**Leesie327 says:** Michael. He saved them from the wreck. Even scraps. Scribbled envelopes. There's mud smudges and water stains on every page, but it's dry. I think he ironed them. I would have lost it all, but he saved them.

**Kimbo69 says:** I can't believe it.

**Leesie327 says:** I don't deserve him. I should be alone, miserable, locked up somewhere banging my head on a wall, instead I'm with this beautiful boy who kisses me when I cry and saves my life every day.

**Kimbo69 says:** Maybe he finally deserves you.

**Leesie327 says:** I'd be so lost without him.

**Kimbo69 says:** Your computer got smashed?

**Leesie327 says:** Everything I took to school was in the back of the pickup.

**Kimbo69 says:** Even your hideous desktop?

**Leesie327 says:** I don't know. It's all gone.
**Kimbo69 says:** I've got all the poems you sent me. Do you want me to email them?
**Leesie327 says:** No. Maybe later. Keep them, okay? I'm not up to email. I've got three hundred unopened messages. All my mom screaming at me, probably. I don't know who else.
**Kimbo69 says:** Did you leave your chapbook from high school at home?
**Leesie327 says:** Yeah. And the dive log Michael gave me. That's safe.
**Kimbo69 says:** Let me know if you change your mind. You should write. You can't do anything else.
**Leesie327 says:** I can't focus. The pain pills they gave me aren't helping much. Wears me out.
**Kimbo69 says:** What are your plans?
**Leesie327 says:** Plans? That's a good one. Today I'm nibbling on toast and drinking tepid water.
**Kimbo69 says:** And Michael's just sitting there staring at you.
**Leesie327 says:** They are all working. I think I'm going to have the place to myself a lot.
**Kimbo69 says:** Is it going to hurt forever?
**Leesie327 says:** Today's a big improvement. I don't feel like throwing up.
**Kimbo69 says:** Try chicken broth.
**Leesie327 says:** There was a chicken wandering down the beach this morning. Maybe I can get the boys to catch it, and I can cook it up for broth.
**Kimbo69 says:** Where the heck are you, girl? Is there even a civilized grocery store? Get that man of yours to buy you some of those little packets of dried up noodle soup. I live on those.
**Leesie327 says:** As soon as I can, I'm going to turn this place upside down.
**Kimbo69 says:** What does that mean?
**Leesie327 says:** It's a pig sty. Filthy. Bare cupboard. Beer and ketchup in the fridge. I need to get HAZ-MAT gear to attack the

guys' bathroom.

**Kimbo69 says:** Don't hurt yourself.

**Leesie327 says:** Too late. Already did that.

**Kimbo69 says:** I got to go, but I need to tell you something... don't know if I should.

**Leesie327 says:** What? You have to tell me now.

**Kimbo69 says:** Have you seen your wall?

**Leesie327 says:** No. I just come straight to chat.

**Kimbo69 says:** Go look at it. People love you, Leesie. A lot of them.

## LEESIE'S MOST PRIVATE CHAPBOOK
## POEM #82, THE WALL

My mouse drifts as far away
from the link to my wall as it can linger.
I thought I was safe here in chat
with online status eternally turned off.
Only Kim can find me.
The wall? Nothing much is ever on it.
It's not like I'm a ChatSpot queen
with thousands of friends.
What did Kim do? She promised.
I'll click her off, too. And that
will be that. ChatSpot?
Who needs it?
Friends? I've even got a new
one of those. Rare thing for me.

*Look at it.*
*Look at it.*
*Look at it.*
No. No. No.

I move the mouse to click
the site closed. My finger
hovers over the mouse pad—
draws a line to the wall
and taps.

The page blooms before my eyes.
Tiny square pictures—roomies
and friends, a girl from my English class,
even kids from home who hated me
and liked Phil—
all saying one thing:

"Leesie, we love you.
Come home."

There's even one from Phil's
glittering Krystal, "Leesie,
I love you. Come home.
We don't blame you."

Tawni says she wants to room
with me next year. Dayla
sends hugs from her and Noah.
Roxi, Cadence and Lily
join the refrain,
"Leesie, we love you.
Come home."

Hardest to read
is from Stephie.
I vaguely remember her
friending me last month
thinking, wow, she's growing up.
On ChatSpot already?

What happened to Barbies?
"Leesie, I love you.
Come home."

Nothing from Kim.
She kept her promise.

Nine pages down
I discover the culprit.
In a few quiet words,
Jaron spills all my secrets
to the world—the accident,
Phil's death, my injuries,
and flight. He asks
them to pray. He asks
them to understand
my grief, my pain, my guilt.
He closes with,
"Leesie, I love you.
Come home."

Never. Never. Never.
You spoiled, self-righteous jerk.
This wasn't your right. I rage
at the screen. This isn't your
story to uncover. Don't flay
me with kindness,
unending understanding.
You aren't my keeper.
Don't you dare remind God
I exist. How can you be so cruel
to break my heart with all
this lost, lost, love?

Come home?

How can I ever?
I killed my brother.
His blood drips in my dreams
My hands are crimson—
never to be white.
You can't love me.
You can't forgive me.
No one can.
No one will.
No one should.

I slam down the screen,
need to get far, far away,
hobble along down to the boat dock.
A white boat crashes through
the foaming break in the reef
into the aquamarine
jeweled water of the safe inlet.
Yes. It's his. That's him
waving, smiling, flexing
his bare pects at me
that sheen with sweat
when he finally hugs me hello
after hefting hundreds of pounds
of gear and tanks out of the boat
and onto the dock.

"I love you," he whispers
and kisses my cheekbone.
"You wanna go home?"

I tense, clench my teeth
and then realize he's talking
about the apartment.
Our home.

My home with my Michael
where I can hide, pressing my face
into his naked chest,
avoiding the questions in his eyes,
barricaded by his strong arms
forever.

## MICHAEL'S DIVE LOG – VOLUME #10

**Dive Buddy:** Leesie
**Date:** 05/10
**Dive #:** 2nd day in the apartment
**Location:** Grand Cayman
**Dive Site:** blow holes
**Weather Condition:** sunshine
**Water Condition:** wild
**Depth:** don't know we're on the shore
**Visibility:** to the horizon
**Water Temp:** feels cold when it sprays us
**Bottom Time:** all afternoon
**Comments:**

After our dive Sunday morning, I'm the last one up to the apartment. Even Leesie goes ahead when I get stuck filling some Nitrox orders. When I get there, it's a pretty cozy scene. Leesie made mac and cheese for everybody.

The guys—even snooty Gabriel—are wolfing it back.

"How did you make this?" Alex scoops up a giant spoonful of golden yellow macaroni. "We were out of milk." She shoves the spoon in her mouth and closes her eyes like the stuff is ambrosia.

Leesie scoops more mac and cheese out of the pot in a new bowl. "I found some margarine behind that giant bottle of ketchup. I used that. My grandma always made it with butter. That's even better."

Cooper's face lights up. "Ketchup. That's just what it

needs."

Alex laughs. "Now you know who owns the ketchup."

"Did you jackals save any for the guy doing all your work?"

Leesie hands me the steaming bowl she just dished. "Of course."

"Thanks, babe." All the chairs are full, so I boost myself onto the counter closest to Leesie. "What did you do with yourself this morning?"

She holds up pruned fingers. Her cast is soggy around the edges. "The dishes."

I swallow my first mouthful of buttery mac. "That took all morning?"

She looks around at the gleaming kitchen. "Did you see the place when you left?"

I take another bite, so I don't have to answer.

"I need to get some rubber gloves." She shakes water out of her cast. "Especially," she talks loud enough for all the guys to hear, "before I tackle that bathroom. What did you guys do in there?"

Ethan points to Brock across the table. "He's got lousy aim."

"No way, brother. That's you."

Cooper raises his hand. "I plead the fifth."

Seth looks up from his bowl. "You're not an American. You can't plead the fifth." I was on the boat with Seth today. He's all right. Not fun like the Commonwealth trio, but he knows his stuff.

Gabriel looks down his long, straight nose, his nostrils flair. "Disgusting." He flashes his playboy pearly whites at Leesie. "You should not go near that room. I don't."

"That's right, eh." Cooper squirts more ketchup in his bowl. "He showers in the buff down on the dock."

Leesie dishes herself a small bowl of mac and hobbles over to the table.

Alex scoots over so she can share her chair. "Don't clean it for them." She sticks her tongue out at all her male roomies. "They don't deserve it."

Leesie perches on the edge of Alex's chair. "But it reeks." She sets her bowl down.

"Keep the door closed." Alex scrapes the last of the cheese sauce from her bowl.

Brock pushes himself back from the table. "No way we'd suffocate."

"Here's the deal." Leesie puts down her spoon and glances around the table, gathering all their attention. "I'll clean it if you'll close the door when you're using it."

Ethan laughs and looks toward me. "Ye've seen a wee more manliness than you're used to, have you?"

"Just close the damn door, okay?" I slide off the counter and cross to the table. "She doesn't want to hear you guys on the john."

Ethan backs off, still laughing.

Leesie catches my eye. Calm down. It's cool.

Yeah, right, babe.

She gets up to clear the dirty bowls. Cooper and Brock rush to help. She flashes her full on smile that makes her beautiful. My smile—that I haven't seen for weeks. At them. "So the big question is—what's for dinner?"

Brock takes a dirty bowl from her. "We usually go out."

Alex stares into her empty bowl. "But there's no place close." She picks the bowl up and licks it clean.

"I can cook if there's food." Leesie gazes out the window to the water that most of us will be diving in again soon. "It gives me something to do until I get this crap off me." She stares down at her blue cast boots.

Alex hugs her. She's big on hugs. "Bonus. I've got the afternoon off. Let's drive down to Georgetown and get groceries."

"It's Sunday." She actually says it. Good sign.

Alex shrugs. "The big stores are open at least until 4:00."

Leesie stares right at me. "Okay."

"I don't think so." I glare back at her, and she gets the message. No tea. No shopping on Sunday. I'm not that dumb, babe. "Better wait until tomorrow. The doctors said to take it easy."

She can't argue that in front of everybody. I don't give her a chance. "Alex, I'll take your afternoon dives tomorrow, so you can go together."

Alex gives me two thumbs up. "Deal."

Leesie won't talk to me. I don't care if she's mad.

Everybody clears out. Alex walks down to the corner store with a shopping list for tonight.

I don't have to dive. Sunday's are slower. Tomorrow I'm scheduled for morning and night. Now I've got afternoon dives, too. Better go nitrox all day. Wouldn't want to end up bent when I'm starting a new job.

I sit down on my cot and pick up the laptop. It's warm from being left on all day. "This is nice. Just us."

Leesie's sulking over by the sink. "Can you help with the dishes?"

"Just a second." I need to check my email. I might have a note from Stan. He promised to let me know if the police are going to lay charges. I flip open the top. The screen dilates onto a ChatSpot wall.

Leesie's.

And a post from Jaron is front and center. I should have thought of that. Told her friends about the accident. I glance up at Leesie. She would have killed me. I read the post again.

*Come home. I love you.*

The guy's got some nerve posting *that*. I scroll up through all the posts on her wall. They all say it. Every post makes me feel worse and worse for taking her away. I didn't steal her. I'm not the bad guy. My fingers are on the keys typing.

Leesie bangs a pot down on the counter. "Are you going to help or what?"

I nix the post, nix the site, jump to clear the rest of the table. "I'll wash."

"You bet you will."

I take the dish cloth from her and reach into the hot sudsy water, pick up a bowl, scrub it and scrub it until she takes the bowl from me. She knows something's up. I don't look at her, keep my eyes on the sink.

She saw that wall. She read those posts. Especially the one from Jaron. Does she regret choosing me? Look where we've ended up. In this hole with a bunch of jerks with bad aim. I can't believe she opened up ChatSpot. I guess she has to when she talks to Kim. I should ask her. Maybe she wants to go home. I saw your wall, babe. Do you want to talk about it? That's it. All I have to say. I saw your wall. I don't want to push her. Upset her again.

Right. Truth is I don't want to take her home. I don't want to lose standing beside her scrubbing dirty bowls. I hand her another overly clean one. "We've got all afternoon. Do you want to do something."

She shifts from one sprained ankle to the other. "I'm kind of tired."

I scrub yellow gunk off a hand full of spoons and think. "How about a drive down to the blow holes?"

"Where you wouldn't stop yesterday?"

"We can sit in the sun and watch the waves crash into them." I hand her the last bowl to dry.

She polishes it up. "Sounds pretty lazy."

"Yeah." I lean against the counter. "I could use a break, too. And we need to get out of here."

Her eyes drift to the bedroom. "Not really."

"Are you kidding?" I throw the dishcloth in the sink. "This place does reek."

She snaps the dish towel in my face. "Good thing I'm an expert at cleaning up after pigs." And she gives me that smile that made me fall in love with her.

I grab the end of the dish towel, pull her close, kiss her, and then hustle her right out of that apartment, so we don't end up where we shouldn't.

# Chapter 11

## UNLEASHED

### MICHAEL'S DIVE LOG – VOLUME #10

**Dive Buddy:** Leesie
**Date:** 05/13
**Dive #:** lost track of how many times we've been here
**Location:** Grand Cayman
**Dive Site:** Rehab Center
**Weather Condition:** nice breeze
**Water Condition:** only one tear
**Depth:** up to my ears
**Visibility:** gorgeous
**Water Temp:** steamy
**Bottom Time:** 20 minutes
**Comments:**

Leesie waits in the garden when I arrive to pick her up at the rehab place after her appointment. I don't know what else they did. Physical therapy exercises? I hope she isn't too tired. I want to take her out to dinner, but she hasn't been able to eat much. I think it's the drugs. Her old ones wearing off or the new ones making her sick.

I spy her yellow dress with the turquoise striped top from

the distance. She's sitting on our bench fiddling with her yellow hat. The first thing I notice is legs. Long, bare ones. "Hey, babe. How'd it go?"

She looks up—jams the hat on her head. I stop and stare. Walk closer. Stare more. They took the metal splint off her face. She's got make-up on and flashes me that smile again. Hair or no, she's beautiful.

"What do you think?" She touches her nose.

I sit down on the bench beside her, cup her face between my hands, kiss her unveiled nose, her cheeks, her eyes. I draw back so I can see her face up close, and my eyes fill up.

Leesie wipes away a tear that escapes out of the corner of my left eye. "What's the matter? Do I look that bad?"

I swallow hard. "It's good to have you back."

Our lips find each other. It's a massive relief to kiss her without that thing on her nose, to rub my nose against hers, to explore every inch of her face with my lips. Her hat comes off while we're making out, and my hand moves instinctively to stroke her head. I haven't touched it since the hair started coming in more. I'm surprised at how soft it is. Like fur. It looks so prickly. My mouth moves there, too.

I rest my cheek on the top of her head and wrap my arms around her. We embrace, zoning into each other while a gentle evening breeze wafts warm sea air perfumed by the gardenia bush a few yards away.

"Look what else!" Leesie whispers into my neck and holds her legs out straight—pointing the toes on her bare feet.

"I noticed that first, babe."

She pivots on the bench and puts her feet in my lap. I pick up the left foot, kiss it, pick up the right, kiss that, too. I kiss her shins and her knees. Her dress is pushed up exposing her thighs.

I pull her skirt down over them and kiss her lips one last time. "We gotta go."

"Can you carry me? I forgot my shoes."

"Nope. If I carry you, I can't be responsible for what

happens when we get back to the car."

"Carry me."

"Watch your step."

## LEESIE HUNT / CHATSPOT LOG / 05/14 2:43 PM

**Leesie327 says:** Guess what? My ankles are better!! I can walk again.

**Kimbo69 says:** Did you go dancing to celebrate?

**Leesie327 says:** Me in a club? That's a joke.

**Kimbo69 says:** Buy something slinky and make Michael take you.

**Leesie327 says:** Michael in a club? That's unthinkable.

**Kimbo69 says:** There's got to be some hot spots wherever you are.

**Leesie327 says:** We're in Grand Cayman.

**Kimbo69 says:** Whoa, that's progress.

**Leesie327 says:** Don't tell anybody.

**Kimbo69 says:** Of course not. Should have a few clubs there.

**Leesie327 says:** Gabriel would know. Don't you have to be twenty-one?

**Kimbo69 says:** Depends on the club. And the country. It was so easy in Mexico. Who you're with counts, too. And the guy checking IDs. Go with Gabriel. He'll get you in.

**Leesie327 says:** Me and Gabriel? I don't think so.

**Kimbo69 says:** You and Michael and Gabriel. Take the whole gang.

**Leesie327 says:** How do you get in? You guys even went in high school.

**Kimbo69 says:** Fake ID. And I don't wear a bra. Low-cut clingy top. Works every time.

**Leesie327 says:** Michael would hate me dressing like that.

**Kimbo69 says:** It turns Mark on.

**Leesie327 says:** And everyone else who looks at you.

**Kimbo69 says:** Who cares about that?

**Leesie327 says:** Michael.

**Kimbo69 says:** Didn't he buy you a bikini?

**Leesie327 says:** And a giant T-shirt to go over it.

**Kimbo69 says:** There's nothing wrong with showing some skin. He's too possessive.

**Leesie327 says:** I'm pretty possessive, too. Alex hugged him last night, and I wanted to slug her.

**Kimbo69 says:** Why did she hug him?

**Leesie327 says:** She hugs everybody—all the time. Uber friendly. Uber nice. I like her a lot. We're going to go buy clothes on Saturday. Michael has to work, but he said I can buy anything I want.

**Kimbo69 says:** Get some really sexy stuff. You're grown up now.

**Leesie327 says:** I'd look ridiculous. I'm sporting a short, short crew cut these days. I've still got a cast on my hand and have to wear this stupid sling on my right arm because of my collarbone.

**Kimbo69 says:** How much longer?

**Leesie327 says:** Three, maybe four weeks. My hand is doing well. The doc said I can use my right hand and arm a little bit if I'm careful.

**Kimbo69 says:** That's progress, right?

**Leesie327 says:** I'm hungry today, too. I got up early and made everybody French toast with extra cinnamon like Michael's gram makes it. I ate two whole pieces.

**Kimbo69 says:** Congratulations.

**Leesie327 says:** The pain seems to be less intense. My pills are strong enough now.

**Kimbo69 says:** The transition has been rough?

**Leesie327 says:** Kind of unbearable.

**Kimbo69 says:** You kept mum about it?

**Leesie327 says:** Michael would have taken me back to the rehab place.

**Kimbo69 says:** But now you're okay?

**Leesie327 says:** Turned a corner. Another week and I can start tapering off these drugs.

**Kimbo69 says:** Be careful with that stuff. My mom's best friend is stuck on them. It's not pretty.

**Leesie327 says:** I hate them. I'm pitching the whole bottle as soon as I can.

**Kimbo69 says:** Good plan. So you're shopping. What else are you doing for fun this weekend?

**Leesie327 says:** Sleep. Eat. Michael has to work. He's off Monday afternoon, though. He promised to take me out in the sea kayak. We want to buy a nice double one to take out free diving when I'm better. We're using the resort's ugly plastic one, but it'll still be fun.

**Kimbo69 says:** You're going to go free diving?

**Leesie327 says:** No. Just paddling in the lagoon here.

**Kimbo69 says:** That sounds romantic—until you capsize.

**Leesie327 says:** Are you kidding? That'll be the best part.

**Kimbo69 says:** Won't it mess up your ouchies?

**Leesie327 says:** I'll tape my cast into a grocery bag. My clavicle bones are stuck back together now. It's just weak. It might jar it.

**Kimbo69 says:** That would hurt, right?

**Leesie327 says:** Maybe.

**Kimbo69 says:** And it'd wreck that thing on you're face.

**Leesie327 says:** That's gone.

**Kimbo69 says:** I think I'd still stay on dry ground.

**Leesie327 says:** You're missing the whole point. He'll have to rescue me.

**Kimbo69 says:** You're going to wear that bikini?

**Leesie327 says:** Nothing but.

**Kimbo69 says:** You're torturing him—you know that?

**Leesie327 says:** He won't do what I want. I'm helping him change his mind.

**Kimbo69 says:** Wake up, Leesie. I know I'm probably not the best one to go and get all preachy on you, but he IS doing what you always wanted.

**Leesie327 says:** That girl is gone forever.

**Kimbo69 says:** You need to find her.
**Leesie327 says:** Why?
**Kimbo69 says:** Because that's the girl he loves.

# Chapter 12

## RIGHT

### LEESIE'S MOST PRIVATE CHAPBOOK
### POEM #83, FUN

Saturday I'm strong enough to don
oversized rubber gloves, fill
a bucket with bleach, dish soap,
and the hottest water, open
the window, flick on the fan
and scrub down every inch
of the guys' nasty bathroom.
I change the water twice,
bleach all the towels
and throw out the rug.
I wipe down mine
and Alex's while I'm at it.

"Now keep it clean!"
I scowl and try to look stern
while I serve the guys
grilled cheeses between dives.

Cooper eats four.
Brock and Ethan two.
Michael one.
Seth says, "Thank you,"
after his third.
Gabriel doesn't show.
"Should I make one for him?"
I sit down with the sandwich
I'm splitting with Alex.
"I don't think we'll see him
much the rest of the weekend."
Cooper tips back in his chair, points
out the sliding glass balcony door.
"Hot babe on our boat today."

I lean around Michael to see
Gabriel sporting Speedo trunks
lingering with a bikini body
wrapped in thick golden hair.
I hold my hand down so
it can't rise to
my shorn head.

"Why do they always go for him?"
Cooper pulls a sad face.
"When they could have"—
he rises, pulls off his shirt—
"all of this?" He turns slowly
so Alex and I can assess.
Alex gives him two thumbs up.
"They must all be blind,
right Leesie?"
I nod. "Especially when you're
sunburnt like that."
He grins, flexes. "So I should

go down there and get in his way?"
Alex and I pull faces at each other.
"Ummm . . . ."
"Traitors."
Michael gets up from the table.
"We gotta go."
He's kind of abrupt, kind of mad,
doesn't kiss me before they leave.

Driving into Georgetown,
Alex and I crack up over
Cooper. "He's always like that.
Sweet. Funny."
"So Gabriel isn't dating
the Governor's daughter
or a supermodel?"
Alex shakes her head, but flashes
me a wicked grin. "He could
date anybody. He's awesome
in bed."

I try not to choke on the sip
of water I just took. Swallow.
Steady my voice.
"You slept with him?"
She nods, bragging. "Oh, yeah."
My eyebrows shoot then "I thought—?"
She shrugs. "Kai and I moved down here
together. Three years I gave that dude.
And that skank Dani steals him. Seth
figured it out first, told me.
Before we could confront them, they
were gone. Our Commonwealth
brothers took Seth into Georgetown
to get him plastered.

That left Gabriel to look after me."
She wriggles, remembering.
"I was crying on his chest,
and then we were kissing, and then
we were in bed. He's one I won't forget."

"Did it make you feel better?"
I blurt it like a fool.
"He got me through the night."
"Are you going out?" I touch her arm.
"Am I in the way?"
She laughs. "One nighter. I'm not
his type." She says it likes she wants
to be. His type.
"What is his type?"
She rolls jealous eyes
in my direction. "Waitresses.
Well-endowed."
"Isn't it awkward now?"
Her face grows puzzled.
"I'm too busy being livid
at Kai to worry about Gabriel."
"Would you do it again?"
I can't believe I asked that,
but I need to know the rules.

"Maybe. It was good.
But in the morning I felt
as bad as Kai and Dani—
the creeps." She punches
the accelerator and shakes
her head. "Yeah. I would do
it again. I'm not going to let
Kai wreck my fun."
Fun? Not love?

Not commitment?
Fun. She pulls in the parking
lot and turns off the car.
"Hey, girl. Let's shop."
Fun.

I buy a white island scarf
with fringe and beads to wrap
my poor head in. It drips
down my back like cloth hair.
Next we find sandals that jingle
with gold charms, a white on white
floral print sundress, spaghetti straps,
and a low, bare back, a padded
underwire bra that gives me
a fake cleavage, low cut clingy T-s,
shortest shorts, and silky thongs that feel
devilish between my fingertips,
another bikini, a gauzy wrap,
and three more hats.

Alex's phone rings. "Dinner?
Tonight? You in?"
I nod, glance down at my bags.
"Sounds like fun."

## MICHAEL'S DIVE LOG – VOLUME #10

**Dive Buddy:** the whole crew plus 2
**Date:** 05/16
**Dive #:** haven't been here for a long time
**Location:** Grand Cayman
**Dive Site:** Rum Point
**Weather Condition:** night
**Water Condition:** placid

**Depth:** 40' when Isadore hits
**Visibility:** dark
**Water Temp:** cold
**Bottom Time:** all night
**Comments:**

Alex and Leesie meet us for dinner at Rum Point. Funky place on the north side with painted signs pointing to Liverpool, Russia, India. Good beach. Restaurant on the sand. Only gets crowded if there's a cruise ship in port. Today's Saturday. We're safe from the masses.

I nod hello to Alex and then get a load of Leesie getting out of the car. She's got a white scarf wrapped on her head like a halo. She's wearing a new white dress that shows her shoulders and back—too much in the front despite her sling. After two weeks here, she's getting tan.

"You like it?" She spins around when she sees me. The full skirt flairs and falls back against her bare legs.

Brock and Ethan come up behind me. "Nice."

Leesie gets pink, and I put my arm around her exposed shoulders and guide her to the big round table where Gabriel and his pickup hangs with Cooper and the chick's friend. I wanted Leesie to be too tired when they called to set this up. No luck.

"This is a first," she says so only I can hear.

"What?"

"I don't think we've ever gone to a real restaurant to-gether."

I pull out her chair and whisper as she sits. "Only your stupid Cougar Eat."

"That doesn't count."

Ethan takes the chair next to her. "What doesn't count."

She gets even pinker. "Nothing."

I squish into the seat next to Leesie. We've got eight around a table for six. Kind of close quarters. Nobody seems to care.

Alex slips into a chair in between Gabriel and Ethan. "Where's Seth?"

Ethan shakes his head. "Couldn't get him to come."

Brock grabs a chair from the table behind us and shoves it in between me and Cooper. That makes us nine. Brock runs his hands through his hair. "He'll be hitting the bars again."

Alex leans forward with her elbows on the table. "And you let him?"

"We can't hold his hand forever."

Gabriel clears his throat and introduces the women but their names go in one ear and out the other. Blonde One and Blonde Two. Both made-up and slinky. Gabriel's is hotter, but Cooper's is hungry.

While I study the menu, Leesie swallows a couple of pills with the ice water the waiter brought before we arrived.

Blonde Two's been staring at Leesie. "What happened to you?"

Blonde One tears her eyes off Gabriel long enough to give us a glance. She assesses me like a piece of meat and then rests her critical gaze on Leesie.

Alex leans around Gabriel, and spits, "Car accident," into the chick's face.

Blonde One backs off. "Too bad." The blondes go back to seducing Cooper and Gabriel.

Alex sticks her tongue out behind her hand.

Silent sparks fly back and forth between her and Leesie. Raised eyebrows. Squints. Stares. Maybe they didn't know these chicks would be here.

I hide in the menu. I haven't eaten here for awhile. I turn to Brock. "What's good these days?"

Brock peals his eyes off the two chicks with his room-mates. "I like the crab."

Crab. No way can I order crab. It's been a year and half since that crabfest on Dive Festiva, but eating it would seem like sacrilege.

"Crab?" Blonde Two pipes up. "Sounds good."

Most of them order it. I order shrimp. Safer. I'd hate to

freak here. Leesie gets a salad. She doesn't say much while we eat. Her eyes keep going to Gabriel and Cooper and those chicks who are falling out of their dresses and giggling at everything Cooper says. Gabriel wears his superior smile. They all crack crab and dip it in butter. Blonde Two feeds Cooper with buttery fingers. He sucks on them staring down her dress.

Leesie's eyes dart to Alex when Blonde One leans over and plants her buttery lips smack on Gabriel's mouth, then excuses herself. Gabriel gets up and follows her down the beach.

I need to bail. All these crab legs are freaking me. I don't want Leesie around this crap. "Let's go. You're tired."

She yawns and nods. "Thanks, Alex." She touches her head wrap. "It was fun."

Alex gives her a thumbs up. "Any time."

"Sorry about tonight." Leesie glances down the beach.

Alex shrugs. "There will be other nights."

Leesie leans hard against me on the way to the RAV4.

I shift my arm to support her better. "Too much. Too soon."

She doesn't agree, but lets me lift her into the passenger's seat. When I get in the other side, she holds out her arms and says, "Do you like me like this?"

I turn the key. "You look like an angel."

She pulls a face. "Guess I shouldn't have bought white."

It's an hour drive back to the apartment. She's sound asleep by the time we get there. I carry her upstairs, lay her on her bed, slip off her sandals and scarf, stroke her soft furry head, tuck her in—dress and all. And she's still sound asleep.

I tiptoe out of her room, shut the door, throw myself down on my cot, wondering how I can get the thought of Leesie in bed alone in the next room out of my head. Isadore pounces. Knew I could count on her.

Crab legs. Giant ones. Walk through her waves. Grasp me with their claws. Pull me off the deck of the boat and down into the water. I fight, choke, sink, surface, kick, thrash, call out to my mother, "Save me. Save me," until a small, pale hand shakes my shoulder. "Mom?"

"Michael?"

It's Leesie, glowing white kneeling on the floor beside my cot like I dreamed her every night back in Tekoa when I fought Isadore nightmares in my dad's old room under that quilt Gram made out of his teenage jeans. I groan and lift Leesie into bed with me, clutch tight to her reality.

"It's okay. I'm here." She kisses away my terror, presses her body to mine.

I kiss her back in a crazy panic. Instinct takes over. I shift to get her body under me. The flimsy cot we're lying on collapses.

She's on her feet, pulling me out of the wreckage. "Let's go to my room," she whispers. "Alex is cool. I'll put a note on the door."

I stumble after her.

In her room, she turns her back to me. "Can you help?" She can't reach the zipper that holds the flowing white fabric around her slender shape.

I press my face into her neck, fumble to find the zipper, grasp it, pull it down—stop. "No, Leese." I step back. "No."

I get out of her room. The apartment. Try to sleep in the back seat of the RAV. Beat myself up for getting so close. Freak. That can't happen again. Freak. Freak. Freak.

I should go back up there.

Tell her to her face.

I get out of the RAV.

Stop.

I know exactly why I want to go back up there, and it's not to tell her, "No."

I stare at myself in the black reflection of the RAV's window. Alex's car pulls into the parking lot. She gets out and opens the passenger door. Seth falls out on her. No sign of the other guys.

I sprint across the lot. "Can I help?" I lift Seth off her.

"Thanks." Alex ducks under Seth's left arm.

I take the right side and get my arm around his back so I can half carry, half drag him up the stairs. "What happened to Brock and Ethan?"

"The bar we found Seth in was having a whisky shot contest. Did you know Scots invented whisky?"

"Nope."

"Ethan couldn't resist the challenge. Brock will get him home."

We make it up all three flights—freak Alex is strong—and dump Seth in his room on his bed. I trip over Gabriel's cot trying to get out of there. He sleeps in there with Seth. Cooper, Brock, and Ethan sleep out in the front room with me.

"Thanks," Alex grabs my arm and guides me out of the messy room. She closes the door. "You're a lifesaver." She glances at the closed door of her and Leesie's room. "You know, if you and Leesie want the room, I don't mind roughing it with the Neanderthals."

I hold up my hands and shake my head. "No. We wouldn't dream of kicking you out."

"I thought you'd be in there tonight for sure. I told Leesie you guys could have it."

"Don't do that again."

"What's with you two? You're engaged aren't you?"

"Long story."

She flicks on the kitchen light. "I'm not tired."

We sit up at the table drinking milk and eating Leesie's homemade chocolate chip cookies. I tell Alex about my parents, how me and Leese met, the whole Mormon thing, Suki, the accident, Phil. It feels good to spill my guts to her. She's freaking easy to talk to.

Her eyes move from her glass of milk to me to Leesie's closed door. "So you guys have never—?"

"Not until we're married."

Her eyebrows lift. "And you're going to convert to Mormonism?"

"No." Freak. I hadn't thought of that.

"She'll marry you now without that?"

"Yeah. I don't know. Everything's messed up since the accident."

She studies me hard—like she's trying to see the gears churning in my thick head. "It's not fair to her if you don't."

"What's that supposed to mean?"

"You said she wouldn't marry you before because you aren't a Mormon. If you marry her now, you're taking advantage of her tragedy. That's so wrong."

"Who are you to judge me?"

"Nobody."

"Do you know what I've done for her? How hard all this is? She won't even tell me about the accident."

"It doesn't look easy for her, either."

Alex doesn't say it, but I can tell exactly what she's thinking. "I should take her home?"

She studies the cookie crumbs on the table, mashes them with her thumb and licks it. "Probably."

I shake my head. "She'd hate me forever."

"If it's right—"

I bow my head until it rests on the table. "I don't know what's right anymore."

Alex puts her hand on my shoulder. "I think you do."

She slips behind the door where Leesie's probably seething mad at me, and I bend back the legs of my stupid cot until it supports me again. I fix the blankets, lie on it—waiting for the crash—pretend I'm asleep when Brock and Ethan stumble in laughing and cursing and peeing all over Leesie's clean bathroom. I want to jump up and start swinging, smashing, bashing their heads together. Instead, I roll over and the freaking cot collapses again.

Brock and Ethan stand there joking while I throw the useless piece of crap off the balcony. I grab a pillow and a sheet and

fling myself on the lounge chair outside. My mind races round
and round.

How could I be so stupid?

How could I think this would work?

This crap apartment.

Cayman.

Running away.

Me and Leesie.

Getting married.

We're nineteen. Legal, but—come on. Get real.

And the Mormon thing.

Stupid Alex.

She is so damn right.

# Chapter 13

## PHANTOM

### LEESIE'S MOST PRIVATE CHAPBOOK
### POEM #84, NOTHING

Michael's quiet, distant—cold?
Working too much.
No time off Monday.
No kayak ride.
No mishap.
No rescue.
He's out late filling bottles,
mixing Nitrox, fixing o-rings.
Misses dinner. Gone early.
I make French toast
adding more and more cinnamon.

He hasn't touched me since
his nightmare, since
he dragged me into his cot, since
I almost won, but lost—lost
too much to try again.
He looks guilty. I feel evil.

I hide that white dress,
the bikini, and the push-up bra—
wear my old T-shirts and ugly capris.
Find his baseball cap and keep
it on my head so he can see I'm his
from this distant strain I can't surmount.

I bake him cookies he doesn't eat,
an apple pie that Cooper smacks his lips
over and says, "Just like my mum's."
The slice I guard for Michael
sits in the fridge day after day,
untouched.

A week. Ten days. Limbo.
Alex drives me to my rehab date,
tells me he told her about us—
He spilled our secrets out
in the middle of the night
all over this stranger?
Good thing I never told her
about the night in that pickup cab
when I screamed at Phil before
I killed him. She wouldn't be
sitting beside me, with sympathy
plastered on her face.
"He's trying to decide." Her eyes
whip to my stunned face and back to the road.
"What do you mean?"
"You need to go home."
"That's none of your business."

Next day, I wash his blanket
and sheet, make up his new cot

all nice for him.
I wash all the clothes jumbled
in the duffel bag he never unpacked.
I fold and put it away in empty
drawers, clean out the bottom of the
bag.

My fingers slip on silk.
I draw out a black bundle.
A turquoise necklace of shell
and beads clatters to the floor.
I jump away quick like it's a snake,
but still its fangs sink deep.

With my broken left hand,
careful not to snag the slick fabric
on the jagged edges of my cast,
I shake out the silk.
A long black skirt,
sexy and Asian, hangs
from my fingertips.

I see it on her—Sukanda
the Seductress—her taking
it off, leaving it on his cabin's
floor to mingle with his
shed shorts.

I search the bag—find sheer
scarves, another skirt.

Suki and Michael?
Suki and Michael?
Pictures don't lie.
They don't lie.

Does he?

An enormous fear rises
from the fabric clutched
in my hands.
Dear Lord, Phil?
You died for this?

*The guy screwed half of Asia by now*
*and you want him back?*
*Open your flipping eyes!*
Echoes fly at me from every direction.
*Open your eyes, open your eyes,*
*your eyes, your eyes, eyes!*
I hurl the fabric at the wall.

Michael's keys shine on the dresser.
I grab them and run.
I pull out into honking cars
and the right lane—wrong.
I swerve hard over to the left
where I should have been
in this upside down world,
floor it up the highway—
away,
away,
just take me away before
echoes catch up to me
and force me to ask,
If all I am is Michael,
what am I now?

Nothing.
Nothing.
Nothing.

A bottle of my pain pills
rolls out from under
the passenger's seat.

Nothing.
Nothing.
Nothing.

## MICHAEL'S DIVE LOG – VOLUME #10

**Dive Buddy:** solo
**Date:** 05/28
**Dive #:** doesn't matter
**Location:** Grand Cayman
**Dive Site:** the whole freaking island
**Weather Condition:** too hot
**Water Condition:** feels like a whirlpool sucking me under
**Depth:** never been this deep
**Visibility:** dark
**Water Temp:** cold
**Bottom Time:** too long
**Comments:**
    I avoid the apartment. Avoid Alex. Avoid Leesie. Avoid
everything. There's enough work to hide in—to bury my resolve
to take her home, my doubts, my desire. The passion that flares
every time I look at her.
    I can tell she thinks I'm punishing her, but it's me that
needs punishment. Every day that passes makes the new dawn
harder to face.
    "We can't get married." I try to imagine myself tell her that.
"I'm not a Mormon. Marry Jaron. He loves you—even thinking
you're sleeping with me, he loves you." But I can't say it.
    "I'm taking you home."
    I can't say that, either.

I dial her dad—hang up when it rings. Six days in a row. On the seventh day, I give up.

I will marry her.

I won't take her home.

I don't even care if she tells me about the accident. Keep it a secret forever, babe. Just be mine.

I'll quit this job, and we'll get out of this stupid apartment—away from Alex and that look she gives me like I'm the world's worst criminal.

She's looking at me like that right now from across the boat. I hustle when we dock, get up to the apartment before everybody. "Babe!" No answer. "Leesie—let's get out of here. We need to talk."

A sheen of black silk bathed in sunlight catches my eye. The skirts I bought Leesie. The pretty scarves. A shell necklace I thought would look cool with her fringed up leather jacket are crumpled on the floor.

I stare at the mess—confused. "Leese?"

No answer.

I look for my keys. They're gone.

Freak. What would this look like to her?

I scoop the gifts into my arms, grab Alex's car keys and head out.

"Where are you going?" Alex blocks my way halfway down the stairs.

"She's gone. I'm taking your car." I push past Alex's stunned face, get in her car, dump my burden on the car seat, and squeal out of the parking lot.

Airport.

Nope.

Our first hotel.

The rehab place.

The beach where she first floated on seawater.

Nope, nope, nope.

She could be anywhere.

I keep pushing west, and north, driving all around the island. Check beaches. Keep driving, driving.

Freak. Why don't we have stupid cell phones that work here? After I find her, we'll get phones. Tonight. No. Better yet, when I find her, I won't ever let her out of my sight again.

When I find her? How am I supposed to do that? Go back to the apartment and wait? No. Not yet. I can't sit and wait. Push on.

It's dark when I get up north to Rum Point where we had dinner with the guys and those sleazy chicks. The place is empty. Cruise ship sheep gone home for the night.

Except there's a girl at a table, slumped over—wearing my old black baseball hat with "Eagle Ray Dive Club" embroidered across the front.

"Leesie," I yell and run over to her. "Thank, God."

I sit down next to her. She doesn't move. There's a pill bottle clasped in her fingers. "Babe." I shake her, pry the bottle from her hand. "Wake up."

Freak.

The bottle is empty.

"Leese, babe, did you take these?"

One eye opens. She sees me. Turns her face the other direction.

"How long ago? You need to vomit. I'm calling Sugar." I grab her arm.

She jerks away like my touch is poison. "I flushed them down the toilet. I can't even kill myself. I was lying here hoping a hurricane would stop by. Instead I get you."

"Leese. Leese. Listen to me."

"No." She stands up and wanders away—to the beach, to the water.

I run after her. "Leese. Listen."

"No!"

# Chapter 14

## GUILT TRIP

### LEESIE'S MOST PRIVATE CHAPBOOK
### POEM # 85, NO

I spin around and scream
in his face, "No, no, no, no!"
sink to my knees in the sand,
bang my head on the ground.
"No."

He's there, beside me.
"Leese, listen."
His hand finds my arm.
I flick it off. "Don't touch me."
I scramble to get away, but he
has me, holds me, won't let me
go.

"No." I cry into his shoulder
and pound his chest with my cast.
"Remember that crazy honeymoon
we made up?"

"No."
"Our deserted island and 24/7?"
"No."
"Remember how I said I'd buy
you seashells?"
"No."
"Every market I went to, I bought
something for *you*."

"For *me?*"

He kisses my forehead.
"For you."
"*Me?*"
"The skirts and scarves—all the stuff
you found—it's not Suki's."
I shudder and he squeezes me.
"I bought it all for you."
He puts the necklace
in my hand and kisses
my trembling mouth.

"Really?"
"Yes."
"I want to believe you,
but—"
He lets go, hangs his head, steps back.
"I've been a freaking moron lately?"
I hold up the necklace to catch floodlights
from the restaurant behind us.
A round shell center pierced
with strands of wood beads
turquoise, round and square,
light and dark.
"It's Cayman colored."

He kisses my fingers. "It is."

I kiss his mouth so I don't cry, turn
and wade into the water.
"Just leave me here."
A few steps take me up
to my knees in soft,
pulsing blue perfection.
Cool. Clear. Enticing.
"Maybe the tide will take me away."
He plunges after me, grabs my arm.
"That's enough. It's over."
I jerk my arm trying to free it.
"I'm too evil to live! I pervert
everything. This gift. Your love."
His grip tightens—
I stare at his fingers and into his eyes,
"You're too good to be near me."
My eyes drop to the cool water
sucking on my knees.
"I killed my brother, Michael."
I take a step deeper.
"I really did. And I wanted to.
I was so mad at him.
We fought—worse than
we ever have over anything.
I screamed, cursed him,
and drove
off the road."

Michael's arms wrap around me.
He presses my head
against his beating heart.
"It's okay. I'm here now."
His voice breaks.

He doesn't move,
doesn't speak,
until he regains control
enough to whisper,
"I'm back."

His two little words unlock
my heart. My body relaxes
against his. "Where did you go?"
He kisses the top
of my furry buzz cut.
"Let's call it a guilt trip."

## LEESIE HUNT / CHATSPOT LOG / 05/30 3:21 PM

**Leesie327 says:** He won't leave my side, and I like it.
**Kimbo69 says:** How's he managing that?
**Leesie327 says:** Took the rest of the week off.
**Kimbo69 says:** They let him?
**Leesie327 says:** Everybody owes him shifts. He's been working too hard.
**Kimbo69 says:** You guys ever heard of the balance?
**Leesie327 says:** Maybe I should lose all hope more often.
**Kimbo69 says:** Hardly balanced! You know Michael isn't your only hope.
**Leesie327 says:** Thanks, Kim. I know I can count on you.
**Kimbo69 says:** I talked to your dad again. He says, "Hi."
**Leesie327 says:** I didn't say you could call him twice!
**Kimbo69 says:** He called me.
**Leesie327 says:** You didn't spill anything, did you?
**Kimbo69 says:** I was so tempted. But that's your job, my friend.
**Leesie327 says:** I don't want to talk about it.
**Kimbo69 says:** Well, you better think about it.
**Leesie327 says:** I'm not thinking about anything ever again.
**Kimbo69 says:** Leesie's getting lazy!

**Leesie327 says:** I'm healing—it takes a lot of energy. I told Michael Phil and I fought before the accident. It did make me feel better to get that out.

**Kimbo69 says:** What? You told Michael you were fighting over him?

**Leesie327 says:** No. Are you kidding? Just that we were fighting.

**Kimbo69 says:** And he didn't ask why?

**Leesie327 says:** Nope. And he won't. Why should that matter? Now he knows why I'm guilty of at least vehicular manslaughter.

**Kimbo69 says:** He doesn't think that.

**Leesie327 says:** I don't know what he thinks. I'm not bringing it up. And he's to sweet to broach the subject.

**Kimbo69 says:** So what have you guys been doing with all this time together?

**Leesie327 says:** Michael slept in today. I sat on the floor and watched his face.

**Kimbo69 says:** Riveting.

Leesie327 says: I had to tear myself away to make him Gram's gooey cinnamon French toast.

**Kimbo69 says:** Gosh, that sounds good. Mail me some.

Leesie327 says: Sure thing. We sat on the balcony and ate it looking out at the ocean. If diamonds were turquoise, it would be this water.

**Kimbo69 says:** Aquamarines?

**Leesie327 says:** Something like that. We talked about Suki.

**Kimbo69 says:** [Insert loud choking sounds here!!] Oh, my gosh—did he finally fess up?

**Leesie327 says:** Yup.

**Kimbo69 says:** The creep.

**Leesie327 says:** No—don't say that. He was a hero.

**Kimbo69 says:** For getting it on with a professional?

**Leesie327 says:** That's a huge lie. Shut up.

**Kimbo69 says:** He didn't sleep with her?

**Leesie327 says:** She enticed him—you saw how gorgeous she is—and he admitted he was tempted, but even though I shoved his ring back in his face like a stupid brute, he didn't do it. He had my ring around his neck. He walked away.

**Kimbo69 says:** You believe him?

**Leesie327 says:** A hundred percent.

**Kimbo69 says:** But they were kissing. The whole world saw the photo.

**Leesie327 says:** The creep she was with beat her up, and Michael took care of her—helped her get back to her people. The Sea Gypsies. She kissed him good-bye. Isn't he amazing?

**Kimbo69 says:** Are you sure he's not making that up to make himself look good? Wanting to do a prostitute doesn't shine in my book.

**Leesie327 says:** No way. I had to pry the story out of him. Now I can tell our kids their dad's a hero. He saved me, too. Don't forget that.

**Kimbo69 says:** You're having kids?

**Leesie327 says:** Lots of them.

**Kimbo69 says:** You going to start that right away?

**Leesie327 says:** Why not? I can't go to school here.

**Kimbo69 says:** He won't let you go back?

**Leesie327 says:** He'd take me to BYU in a second. I can tell he wants to bring it up, but he's afraid I'll flip out again.

**Kimbo69 says:** So you're going to stay in Cayman and have babies?

**Leesie327 says:** I'll go wherever he wants and have babies.

**Kimbo69 says:** You're too young.

**Leesie327 says:** When my mom was pregnant with Stephie, my grandmother always said, "Young bodies are made for making babies." She'd look straight at me and say, "Don't wait until you're over the hill"—glare at my mom—"have them in your twenties."

**Kimbo69 says:** You've got a good decade or more to reproduce.

**Leesie327 says:** But a baby with Michael's eyes would be so cute.

**Kimbo69 says:** And your life would be over.

**Leesie327 says:** Or just beginning.

**Kimbo69 says:** How twisted can you be? The goal is always not to get pregnant, hon.

**Leesie327 says:** Not always.

**Kimbo69 says:** Are you trying to tell me you're knocked up? That was fast.

**Leesie327 says:** No chance of that.

**Kimbo69 says:** Still?

**Leesie327 says:** We made a truce. I promised to stop trying to get him into bed.

**Kimbo69 says:** Crap—he is a hero.

**Leesie327 says:** Yeah. He's guarding my useless virtue.

**Kimbo69 says:** What did he promise?

**Leesie327 says:** To find out how to get married on Cayman.

# GUARD DUTY

## MICHAEL'S DIVE LOG – VOLUME #10

**Dive Buddy:** students
**Date:** 06/01
**Dive #:** --
**Location:** Grand Cayman
**Dive Site:** pool
**Weather Condition:** sunny
**Water Condition:** calm
**Depth:** 10'
**Visibility:** perfect
**Water Temp:** 82
**Bottom Time:** 15 minutes
**Comments:**

Back at work. Three days off with Leesie weren't enough.
I'm teaching today, so I bring her along. Can't leave her alone.
Not yet. Terror too fresh.

The classroom stuff is a good review. She doesn't get in
the pool—but she sits on the edge with her feet in the water and
follows my every move, nodding her head like she's mentally
going through the motions.

I can't wait until she gets that stupid cast off her arm. Then
we'll really dive. One week from today she has an appointment.
I'm taking her for sure. I want to be there. If all goes well, they'll

saw that junk off her hand and not put a new cast back on. Her collarbone seems to be doing well—her arm is out of the sling more than it's in.

It's been over a month since she shaved her head. Her hair is growing fast—almost an inch. At least that's what she says. It's more than half an inch—I'll give her that. Yesterday she searched all over the apartment to find a ruler to measure it. Made me promise to buy her one. Even at half an inch, it's coming in thick enough to give the scar some camo. She doesn't put make up on every day, but the spa ladies at the rehab place gave her heavy-duty stuff that makes a big difference with the part of the scar that marks up her forehead. If she wants to get cosmetic surgery, that's fine with me. Whatever. If it makes her happy, I'll pay for it. I don't care what it costs.

I've got to go under the water with my students. I swim over to Leesie. "We'll be down about fifteen minutes." I don't like not being able to watch her. Since I found her Thursday, I've been with her all day—until I turn her over to Alex—who was stupid enough to take off before I woke up on Saturday.

That scared me. Leesie was fine—up making me French toast, but still. Stupid, Alex. What was she thinking?

Now, Leesie slips off her sling and picks up a mask and snorkel she borrowed from the shop. "Can I watch you from the surface?"

I squeeze her knees. "Sure." Freak, I love her. "Great idea."

She gets me to tape a grocery bag around her cast while my students haul out of the pool, then watch us.

"How come she gets special attention during our lesson?" A middle-aged lady with a giant butt wants to know when I rejoin them.

I grin back at the lady. "Because she's my fiancé." Yeah. It feels good to say that.

The lady shuts up—smiles back at me even. "Congratulations."

"Gear up, guys. What are you waiting for?"

No one says, 'you messing around with your babe'—for that, I'm grateful. Go easy on them. I coach the class of four through getting all their gear on, make them jump in, review descent when we're bobbing on the surface. And then we're down.

Big butt lady gets nervous, but I'm in her face—encouraging her to breathe, in and out, slow and calm—until we wear the panic down. She'll love me after this.

I glance up quick to check for Leesie. She's off to the side watching.

She watches me.

I watch her.

We both hesitate to rock any boats.

She wants me to look up getting married in Cayman. I keep putting it off. I promised her dad to bring her home first. She'll freak when she hears that.

I'm taking Leese out on the boat with me tomorrow. More watching. These students are doing a check out dive in the shallow water inside the reef. The water is way too rough on the East End for her to sit on the boat when we leave the reef's protection on normal dives. She'd be puking her guts up for sure.

She can come with me tomorrow. No prob. I've got morning dives on Wednesday. Then students again in the afternoon. I can bring her along in the afternoon, but what about the morning? Alex is booked on the boat with me. Cooper is captain. Gabriel, Brock, and Ethan have the other boat. That leaves Seth.

Would he hang out with her? Nothing obvious or anything. She'd be ticked if she found out I'd set up a watch dog. I so don't want to ask him. Makes me nervous—yes, jealous. But what else can I do?

## LEESIE'S MOST PRIVATE CHAPBOOK
## POEM #86, CAYMAN PRINCESS

Michael takes my hand
and helps me down
into the boat. Other
passengers clear a lane
for me like I'm royalty.
His princess—with my island
scarf wound round my head,
Michael's Cayman-colored shell necklace
swinging around my neck, his diamond
flashing on my broken hand,
and my old swimsuit giving
me away. It's just Leesie,
people. Move along.

I trip a little so I can fall
against Michael's bare chest.
He gives me a squeeze
and a XXL lady yells,
"Hold it," and snaps our picture.

He lines up his students
along one side of the boat,
sits across from them
and gets down to business.

I sit off to the side
and watch him teach,
watch the muscles in his shoulders
and back ripple when
he stands to reach his wetsuit.
The boat putters a few hundred

feet from the dock while Michael
coats himself in neoprene.
All black—wrapping him tight.
I miss his golden skin but
can't deny he devastates
exponentially more wetsuited.

He hovers over me.
"We won't be down long."
I slip my right hand out of its sling
and rub it along his shoulder and arm
while the rest of the women
watch their prince. "It's cool,"
I whisper. "I'll help Cooper."

Sun burnt, sandy-haired, smiling
Captain Cooper lies on a bench
and follows the one lonely cloud
crossing the sky as he tells me about
Canada and snowdrifts that
don't melt until April.
"I know snow." I hand him a slice
of the melon I chopped for the break.
"Grew up driving in it."
"Cool. Where?"
"Washington."
"State?"
I nod and pitch a melon rind
over the side.
"When you going back?"
My face pulls into a frown.
"Leave here?" My glance
indicates the paradise
of sparkling blue we float in.
"Are you kidding?"

"You can't stay forever."
"Why not?"
"Visa runs out."
"That sucks."
"Not for me. Commonwealth
privileges!"
"Shut up."
"Make me."
I flick a piece of melon
at him and stick my tongue out,
wander to the back of the boat,
try to see what's going on down under.

I've never been so eager to get
in the water, sink into Michael's
kingdom, obey his every command,
trust him with my life
like our pudgy pal and her friends.

Cooper hands me a mask.
"Care for a swim?"
He tapes my cast in bag,
jams fins on my feet,
and comes along so I don't
drown. "He's over there."
He points to bubbles
percolating on the surface.
I swim to them, mask down,
blowing too hard through
my snorkel until
Michael comes into view.
Perfect.
Except I'm here.
He's there.
Gotta change that up.
Soon.
But today, this moment

of jeweled wonder floating
in pure clear ocean
I can watch, wait
and love him.

# Chapter 16

## BACKFIRE

### LEESIE'S MOST PRIVATE CHAPBOOK
### POEM #87, BABYSITTERS

Seth's off this AM,
drunk again last night.
"Can you watch him?"
Alex says through her toothbrush.
I pull a bleck-are-you-crazy face. "What?"
She spits. "Watch him—hang out until we"—
she pauses to rinse—"all get back at lunch."
"What would I do with him?"
I can see Seth through our half-open bedroom door,
awake earlier than he needs to be, turning his nose
up at bacon and eggs.
Alex rinses her toothbrush. "Keep him
away from the beer."
"How am I supposed to do that?"
She gives me a don't-be-this-stunned-this-early
grimace. "Feed him coffee."
"I don't do coffee."
"It's a machine, hon. Already done."
Me serving coffee? To hung-over Seth?
What a joke. Maybe I'll try some.

Or join the guy in a couple of beers.
Michael won't be around to stop me.

The apartment empties out.
Michael's the last to go. He kisses
me good-bye and gives Seth a wave.
Friendly? Weird.
I don't want Michael to walk out
that door and leave me behind
with Mr. Broken-Down-Boozer.
But he does.

I give Seth his coffee, disappear
into the bathroom, take too
long in the shower.
Loud knocking on the outer door
penetrates my steamy retreat.
Somebody's yelling like there's a fire.
I turn the water off, wrap fast in a towel,
drip my way to the door, don't open it.
"What?" I yell at the wood.
"You all right in there?"
Seth's yelling, angry? Still pounding.
"Fine."
The knocking stops. "Oh, sorry."
"And you?" Rude not to play
my part in this strange ballet.
"Fine."
"Perfect. Can I get dressed now?"
"Fine."

I put on my yellow dress with
turquoise stripes, sandals,
the baseball cap that matches,
open the door, peak out—

Seth's sitting in the living room
mess of pulled out couch and unmade cots
sipping a beer.
I begin to withdraw, hide, renege on my promise,
but I push myself forward instead, march
up to him and grab the can. "Alex says
no beer this morning."
He holds out his hand.
"Just let me finish that one.
I don't want to waste it."
I sniff the contents—reeking nastiness—
like grain that's gone bad in the elevator—
fake a smile. "That's okay. I'll drink it."
He's out of his chair, lunges at me, grabs
the can—dumps it down the sink.
"No way, girl. Michael would kill me."
My forehead folds into ugly creases.
"What has he told you guys about me?"
Seth stares at the retreating golden
liquid and mumbles, "That you don't
drink beer, and you're a—"
The guy actually blushes.
I reach over and turn on the faucet.
"What's going on here?"
He pulls the spray gadget free
and squirts the sink clean.
"Michael asked me to—"
"Watch me?" I flip off the water. "That's rich."
"What?"
"Alex asked me to—"
Seth's eyebrows arch, and I start
to see what Dani saw in him.
He grins. "Babysit me?"
Head shakes. Nervous laughs.
"We're officially pathetic."

He crushes the empty beer can.
"Dangerously psychotic."
I take the can and trash it.
We both blurt,
"Who do they think they are?"
He yells, "Jinx."
"You're kidding me."
"You can't talk."
"Nobody's jinxed me since—"

Phil the Pill. A lump gets
stuck in my throat just
above my heart.
Seth's got a pained look on his face, too.
"Damn. Sorry. Dani was goofy like that—
way into kid's stuff—jinx and slug bugs
and—" His voice breaks. "Crap."
I look down at the white linoleum I need
to scrub. "Sorry to remind you."
He takes a minute to get control.
"No one mentions her—I hate that.
It's like she's dead or something."
I close my eyes tight. "That would be worse."
"Maybe not."
"Trust me."

We walk up the highway to East End's
tiny grocery, buy hot dogs, buns,
and a foil pain full of easy-light mini
charcoal that we light on the beach.
I focus on the red glow creeping
through the miniature grill, glance
up at Seth, catch his eyes.
"Did you love Dani?"

His eyes drop down to the caged fire.
"I thought it was just for kicks—until
she left."
I touch his hand. "You should tell
her that."
He jerks his hand away from me.
"How? I don't know where the hell she is."
I speak slowly, not sure what or why,
let the words tumble out.
"But what if she misses you?
What if she's sick of Kai?
What if she made a horrible mistake?
What if *she* loves *you*?"

He searches the horizon for returning
boats, stirs the reddening charcoal.
"The office probably has her address."
I nod, smile. "Don't you have her email?"
"Of course."
"What are you waiting for?"

## LEESIE HUNT / CHATSPOT LOG / 06/05 3:15 PM

**Kimbo69 says:** I can't believe you told Seth to email the slut
who ran off with your roommate's boyfriend.
**Leesie327 says:** I know. I was possessed by something crazy. If
Alex finds out I gave Seth the idea, I'm toast. I'll be sleeping on
the sidewalk.
**Kimbo69 says:** Alex already knows about it?
**Leesie327 says:** Oh, yeah. They all do.
**Kimbo69 says:** Seth told? She must have written back.
**Leesie327 says**: If a guy emailed you that he loves you and life
is hell without you, what would you do?
**Kimbo69 says:** Send him a nice reply saying I'm sorry?

**Leesie327 says:** That's a start.

**Kimbo69 says:** Call him and beg his forgiveness?

**Leesie327 says:** You're getting warmer.

**Kimbo69 says:** Try to see him so I can convince him with my personal charms?

**Leesie327 says:** How about fly back to Cayman and move back in with him as if nothing ever happened.

**Kimbo69 says:** Seth is that much of a sucker?

**Leesie327 says:** It's what he wants more than anything. He took her for granted until she was gone. He won't do that again.

**Kimbo69 says:** Is Alex ballistic?

**Leesie327 says:** It got pretty ugly when Seth told her Dani's coming "home" this weekend.

**Kimbo69 says:** What about the guy?

**Leesie327 says:** Kai? He's staying in St. Lucia. Dani caught him cheating on her. She says he cheated on Alex with a bunch of other girls—not just her.

**Kimbo69 says:** Alex is well rid of the creep.

**Leesie327 says:** She sees that, but not enough to welcome Dani back into the nest.

**Kimbo69 says:** She and Seth should find another place to live.

**Leesie327 says:** No chance of that happening. Seth's kicking Gabriel out of his room to make way for Dani.

**Kimbo69 says:** So where's he going?

**Leesie327 says:** On a cot in the living room I guess. Alex would like him to move in with her, but I'm in the way.

**Kimbo69 says:** Is she making any progress?

**Leesie327 says:** I think so. He got all protective when Seth announced Dani was moving back. He and Alex went down to the beach together—didn't come back until late.

**Kimbo69 says:** Total soap opera.

**Leesie327 says:** Right. Since I caused the problem, I've found the solution.

**Kimbo69 says:** What?

**Leesie327 says:** I looked up getting married on Cayman. If you're a resident, you have to go to the registrar's office and they post a notice in public that you are going to marry. People have two weeks to object. Crazy, huh.

**Kimbo69 says:** Like bans in Jane Austen novels?

**Leesie327 says:** If you're getting married in a church, they still do that.

**Kimbo69 says:** What's your status there? Are you like an illegal immigrant?

**Leesie327 says:** I'm a visitor. I can stay six months. Michael has a temporary work permit. So we're not officially residents. Maybe he is. I can't tell. I think we can get married using a non-resident permit.

**Kimbo69 says:** How does this help the situation?

**Leesie327 says:** Non-residents just have to pay $250, prove their age and citizenship, and they get a certificate. It's easy. Fast. You go to some government office in Georgetown and get it.

**Kimbo69 says:** You're really going to do it?

**Leesie327 says:** I have to convince Michael all this drama isn't good for me. Moving into our own condo would be the only option. He'd do it if we're married.

**Kimbo69 says:** You'll end up convincing him to buy you a ticket home. That wouldn't be such a bad thing.

**Leesie327 says:** That's not going to happen. He loves it here as much as I do. I think he'll work here as long as they'll let him. That's something like eight years. I'm already home.

**Kimbo69 says:** But you have a family.

**Leesie327 says:** He'll be my family. He's all I need.

**Kimbo69 says:** What about your mom's needs? What about your Dad—and Stephie?

**Leesie327 says:** This way they're safe. I can't hurt them anymore.

**Kimbo69 says:** That's stupid. Twisted. Selfish and mean.

**Leesie327 says:** Me.

**Kimbo69 says:** No. It's not you. Not the girl I know.

**Leesie327 says:** But it's who I'll be forever now. I'm scared for Michael. What will I do to him?

## COMPLICATIONS

### MICHAEL'S DIVE LOG – VOLUME #10

**Dive Buddy:** Leesie plus
**Date:** 06/06
**Dive #:** --
**Location:** Grand Cayman
**Dive Site:** the apartment
**Weather Condition:** night time again
**Water Condition:** choppy
**Depth:** manageable?
**Visibility:** too clear
**Water Temp:** getting warmer
**Bottom Time:** not sure--hours
**Comments:**

Seth is supposed to pick Dani up at the airport tonight, but nobody's seen them yet. I take Leesie out to dinner, and when we get back, Alex has Gabriel in the room. There's a note to Leesie on the door. Come back at one.

I steer Leesie out of the apartment before she hears anything. She's never been around stuff like this. I don't like it. "How long has that been brewing?"

"Since Kai left. Gabriel's good at comfort."

"But not commitment." I put my arm around Leesie, and we head down the stairs.

152 / angela morrison

"Alex thinks she can change that."

My hand glides down to Leesie's waist. "He seems to care about her. You should have heard him tear into Seth when we were cleaning up after this morning's dives. Not like him at all."

Leesie slips her arm out of her sling and wraps her fingers around mine. "He's a classic hero. All he needed was a damsel in distress."

I jingle the keys in my pocket. "You want to go for a drive."

She wraps me closer, puts my hand on her stomach. "Nope."

We wander across the beach and down to the dock. She wants to make out, but we need to talk.

I kiss her fingers. "So Alex and Gabriel? Is that going to be awkward?"

She runs the fingers of her casted hand through my hair. "I guess I could take the fifth cot in the living room."

"No way. It's not that serious. They're just messing around tonight. He won't move in with her."

Her eyebrows rise. "You don't know Alex."

I sling both arms around her back. "You don't know Gabriel."

"She got your work schedules changed up, so they're diving together—every shift." She sticks out her tongue at me.

I wrinkle my nose back at her. "She's so not his type."

She leans in close. "But she needs him." Her breath tickles my ear. "That's intoxicating."

I close my eyes and inhale her cocoanut closeness. I miss her sweet banana mango shampoo. "So what do you think we should do?"

She kisses me. "Make out."

"But—"

Her mouth is on mine again. "But nothing."

We kiss for awhile standing on the edge of the dock with the soft night surge swirling against the floating wood and the deep starry night for a backdrop. It's sweet—slow, unhurried, neither of us going anywhere, pressuring each other to do anything else but hold each other and trade love with our lips.

I rest my cheek against her head. "You can't stay in that apartment all summer. It's not good for you."

Her face gets hot. "Maybe I'll learn something."

I grasp her face between my hands and tilt her head back. "I don't want you to learn anything."

Her shoulders rise in a hopeless shrug. "I have to learn sometime."

"I'll find a new place for you to stay."

"Without you?" Her lips find my neck. "No way." She looks down at our feet—mine on either side of hers. "Let's buy our own place."

She pulls me in close, kisses me, won't let me talk.

I turn away from her lips. "But we can't get married."

"Yes"—she kisses me—"we can." Another kiss. "It's easy." She goes in for another kiss, but I pull out of her reach.

She pouts, then flashes the smile I love. "I looked it all up. We could get married tomorrow—well Monday if I didn't have my appointment."

I study her happy face. "Did you plan the whole Dani thing out? Manipulate it all to get me to marry you?"

She laughs. "I'm not that smart. But I am in the way for Alex and Gabriel. We don't have much choice."

"We can't get married."

She kisses me, gets my tongue.

"Stop it, babe." I cover her lips with my fingers, tip my forehead so it touches hers. "I promised your dad I'd take you home before we get married."

The smile drains out of her face. "You what?" She releases me, turns her back, squats down and stares into the dark water.

I hunker down beside her. "When we talked on the phone—I promised him."

She turns her glare on me. "I'm never going home. You

know why. I'll die if my mom finds out Phil and I were fighting before the crash."

"I won't tell her anything." I can't figure out why Leesie thinks that was such a big deal. "Who cares anyway? You guys always fought. What was it about this time? The radio station?"

She turns pale. "I'm not going home."

I lean over and catch her lips. "If you want to marry me, you will."

She moves fast—lies back, jerks me down on top of her. "We can shack up together. I don't care." Her legs wrap around me.

I push up off her. "Nope." I get on my feet and offer her my hand.

She won't take it, lies there looking up at me. "Then what are we going to do?"

"Go back up to the apartment and disappoint Alex and Gabriel."

The clock reads 1:52 AM when I usher Leesie in through the apartment door. All the guys—including Gabriel—mill around the kitchen and living room drinking beer, waiting for Dani and Seth.

"Shhh!" Gabriel puts a finger up to his lips. "Alex is asleep."

Cooper chucks a pillow at him. "Worn out, eh?"

Gabriel catches the pillow, frowns. "She was distressed."

Brock sets his beer down. "And you took her mind off her troubles?"

Ethan looks up from soccer reruns on TV. "She does not need another rascal breaking her wee heart."

"I'm well aware of that." Gabriel lets the pillow drop from his hands.

Cooper stands. "Then what the hell are you doing?"

Gabriel rifles his fingers through his black play-boy hair. "She wants me." He rotates, gathers everyone's eyes. "What am I supposed to do? Turn her down? Humiliate her?"

"You're taking advantage of her." Cooper gets right in Gabriel's face. "Not cool, dude."

Gabriel puts his hand flat on Cooper's chest and pushes him back. "I'm trying to make her happy." He sits down on the couch.

Brock cocks his head. "You care if she's happy?"

Gabriel's face softens. "I do. I care." He see's Alex's face peeking from a crack in her and Leesie's bedroom door, turns, and addresses her. "I care very much."

Alex slips through the door, crosses the room to Gabriel, climbs on his lap, and hides her face against his neck. Gabriel's arms go around her, protecting, a hand strokes her head, and he kisses her forehead.

Leesie smiles, goes to the fridge and takes out butter and eggs. "I need brownies. Anybody want to help?"

I crack the eggs. Leesie melts the butter and chocolate on the stove. Brock turns on the oven. And Cooper and Ethan measure flour and sugar.

A half hour later, we're crowded around the table, eating hot, gooey brownies—same recipe that she made when I met those jerk missionaries back at BYU. The guys traded their beer for milk. The apartment door opens and a half-drunk Seth leads in a very drunk blonde girl spilling out of her fuchsia halter top and matching mini skirt. Dani.

Alex gives her a brutal, loathing glare and stalks into her and Leesie's bedroom.

Gabriel stands up. "Hello, Dani." He speaks in a solemn voice and goes after Alex.

Dani giggles and punches Seth in the arm. "You're right, Sethie. They all want me back. " She stumbles. Seth catches her—stumbles, too.

Cooper and Ethan leap to help them. "It's cool, Dani," Cooper says. "We're glad you're back."

"Liars." The giggle dissolves to tears. "She should be mad at Kai—not me. It's his fault."

Brock pats her arm. "If you promise to make this pathetic bloke happy again, we'll all be thrilled with your return."

She beams at Seth. "So it's true? He can't live without me?"

Seth plants a loud smack on the side of her face. "You're never getting away from me again."

She kisses him, and Brock and Cooper hustle them into their room and shut the door.

Leesie leaves the table with the dirty plates balanced on her broken left hand.

I gather up the dirty glasses and join her.

She dumps her sling on the counter and whispers so only I can hear. "Dyed hair. Long, though. Pretty."

"Uh-huh."

"And those"—she rolls her eyes dramatically—"weren't real."

"I didn't look." I concentrate on scrubbing the plate in my hand.

Leesie elbows me. "Yes, you did."

"They weren't so big."

"So you admit it?" She pulls the sprayer gadget out and rinses the plates I washed.

I nuzzle the side of her head. "Sorry. I won't ever look at those again."

"Or any other girl's frontal zone." She turns to me holding the sprayer like a weapon.

I hold up my hands. "For the rest of my life?"

"Yes. This is all you get." She drops her hands to I can assess my fate.

I put my hands on her waist and whisper, "You know I'm a small breast guy."

"There's no such thing." She glances down at her white T-shirt. "Should I get them fixed? Look like that?"

"No way, babe." I hug her. "I want 'em real."

Leesie still has the sprayer in her hand, and somehow it

gets pressed and soaks my back. I wrestle it away from her, making sure I douse her front.

She hides against my chest and whispers, "Do you want to go back out to the beach?"

"Yeah." It's too late, we're too tired, too turned on, and feeling her up is a huge sin, but we'll just roll around in the sand—make out some more—that's it.

She takes my hand, walks backward to the door so I get a good view of her wet T-shirt, pulls me forward.

Gabriel opens the bedroom door. "Leesie?" he calls. "Alex needs you."

The teasing excitement drains out of her face. "Sure. I'm coming." She kisses me goodnight and disappears.

## LEESIE'S MOST PRIVATE CHAPBOOK POEM #88, GOOD THING?

Alex sobs curled in a fetal
ball on the bathroom floor.
Gabriel picks her up,
tucks her in bed,
wipes her face
with tissues. "Come on,
now, my treasure,
enough."

I relieve him of the box
of tissues. "Let her cry."
His handsome face
shows doubt. "Are you sure?"
I nod and sniff, blinking
back my own tears that threaten
to break through the stone
I've buried my heart under.

Gabriel bends over and kisses
her forehead. "Goodnight, my Alex."
He retreats elegantly, looking every bit
the millionaire playboy caught
in caring that's morphing to love
with every tear Alex sheds.

Once he's gone, she groans, hiccups.
"I can't stop. I keep trying.
Gabriel saw me like this.
How hideous am I?"
I give her a fresh wad of
soft whiteness to staunch
the hot snot dripping down
her chin. "He loves you like this."
"I wish." She buries her face
in the tissues.

"Cry, Alex. Don't stop.
Even I still believe
in the power of tears."
She sobs and sobs,
mourning her hurt, her loss,
melting into new found
tenderness that tinges her pain
with promises of joy,
flutters of hope,
and the dawn of love.

In the morning, she meets
Dani with coolness, but doesn't
tear all the hair out of her head
or stab her with the knife Alex
wears strapped to her leg when she dives.

Gabriel whisks her away
for a day off in the sun, lazing
on beaches and sipping icy fruit froth.

Dani's got double shifts
until hell freezes over
to make up for leaving
everybody high and dry.
Seth's working with her.
The boys have the other boat—
which leaves me my Michael
to dote on all day long.
Bonus.

We leave the dishes undone
and the place a wreck,
drive down to the blow holes,
buy spicy grilled chicken
from a roadside stand,
eat it, sitting side by side
on the bare coral shore
as waves crash against the cliffs
and force water in the cracks
and up through the spouts
to spray white and pure
high into the air.

He picks up a drumstick.
"I'm sorry about last night."
He bites and chews. "Good thing
Alex needed you."
Good thing?
Bad thing?
It used to be so easy
to spot which was which.

I've opened the door
to bad thing.
Crave it more and more
every day. Would it
be so bad? Or would
it be the best thing
that ever happened to me?

I lean my head against
his shoulder. "If we would
have gone down to
the beach—?"

His eyes move away
from the intensity of mine
and gather the spectacle
of the ocean's purity.
"I don't know, babe."
He shakes his head.
"I don't know."

# Chapter 18

## I KNOW

### MICHAEL'S DIVE LOG – VOLUME #10

**Dive Buddy:** Leesie
**Date:** 06/08
**Dive #:** last time here
**Location:** Grand Cayman
**Dive Site:** Rehab Center
**Weather Condition:** sunshine
**Water Condition:** 2' swells
**Depth:** on the surface
**Visibility:** 100+
**Water Temp:** fine
**Bottom Time:** the rest of the day
**Comments:**

Diving this morning. Seth and Dani. She ran the show. Whatever else you say about her, she knows her stuff. Great with the people on the boat. Not just the drooling guys. Even the kids and their moms.

I'm off this afternoon to take Leesie to her appointment at the rehab place. She got all dolled up for the nurses. Pretty white dress and the hip white scarf twisted around her head—I hadn't noticed the silver and white beads tied onto the fringe. Lots of makeup. The only color she's got on is the bead and shell necklace she thought was Suki's. I love that she wears it.

"Ah, Sugar, look at you!" Her favorite nurse greets her with a hug. "So pretty! Better, no?"

Leesie blinks, getting emotional. "No more pills." She's refused to even take over-the-counter pain pills since that night she flushed her drugs down the toilet at Rum Point.

"Good for you." Sugar pats her back.

We wait for the doctor in a treatment room. Leesie's nervous. "What if it's not fixed right?" She holds up her hand, twists it trying to see under cast and inside to the bones.

I take her hand. "Don't worry."

"What if he says I have to keep wearing the cast?"

"Then my plans for tomorrow are wrecked." I want to get her in the water so bad.

"Here, take my ring. I don't want cast-dust on it."

I take her hand and slide the ring off her finger and put it in my pocket.

"Do you think they're fat now? My fingers?"

I bring her fingers to my lips and kiss them. "Your fingers are fine."

She tips her head to rest against my cheek. "I love you."

"I know."

She sticks her tongue out at me, and the doctor walks in. Leesie gets cherry red and flustered, but the dude has his nose in Leesie's chart.

"Let's see what we've got now." He directs Leesie to perch on one of those doctor's office exam tables. He checks how the wound on her head is healing. "Any headaches?"

"Only him." Her eyebrows rise in my direction.

The doctor laughs. "How's your nose?" His expert fingers press along the ridge of her nose, stop at the slight bump from the break. "Is it still tender here?"

"Not very."

"Any nosebleeds?"

"No."

"Good." He unlatches her sling and pulls it off.

The dress is bare on top, shows how tan she's getting.

The doctor runs his fingers all along her collarbone—spends extra time around the break. "This has healed nicely. Have you been using your arm?"

"Some." She looks down at the white skirt of her dress draped over her knees.

"A lot." I fold my arms across my chest.

She glares.

"Good." The doctor helps her put the sling back on. "Wear the sling as needed for another two weeks. But you can take it off for exercise. Swimming would be good. Are you doing your exercises?"

"Yes. Every day."

That and more. She works out until she hurts. I think she wants to be buff like Alex. I got to change her mind on that one.

The doctor finally gets to her hand. He rolls a wheelie table in front of her and takes an electric saw with a round whirling blade out of a drawer. "Rest your hand here." He puts on safety glasses and revs up the saw. "Hold still."

The blade whirrs and kicks up a billow of white dust. It's hot in the room. Airless. A vision of him cutting her hand right off invades. I breathe faster and faster like a newbie diver in panic mode. Choke on the dust.

Leesie stops the doctor with a touch on his shoulder. "Are you all right?"

I wipe my face. "Fine."

"Good—look." She holds her hand up so I can see her cast hangs on by a mere half inch width.

The doctor puts down the saw and opens a drawer. "I'll use my scissors on that. Don't want to slice open your hand."

He didn't need to say that.

I take a deep breath, move closer for a better view. Snip.

Snip. He pulls the cast off and her hand is free.

Pale, clammy, greenish contrasted with her tan fingertips. She turns it over. Four faint scars curved to fit my fingernails emerge and memory blurs my vision. She's holding my hand for the very first time, talking about angels, and I hang on to her so tight I hurt her.

She sees them, too. Remembers? I hope so. I need her to remember the power and conviction she bathed my wounds with that night. I wish I could bathe hers like that now.

Not my element.

Saltwater, though. Healed me up fine in the end. It should work for her, too. A good place to start.

Tomorrow.

## LEESIE'S MOST PRIVATE CHAPBOOK
## POEM # 89, SALTWATER WONDER

Water closes over my head.
My pulse rate triples.
Michael, his face inches
from mine as we sink
together, motions slow,
take it slow, slow, slow.

I swallow, and my ears pop
like we practiced yesterday
in the pool, swallow again.
No pinching my nose and blowing
like I learned with him back
in SLC in that hotel pool—
he's worried about pressure
on my weakened nose.

To avoid strain on my newly

healed collarbone, Michael
geared me up in the water,
kicking tanks and weights to where
I floated and gently wrapped me
in the complex web of equipment.

He motions, Okay?
I nod—remember to return
his signal, swallow again
and bump my leg into his
on purpose. Private lesson today.
No other students.
Just him and me, coral
and aqua water. Stray fish
staring at me like I'm an alien.

Alex with her students stir
up the sand on the other side
of the boat.

I'm in a new world with
Michael—his world
where my heart races
and I want to kick free
and swim for blue skies,
his world where bubbles
he exhales break around me,
calm my soul enough to pass off
skills kneeling in the sand,
wetsuited knees touching,
gauges checked, masks cleared,
air supply recovered, buddy
breathing.

Buoyancy balanced, he

leads me on a swim around
that replaces final fearful
wisps with wonder.
Is this really just under the surface?
Or did he transport me?
Am I on the moon? Mars? Venus?
A purplish world where
large flat fans screen the water
in lazy rhythm, fantastical formations
top every coral head.
A kingdom of tiny bright subjects
whiz in and out of their intricate
castles. Yellow. Blue. Black. Orange.
Vivid in tubular rays descending
from our own bright sun,
revealing their hidden playground.

Too soon we're on the surface.
Too soon Michael unsnaps my B.C.
and unsnugs the Velcro cumberbun.
Too soon he boosts me back into the boat.
Too soon he reads the delight
in my face.

"Can we go again?"
I'm dying for another taste
of this mystery he loves so much.

He crushes me close, wipes a tear
from his eye before it can fall.
"Sure, babe." He whispers,
"I love you."
I blink, sniff, and manage to say,
"I know," before his lips
take my breath away.

# MERMAID?

### LEESIE HUNT / CHATSPOT LOG / 06/12 9:18 PM

**Kimbo69 says:** Where have you been?
**Leesie327 says:** Diving every day.
**Kimbo69 says:** Doesn't it scare you?
**Leesie327 says:** Not anymore. I love it. I love it. I love it.
**Kimbo69 says:** You love it?
**Leesie327 says:** I'm totally certified now and I love it.
**Kimbo69 says:** Are you sure you didn't mean certifiable?
**Leesie327 says:** I love it.
**Kimbo69 says:** What's the appeal?
**Leesie327 says:** Michael in a wetsuit.
**Kimbo69 says:** Doesn't impress me. I'm into skin myself.
**Leesie327 says:** Work with me, my friend. I'm doing the best with what he'll give me. I especially love it in between dives when he peels his wetsuit half-off and lets it hang around his waist.
**Kimbo69 says:** Hmmm…the best of both worlds.
**Leesie327 says:** Sigh.
**Kimbo69 says:** You go diving every day just to see him in a wetsuit? That sounds like too much work. Doesn't he walk around the apartment in boxers—a swimsuit at least?
**Leesie327 says:** Rarely shirtless.
**Kimbo69 says:** Too much temptation?
**Leesie327 says:** The rest of the guys do.

**Kimbo69 says:** Massive skin alert. Can I come visit?

**Leesie327 says:** It makes me nervous.

**Kimbo69 says:** Overheated.

**Leesie327 says:** Maybe that's it. Gabriel's the worst.

**Kimbo69 says:** I thought they were all hot.

**Leesie327 says:** He's the only Speedo king.

**Kimbo69 says:** Pictures, girl. I need pictures.

**Leesie327 says:** Mark wouldn't care?

**Kimbo69 says:** You should see what he looks at. No, you shouldn't. It's gross.

**Leesie327 says:** Well….my new phone does have a camera.

**Kimbo69 says:** Yes! Promise?

**Leesie327 says:** It shouldn't be hard. He's always in our room.

**Kimbo69 says:** Lucky Alex.

**Leesie327 says:** When they want to be alone, Alex shuts the door, and Michael and I get out of the apartment.

**Kimbo69 says:** Michael's a prude?

**Leesie327 says:** He doesn't want me around their influence. But Gabriel barges in every morning to wake Alex up. I've got zero privacy.

**Kimbo69 says:** Privacy is highly over-rated. You'll get used to not having it.

**Leesie327 says:** I can't say anything to Alex. She's so happy. And Gabriel's too romantic for words. Yesterday, he brought her breakfast in bed and called her "mi cielo."

**Kimbo69 says:** What does that mean?

**Leesie327 says:** That's what Alex said. And he murmured in that sexy accent of his, "There is no English for this. It means you are my heaven. Being with you is like being in heaven."

**Kimbo69 says:** You should write that down.

**Leesie327 says:** I just did.

**Kimbo69 says:** How did Alex react to that?

**Leesie327 says:** I had to leave the room quickly.

**Kimbo69 says:** What about Seth and Dani?

**Leesie327 says:** Don't see them much. They have to work all the time. And when they get off, they go into town to drink.

**Kimbo69 says:** I thought he drank because she left him.

**Leesie327 says:** Me, too. Now they hit the bars because she's back.

**Kimbo69 says:** Maybe he just drinks.

**Leesie327 says:** You're so perceptive.

**Kimbo69 says:** What's your plan—now that you're no longer handicapped.

**Leesie327 says:** Keep diving.

**Kimbo69 says:** That's it?

**Leesie327 says:** That's about all I can handle. Dive with Michael. Every day.

**Kimbo69 says:** You can't do that forever.

**Leesie327 says:** I can try.

## LEESIE'S MOST PRIVATE CHAPBOOK
## POEM # 90, ICE

Michael's on the balcony,
checking email before
he has to head out.
I fiddle with French toast,
pout, not going with—
boat's full.

We're out of eggs now,
bread, butter and bacon.
A walk to the store.
An hour on the beach
to work my tan
and pump Alex's free weights.

"Leese, there's news."
His voice finds me,

draws me to him.
"From who?"
He closes up his laptop.
"Stan the Man."
His wizardly lawyer—
mine now, too.

Fright grips me
like all of the sudden
I grip Michael's arm.
My stomach turns upside
down and a cold chill
in my veins makes
all my healed hurts
pulse together with pain.
"What?" Is all I can mumble.
Manslaughter? Vehicular homicide?
Reckless endangerment?
Will there be a trial or will
I just go to prison?

Michael trades me for the computer
on his lap, barricades
me in his arms. I take cover
in his the soft cotton T-shirt
hiding his chest.
He strokes my head. "Good news."
"Do the police want me back?"
"No."
"Stan can deal with the trial
without my presence?"
"What trial?"
"Tell me the charges."
"Driving too fast for conditions.
He already paid the fine."

I close my eyes tight, and my hands
ball up with bits of Michael's shirt caught in them.
"You're lying. Tell me the truth."

He kisses the scars on the back
of my left hand where his ring shines
"There was ice on the road."
I sit up and concentrate on his deep gray eyes.
"Ice?"
He presses his face alongside mine.
"The police say that's why you crashed."

"Ice?" I pull away from his tenderness.
My face knits into confusion.
"We were fighting—
like I told you—an awful fight—the worst.
I lost control. That's why
we crashed. It's my fault.
I killed him.
I murdered my brother.
Not the ice."
Michael's hands cup my face.
"I believe you, babe. I do.
But ice was
on the highway, too."

My eyes blink, and I shiver.
"All hail—the Ice Queen cometh."
Bitterness drips from my lips.
"Hush, babe. Don't."
He presses my head back down
to his chest. Holds me tight.
"Let's call your dad tonight.
It's time to mend more than
broken bones."

"No." I curl close to him,
trying to steal the warmth
from his body. Ice. I shiver.
He squeezes me. "Think about it."
"No."
He cradles me, kisses me,
leaves me curled
tight in a fetal prison
on the chaise lounge
contemplating the possibilities
of ice.

# Chapter 20

## SLIP-UP

### MICHAEL'S DIVE LOG – VOLUME #10

**Dive Buddy:** Leesie
**Date:** 06/17
**Dive #:** --
**Location:** Grand Cayman
**Dive Site:** kitchenette
**Weather Condition:** steamy
**Water Condition:** steamy
**Depth:** an inch too far
**Visibility:** clearing
**Water Temp:** hot
**Bottom Time:** two minutes too long
**Comments:**

I'm lying on my cot in the living room trying not to wake up. I dozed again after everyone left for the 8 AM dive. I'm teaching at ten. Get to sleep in.

The scent and sizzle of bacon Leesie's frying up in the kitchen seems worth opening my eyes for.

"Hey, sleepyhead." She sounds upbeat this morning. Maybe I can get her talking about the accident again. She needs to believe Stan and the police. Ice on the road. Not merely a mindless fight. There's something she's left out of her story that I got to know.

I sit up, rub sleep gunk out of my eyes.

She calls, "You want some of this?"

I stand and stretch. "You know I do."

"Get over here and earn it then."

I stumble through the chaos of all the guys' beds and clothes to the kitchenette where she's working in front of the stove. She's wearing bikini bottoms and a tiny tank top. "You're looking good this morning." I hope she didn't wear that in front of the rest of the guys.

She tosses me a glance over her shoulder and sees that I can't take my eyes of her butt. She giggles. "You're a mess."

"Are you going to feed me like this every morning after we're married?" I rest my hands on her hip bones and kiss her neck.

She tilts her head to reveal more neck, and I keep moving my lips along it, slip my mouth to her shoulder.

"Naw—I'll put you on tofu—don't want you getting fat."

My hands drift to her stomach. "You're in no danger of that." I close my eyes—caress her skin—enjoy the subtle changes I discover. "You taste good, too." I chew on her neck some more.

"That's the bacon."

Banter. That's all I get from her the past couple days. She won't be serious—won't accept the news we got from Stan for what it's worth—won't call her parents—won't let me. She's still the guiltiest person in the universe. Won't let it go. Blames herself even more now. As soon as we're done here, I'm going to ask—freak. I sucked too long on her neck. I rub the raspberry spot. "Sorry, babe." I kiss it.

She reaches back and strokes my cheek. "I'm a marked woman now."

"I didn't mean to."

She turns a piece of bacon over with a fork. "Mean the next one or you don't get breakfast."

"Babe!"

She holds a crispy piece of bacon up and wafts it close to my nose. "Get to work."

I catch her mood. What will it hurt? "Okay. Okay." I rub her bare shoulders and plant a kiss in the middle of her back. "Where do you want it?"

She tips her head the other way and points to the spot where her neck and shoulder meet. "Let's see how long you can hold your breath."

I laugh, hug her from behind, and start my free dive breathing cycles.

"Stop stalling."

I blow air out all over her neck.

She wriggles with pleasure.

I inhale, inhale, pack it and then slowly, gently I place my lips back on her skin.

She melts into me.

My hands go back to her supple stomach. She feels so good. My lips suck harder and harder on her soft skin. She reaches up with one hand and combs her fingers through my hair, turns off the stove top and pushes the frying pan off the heat with the other.

She's got both hands in my hair now—won't let me stop sucking on her neck. Not like I want to. I close my eyes. Immerse in the moment. My hands stroke her stomach with more and more intensity, drift to her ribs, higher—

Freak.

I touched her.

I dart away and stare at my hands. "I'm sorry, babe. I'm sorry."

She slumps over the stove. "Did I gross you out that much?"

"What? Stop it. That's stupid." I look up. "I just made you sin."

She turns around. "Come back." She laughs. "Let's sin some more."

I hate that laugh. It's so not her. "Be serious. What do we do now?"

She walks towards me. "Whatever you want."

I back up with my hands out in front of me to ward her off. "I mean to fix it."

"Don't bother." She's close now. I could touch her if I dared. "Nothing can fix me."

"There was ice on the road, Leese. You're not a murderer."

"Shut up. You don't know."

"I'm calling your dad." I head for my cell phone, but she gets there first.

She backs away, clutching the cell phone to her chest. "You're so not calling my dad."

I close my eyes—can't look at her another second, or I'll be all over her—try hard to think. What do we do? There's something important I can't quite remember. The red face of the president guy from her church back home—Jaron's dad, no less—forms in my brain. I remember how angry I was when she told me she talked to him after our break up—told him about that night after the dance down by the pig barn when I marked up her stomach like I just stained her neck. "How about we call your president guy, then?"

"Jaron's dad? I'm not confessing to him."

My eyes open. I step towards her with my hand out for the phone. "But this wasn't just making out or giving you a hickey. I crossed the line. Major sin—that's what you used to call it."

"It doesn't matter any more. Why don't you believe me?" She puts the phone behind her back.

"Because I'm still listening to the old Leesie."

"Don't—she lost."

"Let's find her. Please. Can Jaron's dad help?"

She scowls. "I don't live there anymore. He's not my branch president."

"Is there one here?"

"No."

I pick up my laptop, flip it open, type, "Mormons in Grand Cayman" in the Google box. Yes. "Look, babe."

She won't.

There's a picture of a small, gray boxy church with an unmistakable Mormon steeple. And a phone number.

I snag Leesie's phone out of her room. Dial. Get somebody's wife.

But she says he'll be at the church tonight.

## LEESIE'S MOST PRIVATE CHAPBOOK
## POEM # 91, A BARGAIN

I want to steal the keys,
the car, and run,
but Michael makes me go with him.
I sit in the back of the makeshift
dive classroom, with my head
buried in my arms resting
on the folding table, and listen
to pens scratch and Michael's voice
teach dive physics—one atmosphere,
two atmospheres, three atmospheres,
four.

I'm angry—want to hate him,
but his voice feeds my weakness,
my wanting, my worship, my desire.
I dream his body, his hands on mine.
No retreat.
Only surrender.

It's a relief to cool
down in the pool
after lunch, swim laps

with his students,
help them and win
a smile from Michael.

A smile that says,
I love you,
I want you—
just do this one thing.

I shake my head.
No, Michael, no.
No.
No.
No.

# A GAMBLE

## MICHAEL'S DIVE LOG – VOLUME #10

**Dive Buddy:** Leesie
**Date:** 06/17
**Dive #:** --
**Location:** Grand Cayman
**Dive Site:** East End Pool
**Weather Condition:** sunny
**Water Condition:** turbulent
**Depth:** 10 ft.
**Visibility:** shifting
**Water Temp:** thermocline
**Bottom Time:** most of the day
**Comments:**

After a long afternoon of back-to-back pool sessions, I hustle Leesie up to the apartment. "We need to hurry." The president guy's wife said we could see him at seven. It's almost six. She said the church is close to the grocery store on the way out of Georgetown—about forty-five minutes drive. Funny. I must have driven by it a hundred times and not noticed.

"You can't make me go." Leesie stomps across the apartment into her and Alex's room and slams the door.

I'm on her heels. "Please, babe," I croon into the door. I try the knob—not locked. I push open the door. What the heck.

Gabriel's always in there. Why not me?

She's sitting, scowling on her bed. "You can't make me tell him anything."

"If you won't"—I close the door behind me so the entire apartment full of tired dive guides won't hear all our personal business—"I will. I need help."

"Divine intervention?"

"Whatever it takes."

"I don't want to talk to a stranger."

I sit next to her on the bed. "What you and I *want*"—I put my hand on her knee—"is massively irrelevant."

"You want—?" She glances down at the bed.

"That's what I've always wanted. You know that. I don't believe any of this stuff."

"But—"

"But you do. So it's important. More important than what *I* want."

She rests her head on my shoulder. "This is useless. Believe me. He'll shake his head and show me the door."

"I don't think so." I put my arm around her. "I've got a feeling—"

She sits up, ducks my arm. "That's rich. You're getting revelation these days?"

I hate the tone in her voice and the look she gives me. I glance down, find her hand, grasp it in mine. "Something in my gut says we need to do this. Please, get ready."

"What do I get if I go? It's going to be humiliating."

I press her hand. "You're wrong."

"Want to bet?" She makes a sound half-way between a snort and a laugh.

"Sure." I lean forward and kiss her forehead. "If it will get you in the shower."

She kisses me. "You could get me in the shower."

"Freak, you're wicked."

"You love it." Her lips are on mine again.

I want to lie down with her in that bed and forget all about that guy at the church, but I disentangle myself and stand up. "What's the bet?"

She runs her hands over the sheets. "If I'm right, we come back here and lock Alex and Gabriel out of the room." She wrinkles up her nose. "No. Not here. If I'm right, we find a dark, lonely beach."

"And if I'm right?"

"We'll get married tomorrow."

I take her hand and pull her to her feet. "If I'm right— getting married?" I start to lose it and have to turn away from her. "You might not want to anymore."

She hugs me from behind. "Nothing can ever make me not want to marry you."

I turn around and clutch her hands in both of mine. "We both know that's not true."

"You're going to risk us"—light plays on my diamond on her finger, mesmerizing us both—"for a stupid feeling in your gut?"

"Here's the bet." I kiss her one more time. "If I'm right tonight, babe. You gotta call your parents."

## LEESIE'S MOST PRIVATE CHAPBOOK
## POEM # 92, CONFESSION

"Look at that! There it is."
Michael turns his rental RAV
in the parking lot next to
the Grand Cayman Branch
of the Church of Jesus Christ of Latter Day Saints.
He parks, turns off the ignition.
"Weird we never saw this."
I stare at the building—not a big chapel
but way nicer than where we meet back home.

"I guess we weren't looking."
He squeezes my shoulder.
"We've found it now."

We find our way in, find
President Bodden waiting in his office.
He stands—taller than Michael—
gray touching the close cut
fuzzy black hair at his temples.
"Sister Hunt?" His voice echoes
the Cayman richness of my doctor's
accent.
I nod.

My hand disappears into the warmth
of his huge black hand. He releases
me and turns to Michael. "I didn't
catch your name. Brother—?"
"Michael." He shakes President Bodden's hand.
"I spoke with your wife."
"Well. Come in. Come in." President Bodden
stands aside, holding open the door.
I hold Michael back. "He's not a member."
President Bodden's shoulders rise and his hands
motion welcome. "I can talk to you both."
"Not tonight." I'm worried Michael will say too much
or I will. I've promised to talk, but if I start,
will I ever stop? There is too much Michael
shouldn't hear—can't hear—ever. "Wait, okay?"
He smiles courage at me and backs off.

I close the door, turn to the office.
President Bodden sits and folds his large hands,
that seem made for putting on heads
to channel God's power into the afflicted,

on top of his desk.
I take the chair he offers.
"How long have you been on Cayman?"
I count back—takes a moment to assess
the time. "Almost eight weeks, I guess."
His silvery eye brows rise and fall.
"I'm sorry we haven't see you on Sundays."

I stare at my toes sticking out of white sandals
resting on the standard blue Mormon church carpet.
He continues. "When is the last time
you took the sacrament?"
"The Sunday before I left BYU."
His hands come off the desk, he sits straighter, his brow
creases. "You're a BYU student?"
"Was," I whisper as the twin marks on my neck
pulse redder and redder. "I was."
"The Lord gave you that great privilege,"
he tries not to let his disgust linger in his voice,
but fails, "and this is how you show your gratitude?"

He thinks I'm a slut breaking the honor code.
Fine that's just what I'll be. I stand up.
"That's why I'm not going back."
He stands, too. "Do you know how many
righteous youth want to go to BYU and can't?"
I nod, hand on the doorknob. "I get the message."
"No you don't. Sit down, Sister Hunt."
No one could resist his tone. I obey.

He sits, too, and glances at the ring glittering
on my finger. "Are you living with that young man?"
I pick tissues from a box on his desk. "Michael. Yes."
"Sleeping with him?"
"No."

"Let me be clearer. Have you had sexual
intercourse with him?"
"No." But I want—I really, really want to.
I don't say it aloud, but he hears.

I concentrate on mangling the tissue.
"Are you humping?"
"No."
"Petting?"
"He touched my breasts for half a second
this morning. Freaked out. That's why I'm here."
"You didn't freak out?"
"No."
"You don't sound very repentant, sister."
"I'm not."

His eyes squint into concentration
on the shredded tissue I'm littering
his desk with. "But you said he's not a member."
I push the mess towards him and sit back.
"He knows the rules."
"God's commandments."
"He doesn't believe in God, so I called them rules for him."
His eyes move from one bright red Michael bite
on my neck to the other. "You're living together
but not intimate at all?"

I look him square in the eye. "It's an apartment.
Nine of us. Six guys. Three girls.
I share a room with a girl."
"And your parents approve?"
I have to look away.
"My parents don't know."
He closes his eyes a moment,
and a familiar feeling comes into the room.

His eyes open as he says, "You'll have to move out."
I push away the enticings of salvation that float
above my head. "I can't. I won't."
President Bodden's eyes graze me
with infinite sadness.
"I can't help you then."

I rise, get the door open this time.
"Wait—Sister Hunt."
"I don't have anything more
to say."
President Bodden follows me to the hall.
"I want you to know, Sister Hunt.
The Lord loves you."

Michael sees, hears—
more than I want.
I rush to him. "I was right."
He takes both my hands.
I squeeze his hard and whisper,
"You owe me now."
Surprise, disappointment,
or surrender? I can't read him.
"Are you done?"
"Yes."
"No."
The power in President Bodden's voice
forces Michael's eyes away from me
to my judge in Israel.
"Did she tell you"—Michael's arm
surrounds me, and his voice drops
to holy levels—"about
the accident? Her brother?"

# GUILTY

## MICHAEL'S DIVE LOG – VOLUME 10

**Dive Buddy:** Leesie and President Bodden
**Date:** 06/17
**Dive #:** first one here
**Location:** Grand Cayman
**Dive Site:** Cayman Branch of the Mormon Church
**Weather Condition:** nice
**Water Condition:** fine
**Depth:** hard to tell
**Visibility:** clearer
**Water Temp:** warm
**Bottom Time:** 45 minutes
**Comments:**

Leesie's back in President Bodden's office. I'm in there this time. Leesie glares at me like I'm the biggest snitch in history. The guy sits back in his chair and looks from her to me.

A picture of Jesus wearing a red robe standing in front of a door, knocking, hangs on the wall above President Bodden's head. I don't know anything about this Jesus stuff, but I do know I need help. I hate when she's deceptive. Freak. She flat-out lied to me out there. This isn't the girl I fell in love with. Maybe this guy and his Jesus picture can help me find her again.

Who knows what she told the guy. Nothing good. For all

I know she told him we're doing it ten times a day. The look
on his face got to me. It wasn't disgust or loathing, though. It
was pain. Sorrow. Like he'd lost a child. His voice was full of
love—calling her back. He says it again, "The Lord loves you,
Sis. Hunt."

She pulls her scarf off her head. The long scar shows
through her inch-long hair-do and creeps down her forehead. "I
drove my brother off a cliff and killed him."

I reach out and put my hand on her arm. "There was ice on
the road. She was hurt really bad."

"We were having a huge fight." She closes her eyes. "I was
mad enough to shoot him. And driving way too fast. I killed him.
Manslaughter, at least."

"He didn't have a seatbelt on. It was an accident."

She shoves my hand off her arm. "Don't tell me it was
just an accident. Don't tell me I'm not guilty." She clasps her
hands together and leans toward President Bodden. "He doesn't
understand. I'm lost. Murder." Hysteria grows in her voice. "No
forgiveness in this life. Read him that scripture!" She hides her
face in her hands.

I lean over and grasp her shoulders, try to calm her. "In the
hospital, she went on and on about stoning. You guys don't do
that do you?"

"No. That's biblical." President Bodden rises and comes
around the desk, stands next to Leesie but doesn't touch her.
"Sister Hunt?"

"She told me—"

She drops her hands. "That's enough, Michael."

I put my hand over hers. "She told me the rules don't
matter any more. That she was lost forever, so it would be
okay—"

"And you—?"

"Didn't believe her."

"You protected her?"

"From me." I feel like scum.

Leesie's glittering eyes attack me then President Bodden. "I did everything I could to get him to sleep with me. And I'm not giving up."

"Sister Hunt!" President Bodden's eyebrows jut out. "Why are you tormenting this young man who obviously loves you? That is cruel."

Leesie starts, shakes her head wildly. "I don't know. I don't know. It's all I can think about. Every day. Every night." Her eyes swim with tears. "I've made it so hard for him. I am cruel. It's evil I know. That's who I am now. It's hopeless, President. I am lost." Tears stream down her face. "You can't find me."

President Bodden sits down behind his desk, reaches the box of tissues and hands it to Leesie. He doesn't say anything—lets her cry.

I try to comfort her, but she pushes me away. She finally blows her nose and says, "It's eating me up, President. What do I do? I can't live like this. We need to sin and get it over with."

"The guilt you are feeling is real. I'm not going to tell you, you did nothing wrong. We both know that isn't true."

I glare at the guy. "But it was an accident." What's with him?

"Guilt is a warning flag that leads us to repent. It is a gift from God. It will wrack your soul until you turn back to Him. But if you don't turn back to Him, it will eat you up from the inside out." The expression on his face reminds me of Leesie's dad. "And then you'll become hardened. Past feeling. All you'll want is sin. What you've told me tonight, Sister Hunt, concerns me greatly. You've given your guilt to the adversary."

The adversary? "What's that?"

"Satan. She's under his influence now."

I stare at Leesie wondering if she'll go all Carrie on me. "What is she guilty of?"

He watches emotions play across Leesie's face. "She can tell you."

Leesie sits up, lets me take her hand, squeezes her eyes

shut, and whispers, "Anger. Blinding anger and hatred toward my brother. That cost him his life."

President Bodden nods. "Go on."

Her eyes open. "Hurting my family. Recklessness." She fights down a sob. "I am responsible for that accident."

President Bodden studies her face. His voice is hushed, holy. "But you didn't murder your brother, did you?" His words open Leesie's heart. There's a power under them that even I feel.

Leesie looks at me and dissolves in a pool of sobs. "No." She falls into my arms. "No, I didn't."

## LEESIE'S MOST PRIVATE CHAPBOOK
## POEM #93, SHE COMES TO ME 2

Crying on Michael's chest
the wall I built to keep out the light,
cracks, splinters
and in cleansing white glory

*She comes to me,*
*a pure and shining presence,*
*knocking on my soul.*

"Sister Hunt?"
My grandmother smiles on my heart.
President Bodden's voice filters through
the rapture I'm encased in.
"Do you know your
very worst sin?"

*defogged, unfuddled*
*reveling in perfection*

I sit back from Michael,

wrap my arms around my chest
so I don't fracture into millions
of pieces at the exquisite force
so intense, so unearned, so blessed.

Along with my grandmother
blooming in my heart,
there's whisperings of something
that can only be Phil.
*I'm sorry Leesie. I love you.*
I bow my head and whisper,
"Me, too."

Michael rubs my back.
"Are you all right, babe?"

*spilling joy that*
*embraces my sorrow*
*they smile*
*and wave*
*farewell.*

Tears flow like water pounding
from a spout, splashing, gurgling
filling a baptismal font like the one
I stood in at eight with my father's
hands full of power to cleanse me.
President Bodden's voice extends an iron rod
to rescue me from endless wanderings
in a faceless field full of the lost.
"Your worst sin, Sister Hunt, was to believe
your Savior has power to save everyone—
but you."

I grasp Michael's hand and meet the man's gaze.

"I testify to you,"—his words soft but strong,
pierce my stubborn, stone heart—
"He loves every vile murderer in every
penitentiary and somehow, someday
in the great Eternal realm, they will all
find their own salvation through Him."

I rest my head against Michael's cheek.
He strokes my face and whispers, "Listen
to him, Leesie. Listen. You need this."

I study every word President Bodden's mouth
creates. "He waits with open arms,
spread wide to welcome you home
with love and forgiveness if you will
repent."

Emotion overtakes me once more.
I sob with my head down on the desk—
tears—the only offering I have left to give.

## MICHAEL'S DIVE LOG – VOLUME 10

**Dive Buddy:** Leesie
**Date:** 06/17
**Dive #:** --
**Location:** Grand Cayman
**Dive Site:** highway to East End
**Weather Condition:** clear skies
**Water Condition:** salty
**Depth:** heart to heart
**Visibility:** full of stars
**Water Temp:** hot
**Bottom Time:** 53 minutes
**Comments:**

Leesie's calm as we drive home. Before we left the church, President Bodden rattled off a list of what she needs to do. Assignments. In real life he's a teacher. Grade school principal. He does the church stuff as a volunteer. Their whole church runs like that.

First on the list. Leesie's supposed to "pray until her knees wear out." And I'm supposed to pray with her.

Second, read her scriptures. I saved them for her. She hasn't unpacked them. Don't know if she even saw them. I know she found the sheets of poetry I scavenged off the side of that mountain. She's got them hidden in a drawer. Maybe she's ready for those now, too.

Third, go to church this Sunday. He said she could take the bread and water thing they do. That shocked her. She figured she wasn't "worthy."

Fourth, move out of the apartment. That's the big one. He's going to try to find her a place tomorrow. We're meeting him at the church with Leesie's packed bags. I wanted to protest—but with everything going on at that apartment with Seth and Dani and Gabriel and Alex, I have to agree. She needs to get out of there.

The last assignment? Apologize to everyone she's hurt.

She starts with me. "I'm sorry." That brings tears close to the surface again. "If I really loved you"—her lip trembles—"I wouldn't have made it so hard for you."

I tilt my head until it touches hers. "You don't have to go there."

Her hands cling on my driving arm. "I do. I was awful. But I do love you—even if I didn't act like it. I'm sorry."

"You are ten times forgiven." My eye moves from the road to her eyes and flicks back. "Am I doing it right?"

She kisses my arm.

She hangs on me the rest of the way home.

When we get back to the apartment, she takes her phone out on the balcony where the signal is best and keys in a phone

number she knows by heart. "Hi, Mom. It's Leesie."
She pulls the sliding door shut and turns away.

# Chapter 23

## REUNION

### LEESIE'S MOST PRIVATE CHAPBOOK
### POEM #94, TOGETHER

I'm crying so hard
I can't speak.
Mom gets Dad on the phone.
We all three cry
together.

The call lasts
minutes?
hours?
forever?

I hang up and don't
know if I even told
them anything.

"I'm sorry."
I got that out.
"I love you."

We all said that.

"Whenever you want to come
home, Leesie-girl, is fine with us."
That was Dad.
How does he know
I'm not finished here
when I don't even know
myself?

"Give Michael our love"—
is all I remember from Mom.

And Dad's, "Tell him
we'll be proud
to call him son,"
made my heart burst.

I sop my face
with the last three
tissues on earth
and stare out at the stars
and moon shining hope
on the water.

My cell rings.
It's Dad saying,
"By the way, Leesie"—
he's that sweet, sheepish
farm boy my mom fell
in love with—
"Where are you?
We forgot to ask."

# YOU

## MICHAEL'S DIVE LOG – VOLUME 10

**Dive Buddy:** Leesie
**Date:** 06/17
**Dive #:** --
**Location:** Grand Cayman
**Dive Site:** the balcony
**Weather Condition:** night but still hot
**Water Condition:** we can hear the waves breaking on the reef
**Depth:** enveloped both of us
**Visibility:** it's dark but I can see farther than I have for a long time
**Water Temp:** perfect
**Bottom Time:** 67 minutes
**Comments:**

Everyone else is asleep when Leesie slides back open the balcony door. I'm awake in my cot. "Babe," I whisper, get up, trip over Ethan. He curses me, rolls over, farts.

This could be Leesie's last night here—last night with me. For all I know, her parents want her to get on a plane tomorrow and go home. I'll quit, go with her. They're okay here with Dani back. I hate to bail and leave them short-handed, but Leesie comes first. Maybe if I deliver her looking so much better like she does, it'll get me on her parents' good side. I did call her dad—and he was grateful—but I also stole their daughter. Do they understand why I did it? What did Leesie tell them?

And then there's Mr. Branch President dude. Who knows what crazy stuff he's got in store. Probably, same idea. An airline ticket home. Best I can imagine is an apartment I can rent for her. A marriage license? If he insists, I'm not going to debate it. Not any more. It's out of my hands. It's all up to her now.

I reach Leesie. She's pretty much drenched in tears and other facial fluid. "You okay?"

She holds her hands out for me and starts crying again. I step into the warm night air on the balcony. "Hey, hey, hush now. I'm here." I fold her up in my arms. "Are they making you come home?"

Her voice squeaks through her tears. "Dad says I can stay here as long as we need to."

I close my eyes, don't want to say this. "I can take you home tomorrow. Just say the word."

A shudder moves through her body. "Let's talk to President Bodden first."

"Does your dad have a shot gun? What about his razor knife? Is he buying new blades?"

She shakes her head—trying to remember. "He said something sweet about calling you, 'son.'"

"He always does that."

"He meant it different this time."

I rest my lips on her soft, furry head. "What does that mean?"

She bites her trembling lip. "I think it means you can't get rid of me no matter what."

"Even if I'm not a Mormon?"

"My dad's got a lot of faith." She sniffs and loses it again.

I'm not sure what that's supposed to mean. So far—it's all good. "Were they angry?" I sit on the chaise lounge and pull her down beside me.

She shakes her head and squeaks into my shoulder. "We

were all devastated together."

I stroke her head. "You've been holding it in."

"It's coming out now." She wipes her hand down her face. "All over you."

I squeeze her. "Any time, babe."

"24/7?"

"If that's what it takes."

"I don't deserve you."

"I don't deserve you."

"No way we're even."

I kiss her nose. "Don't worry. I'll collect."

"Michael!" She slugs my arm.

I love every note of her protest. I kiss her to make sure. All her old barriers are back up. "Freak." I rub my face against hers. "You're back. You're really back."

She manages to add a trembling smile to her tears.

"Will you tell me something?" I've been patient—haven't questioned her story about the accident.

"Anything." She kisses me. Her lips are hot and salty.

I swallow my suspicions. It's nothing really. Her story makes sense. Mostly. She's like a fresh born butterfly with wet wings. I don't want to crush them while she's getting ready to fly.

## LEESIE'S MOST PRIVATE CHAPBOOK
## POEM #95, REDEMPTION?

Hesitation clutches my stomach
before I enter President Bodden's office.
Does lost Leesie lurk in the corner
where Grandma and Phil's heaven sent
light left her licking her wounds
and planning a counter offensive
to retake my soul at dawn's first light?

Michael guides me through the door—
my buffer, my strength, my hero.
The room feels sweet, inviting, holy.
I whisper a prayer of thanks as I sit.
The Spirit washes over me in healing
waves. *Slowly, slowly.* It whispers. *Go slowly.*

Michael reports my phone call home.
He knows unstoppable tears will
pour from me again if I try to speak of it.
I stood in the shower for a half hour
last night before I stopped sobbing
enough to sleep.
President Bodden leans forward,
hands clasped, eyes concerned.
"Are you leaving us then, Sister Hunt?"
Is he disappointed?
"My dad said"—I swallow and sniff,
blink watery eyes—"I can stay if I need to."

President Bodden smiles. "The Lord works
in mysterious ways."
Michael doesn't understand. "I can take
her home whenever she wants to go.
She's known that from the start."
"I appreciate that." President Bodden's voice
calms the water. "I have an opportunity
for Sister Hunt to consider."
I sit up straight and try to focus.
"Like a place to stay?"
"Like a job?" Michael's voice
and concern entwine mine.

President Bodden's mouth splits into a welcome
grin. "Let's call it a service project."

Michael frowns back at him.
"That's what she called me."

"A sister in the branch—
we all call her Aunty Jaz—"
Michael's eyebrows shoot up.
"Aunty Jaz is a Mormon?"
"You've had her fish?" President Bodden closes
his eyes to savor a succulent memory.
Michael does the same.
Inhales a phantom scent.
"It's the best."

The story unfolds—
Hot oil. Burned foot. Blisters.
Bad infection. Diabetic. Not healing.
Released from the hospital but needs
help round the clock. Sisters
have taken turns all week.
Her daughter in the states
just had twins. Her son on
Cayman is court-ordered
to keep his distance.
Fish shack closed. No money
coming in now for weeks.
"We're looking after her utilities
and food, but hiring a companion
is beyond what we can do."

I sit up tall, straight, feel the Lord's
hand redeeming my life.
"I can do it. I can. I took care
of my grandmother."
President Bodden holds his hands up,
slow down, girl, slow down.

"You'll have to cook and clean.
She does have a nurse
stop in to dress the wound
and bathe her."
"Yes, yes, yes, please let me try."
I've wallowed in guilt day after day
week after week, months now.
I can serve, Lord. I can.
Thank you.
Thank you.
Thank you.

"Are you sure, Leese?"
Michael's hand rests on my knee.
I nod. So sure.
His eyes turn to President Bodden.
"What about the son?
Will she be safe?"
"Aunty Jaz hasn't heard
from him in two years."
How sad. Poor Aunty.
If not for Michael—that could be me.
Estranged forever. But now I'm released.

"You should pray about it, Sister Hunt."
I make a strange sound halfway
between a laugh and a sob.
"I already did. I'm ready now.
But, first, President, will
you give me a blessing?"
I need Michael to see this,
to feel this,
to know the power
he's brought back into my life.

President Bodden blinks his eyes
to ease the water that fills them.
"I'd be honored."

## MICHAEL'S DIVE LOG – VOLUME 10

**Dive Buddy:** Leesie
**Date:** 06/18
**Dive #:** --
**Location:** Grand Cayman
**Dive Site:** Mormon Chapel
**Weather Condition:** intermittent showers
**Water Condition:** calm for now
**Depth:** no longer flood stage
**Visibility:** remarkably clear
**Water Temp:** 80
**Bottom Time:** another half hour
**Comments:**

Leesie wants one of those blessings things like her dad and
Jaron did back in the hospital before I take her to Aunty Jaz's.
All the sudden she's moving in with a sick old lady. Aunty Jaz's
fish shack was my dad's favorite place to eat on the island. A
dump from the outside, but the best fish—spicy and moist. It's
sad she had to close the place. The woman's a perfect stranger to
Leesie. But the way her and President Bodden talk about Aunty
Jaz, she's close as a real aunty. Sister this and Brother that. I got
used to that when I was in Provo before Christmas last year, but
it still sounds weird. Especially, Brother Walden. That sounds the
weirdest of all.

I don't mind slowing down. Making sure Leesie thinks this
through. If this blessing deal gives her a chance to do that, cool.

President Bodden invites a second dude to join us. This
guy is short, sunburned, mostly bald with a buzzed blonde fringe.
President Bodden wears a dark suit, white shirt and tie, but this
guy's got on tan Dockers and sandals with his obligatory white

shirt and tie. He smiles at Leesie, runs his hand over his head. "I like your do." He speaks with a British accent.

"This is Brother Clark." Pres. Bodden's eyes rest on my face. "He'll assist."

Brother Clark has a silver cylinder on his key chain like Jaron did. I feel totally useless. If he was here, he could do this for Leese—instead of these strangers—"brothers" or not.

Brother Clark opens the cylinder. "This is olive oil, like they had at the time of Christ, that has been consecrated"—he notices the puzzled frown creasing my forehead—"blessed for the healing of the sick."

"She isn't sick."

The two men stand on either side of Leesie's chair. President Bodden grasps the back of it. "Physically, she is well. But spiritually . . . "

Leesie whispers, "I've got a long way to go." She closes her eyes.

"Can I stay?"

"Please do, Brother Walden."

Brother Clark puts a drop of oil on Leesie's head. He and President Bodden place their hands on her head, too. Brother Clark says a few rapid words I don't catch, their hands lift off Leesie's head a beat and then rest down again.

"Leesie Marie Hunt." President Bodden's rich Caymanian accent fills the room. "By the power of the Holy Melchizedek priesthood which we hold, we place our hands on your head and give you a blessing. . . . "

The rest is intimate, personal, holy. I don't feel right writing it down. I couldn't if I tried. He blessed her with health, strength, and the power to conquer temptation. Does that mean me or just sinning with me? I get a strong impression that it doesn't mean me.

He says stuff about the accident and Phil. Her family loving her. God loving her.

And then he says, "You've found the love of a valiant son

of God. Cherish that love. Build upon it. Eternal happiness can be yours." My first thought is he's talking about Jaron. Dump this jerk and get home to your destiny. Then a powerful force hits me in the heart, and I know that it's me. President Bodden is calling me that. A son of God. Valiant. Me?

I don't recall anything else in the blessing after that.

Leesie can be eternally happy with me? I didn't think that was possible. I thought I was against all the rules—even if we got married.

*I can't marry you if you're not a Mormon.* How many times has that echoed in my mind since I proposed the first time, and she threw my ring back at me? That's not fair. She cried. It hurt her as much as it hurt me.

What's changed now?

What's so different?

That power speaking to my heart whispers—

You.

# Chapter 25

## JAZZED

### LEESIE'S MOST PRIVATE CHAPBOOK
### POEM #96, AUNTY

Michael drives me to a world
I didn't know existed on Cayman.
Narrow roads, no sidewalks.
Cinder block walls, corrugated
metal roofs, wire fences.
Fat chickens and skinny dogs.
Laundry outside drying on lines
strung from trees, baking
in the hot Cayman sun.

No manicured resort lawns
and tropical gardens. No beach,
no sand, no ocean.
Jungle-like growth encroaching
each habitation, green upon green
punctuated by scarlet bougainvillea
in rampant profusion climbing
telephone poles, fence gates,
houses and engine-less cars
rusting in the front yards.

Dusty black children play
in dirt yards.

Aunty Jaz's fish shack is truly
a shack. Vines entangle the tiny
structure as if they'll pull it apart.
President Bodden told us she lives
in rooms behind it.

Michael parks in front.
"Are you sure, babe?"
He looks up and down the street.
"This part of the island
isn't what you're used to."
A rooster struts across the road.
"I come from a farm full of pigs.
My grandma had chickens."
He frowns, uncomfortable.
"But every body here is—"
"Poor?"
"A different color."
I frown right back.
"Those cute kids over there
don't scare me."
His hand rests on my head.
"I'm not leaving you here
until I know you're safe."
I lean over and kiss him.
"Deal."
I climb out, and a small boy
with a huge dog calls from across
the street. "Aunty Jaz is sick.
No fish, lady."
I cross the street and pat
the mutt's head. "Hi, I'm Leesie.

I'm Aunty Jaz's friend."
The kid's lower lip juts out.
"How come I never see you before?"
The dog growls.
I recall my hand. "I'm a new friend."
"I thought so."

Michael won't unload my bags
until we check things out.
We pause in front at windows
closed with heavy wooden shutters
painted yellow and purple.
And a locked pink door.
"Around back," the boy yells.

"Keep behind me."
Michael shields me with his body,
quietly creeping, in case
we're attacked by—
the two large, laughing women
we find on a screened porch.

"Don't make me laugh, sister,"
a gray-haired one shrieks,
"it hurts my foot."
"Laughing hurts your foot?"
"Everything hurts my foot."
They see Michael and stop.
"Aunty Jaz?"
She frowns. "The restaurant's closed
young man."
I step out from behind Michael.
"President Bodden sent us."
Her hands flap up and down.
"Mercy, where's my manners?

You'll be Sister Hunt?"
I can't help but smile back at her.
"Leesie, please. Can I call you
Aunty Jaz?"
"Only if you come right here"—
she holds open her arms—
"and give this old soul a kiss."

The other lady opens the screen
door wide, beams and nods.
I go right up to Aunty Jaz,
lean over, kiss her sunken cheek.
She hugs me to her expansive bosom.
Her eyes move from the ring
on my finger to Michael and back
to me. "I bet you got a good story for me."
"Leesie's a poet."
Michael stands in the doorway.
"You don't say." She moves
over so I can sit beside her
on the sagging couch.
"I'll be having that after dinner then."
A void in my soul makes my head drop.
"I can't. Michael saved some rough scraps,
but all my good stuff is lost."
Aunty Jaz's shoulders heave up and down.
"Write me more then—after dinner."

"Excuse me." Michael disappears,
returns with my bags.
He pulls the scribbles he rescued
out of the side pocket, dumps
them in my lap. "Time you got to work.
I'll leave you the laptop."
I pick the bundle up,

stare at it. "So I can stay?"

He nods. "I have a good feeling about this."

He turns to Aunty Jaz. "My dad loved
your fish fry. Do I get a kiss, too?"

Aunty Jaz grins and puckers her lips.

Michael kisses her cheek like I did.

She kisses him back. "Sit down, boy.

Sit down and we'll have us a visit.

I've a good feeling about you, too."

## LEESIE HUNT / CHATSPOT LOG / 06/23/2010 3:17 PM

**Kimbo69 says:** You moved away from all those beautiful boys
before I could come visit?

**Leesie327 says:** Poor Mark. Do you drool like this when he's
around?

**Kimbo69 says:** We have a mutual agreement about eye candy.

**Leesie327 says:** You'll love Aunty Jaz.

**Kimbo69 says:** Why do they call her that?

**Leesie327 says:** Her name is Jasmine—like the flower.

**Kimbo69 says:** Does she smell good?

**Leesie327 says:** Michael thinks it's a sign from his mom. She
used to wear gardenia perfume. It's like one tropical flower to
another.

**Kimbo69 says:** He's getting as crazy as you are.

**Leesie327 says:** He took us to church Sunday. I didn't even ask.
All the sudden there he was in front of Jaz's shack, honking the
horn of a used car he bought because the RAV he'd rented was
too hard for Aunty Jaz to get into. He wore a brand new white
shirt and that Valentino tie I Ebayed for him when I made him go
to that dance with me. He took it to Thailand. The tie. Figure that
one.

**Kimbo69 says:** He went to church with you?

**Leesie327 says:** It took both of us to get Aunty Jaz in the front seat of the car. It was worth it, though. She was so excited to be going to church again. She used to take a bus. Can't now with her foot.

**Kimbo69 says:** Is her house really a shack?

**Leesie327 says:** Pretty much. There's running water, a real toilet, electricity—no AC. We spend a lot of time on the porch.

**Kimbo69 says:** How sick is she?

**Leesie327 says:** I have to make sure she eats and gets her insulin shot. We test her blood sugar, too. The nurse came Friday, and I helped her change the bandages on Jaz's foot—it's bad.

**Kimbo69 says:** I'd hurl.

**Leesie327 says:** I'm tougher than you.

**Kimbo69 says:** It sounds like you like this stuff.

**Leesie327 says:** I do. I've got something to do other than flail myself with guilt over the accident or fantasize myself crazy about Michael.

**Kimbo69 says:** You've stopped fantasizing about Michael?

**Leesie327 says:** I'm trying—it's not easy.

**Kimbo69 says:** No fantasizing? That's not healthy.

**Leesie327 says:** I've got to repent.

**Kimbo69 says:** Even your thoughts?

**Leesie327 says:** Yeah. That's the hardest part. He walks into the room, and I have to start all over again. Let those thoughts go wild, and it's hard to tame them.

**Kimbo69 says:** I'll never figure you out.

**Leesie327 says:** It's not such a mystery. If I can't sleep with him, it makes it worse if I'm constantly thinking about it. Duh.

**Kimbo69 says:** Are you still getting married?

**Leesie327 says:** I hope by the end of the summer like we planned. I'm never giving him his ring back. He's stuck with me.

**Kimbo69 says:** That doesn't sound too definite. What's wrong?

**Leesie327 says:** Nothing. I have to go home first—he promised my dad.

**Kimbo69 says:** Can you do that now?
**Leesie327 says:** I've been on the phone with my parents every day since that first call. I think I'll be ready. I have to be ready. So we can get married.
**Kimbo69 says:** Is Michael pretty stoked? It's what he wants, isn't it?
**Leesie327 says:** We're not talking about it. There's still one big complication.
**Kimbo69 says:** You're holding the Mormon stuff against him?
**Leesie327 says:** That doesn't matter to me anymore. I just want him.
**Kimbo69 says:** Tell him then.
**Leesie327 says:** I tried—and I choked on the words.
**Kimbo69 says:** He deserves this, Leesie. Don't be such a wimp.
**Leesie327 says:** I know. I know.
**Kimbo69 says:** How often do you get to see him?
**Leesie327 says:** He drives all the way over here every night after work. Hangs out until midnight and then goes back to East End. That's a lot of driving.
**Kimbo69 says:** I'd call it devotion.
**Leesie327 says:** Aunty Jaz told me her husband got baptized twenty years after they married. I'd wait that long for Michael—I would.
**Kimbo69 says:** What if he never gets baptized?
**Leesie327 says:** He brought me back. He must believe a tiny bit.
**Kimbo69 says:** He knows you need it—that doesn't mean he believes it.
**Leesie327 says:** I know. That's why I'm too afraid to even bring it up. After all we've been though, I can't risk offending him.
**Kimbo69 says:** You've got to talk to him.
**Leesie327 says:** I think I'm going to watch and wait. Nothing else feels right.
**Kimbo69 says:** That's it?
**Leesie327 says:** And pray.
**Kimbo69 says:** Pray?
**Leesie327 says:** Pray. A lot.

# Chapter 26

## JAZ'S TEST

### MICHAEL'S DIVE LOG – VOLUME 10

**Dive Buddy:** Leesie
**Date:** 06/25
**Dive #:** first one in the new kayak
**Location:** Grand Cayman
**Dive Site:** Turtle Reef
**Weather Condition:** sunny
**Water Condition:** calm
**Depth:** 50 ft.
**Visibility:** 80 ft.
**Water Temp:** 82
**Bottom Time:** 4 minutes at a time
**Comments:**

I lucked out. It's slow today. The new kayak I ordered is in at the scuba shop downtown. Aunty Jaz's nurse comes Thursday afternoon. Which all adds up to me and Leesie paddling out to the mini wall off Turtle Reef. Jaz lives in West Bay. Close to where I certified to free dive as a kid. North Wall is close, too. Great diving. Too bad I'm down in East End, but we'll make it work. I bought a car. It's cool.

Okay, I lied. I'm doing all the paddling. Leesie's facing me instead of turned around in paddle ready form. She's lying back on the rugged black nylon the boat's made out of, eyes closed, fingers trailing in the water. She wore an old one-piece swimsuit with a t-shirt over it. I'm wearing swim shorts and a rash guard so I don't get burnt. Too warm today for wetsuits—even a dive skin.

I hold the paddle so it drips on Leesie's face.

Her eyes open. "Are we there yet?" She wipes the drops from her face.

"No."

Her eyes close again. "When can we go swimming?"

"Can we talk first?" We haven't talked alone much since she moved to Aunty Jaz's.

"I'm hot." She sits up and drops her head on my shoulder.

I lower my paddle. "Let's swim then."

She slips out of her t-shirt and hits the water before I can even stow my paddle. I hand her fins, snorkel and mask. "Babe, you gotta wear this stuff. You're in the ocean."

She takes them and smiles. "Have I told you I love you?"

"Not today." I slide into the water and kiss her.

She pushes me away. "That's so dangerous."

"I know." I hook one arm on the kayak and watch her. "I'll be good."

Her face gets bleak. "I'm not worried about you."

"You're going to flip out and attack me?"

That coaxes a faint smile. "Yeah. Brace yourself."

I maneuver the kayak between us. "How's this?"

She hooks her elbows over her side and stares across at me with her chin propped on her fists. "Perfect."

"How's it going, babe? All that stuff President Bodden told you to do?"

"Okay, I guess."

I frown at her. "You didn't eat the sacrament thing Sunday."

"You saw?"

"The pres said you should."

Her eyes study the bottom of the boat. "I know. I need to do it, but I'm scum. It felt wrong."

"Hey." I lift her chin. "Why?"

"I listened to the wrong voice." Her masked eyes search for mine. "I felt horrible that I didn't take it. This Sunday for sure I will. Will you drive us again?"

"Of course." I rest my hand on her shoulder.

"It's not too boring?"

I squeeze her arm. "How's the other stuff going?"

She inhales deeply, slips her mask up on her forehead. "I emailed Krystal yesterday. I haven't heard back. That's the last apology I can think of."

I push my mask up, too. "What about all that praying?" I stroke her cheek.

She leans against my hand. "I'm doing that, too."

"President Bodden said I should help."

"It's okay, Michael." She slips from my touch. "I can handle it. I know all this stuff makes you uncomfortable."

I don't know what to say to that. Am I relieved? Or upset that she's blocking me out? I pull myself into the kayak and help her back in. She picks up her paddle. We stroke in sync a few minutes up-current along the mini-wall to a good free diving spot. I rest my elbows on my paddle and lean forward so I can whisper to Leesie. "It doesn't."

She cranes her neck around. "What?"

I stroke her slicked down wet head. "Your church stuff. It doesn't make me uncomfortable anymore."

She bows her head.

I wrap my arms around her. "You're praying right now, aren't you?"

"Just saying thanks."

"Let me hear."

She twists to face me, takes hold of my hands and bows her head again. "Dear Heavenly Father, Thank Thee for Michael."

I rest my forehead against hers. "That's what you pray?"

"All day. Every day. 24/7."

Then we get in the water, and I feel like everything is slow motion. Breathing down for a free dive, falling through the water to the wall, floating with a couple angel fish, kicking with my huge free dive fins to get back to the surface and Leesie. It's like a dream. My mom is there all around me—in every drop of water, every smile Leesie gives me, every ray of sunshine that lights the ocean we dive through.

I get Leesie to try a few free dives. She's awful at it—can't hold her breath. She tries, though. We stay out on the wall until I'm almost too tired to paddle back in. Leesie's tired, too, but she's good with a paddle.

When we get to Aunty Jaz's, I corner Jaz on the porch while Leesie's changing. "How do I know that what I feel is what you guys say it is? It feels like my mom. You know she died?"

Aunty Jaz shakes her head. "I'm sorry, sweet boy." She pats my knee.

"Me, too. What Leesie says is your Holy whatever feels to me like whispers from my mom. I know that's real. Why should I believe the way you guys explain it?"

Aunty Jaz hands me a Book of Mormon she was reading before I sat down. "Turn to the back. It's marked." She leans across me, flips the pages to a couple underlined verses.

It says if someone reads the book and asks God about it, He'll tell him if it's true. "That's it?" I look up at her. "I just have to pray?" That's kind of their answer for everything.

Aunty Jaz grins and winks at me. "Read that book and pray."

I close it up and hand it back to her.

She pushes it to me. "You keep it. My gift."

"Are you sure?"

"Of course."

I put it away before Leesie returns.

Read the book and pray.

How hard can that be?

# LEESIE'S MOST PRIVATE CHAPBOOK
## POEM #97, SABBATH SURPRISE

Sunday.
Church.
Michael holds the silver
bread tray for me until
I take
a tiny white crumble
and put it in my mouth.

I chew slowly, waiting
for a lightening bolt
to fry me in my seat.
I close my eyes, feel
Michael's fingers winding
around mine.

Did You know he would
be such a miracle?
The heavens don't answer.
I'm left to ponder until it's
time for the water.

I don't hesitate at this
second emblem of renewal.
I feel it washing me inside
as it trickles down my throat.

Michael senses success,
squeezes my hand.
He cares so much
that I find my way
back to a Savior

he doesn't
admit exists.

Is he pretending?
Is this all show for me—
so I can get that crutch
back under me?

I want it to be
as real as the intensity
his gray eyes reveal
when he catches mine
and smiles.

After dinner at Jaz's,
while she snores on the couch
with her bandaged foot propped
on a tower of pillows balanced
on a wispy coffee table,
Michael sits beside me
on the step that leads to
a kitchen full of dirty dishes
that I need to wash.
I lean into him and inhale
his presence.

His lips rest on the top of my head
for a moment and then
he carefully places an open
Book of Mormon in my lap.
"I don't get this part." He
points to a verse.
"Can you help me?"
I sit up, study his face.
My eyes find his and hold them.

"You're reading this?"
Tears threaten and a lump
in my throat chokes off my words.
He did this on his own? all alone?
Without me?


I sniff and pull a ragged tissue from my pocket.
He kisses my forehead. "Aunty Jaz told me
about the test at the end."
I try to stay calm, match his nonchalance,
focus on the page open in my lap—
Lehi's dream? My fingers smooth
over the page as my heart
beats loud enough for him to hear it.
"What do you think so far?"


"I don't know I just started."
His arms go around me.
"More action than I expected.
I thought holy guys were wimps."
I snuggle into his embrace. "Not Nephi."
"Yeah." He raises a hand to his throat.
"That dude's dangerous."
"We don't chop off heads at midnight."
He laughs and stretches his legs out.
"Do you think I'm Laman or Lemuel?"
"The bad boys?" I frown at him. "No way."
"Who then?"
"Sam?"
"No."
I hunch over thinking, with elbows
on my knees and my chin in my palms.
"I know"—I sit up and twist to face him—
"You're Zoram." He looks puzzled.
I flick the pages back, searching.

"The guy they capture and force
to come along. Here." I point to the verse.
He reads and shakes his head. "That's what
I thought. Join us or die."

I lean close and press my lips to his.
"That's not your choice."
He holds my face against his.
"Join us or lose you."
I kiss him again.
"That's not going to happen."
"Even if," he murmurs across
my mouth, "this test is a flop?"
I bow my head onto his shoulder.
"Have you prayed yet?"
"I'm on page fourteen."
I look up. "So?"
"Don't I have to finish
the whole thing first?"
I take his face between by hands
"Pray ever time you open the book."
He leans forward and kisses me.
"Like now?"
We kiss again. "Uh-huh."
He sits up, serious now.
"Can you do it?"
"No." I push his hair out of his face.
His eyes move away from mine.
"You know I don't believe
I'm talking to anybody."
I take his hands and whisper,
"Then what will it hurt?"
He bows his head, closes his eyes.
"Dear Leesie's God-guy,
Can you get her to explain

this dream bit to me? Amen."
I squeeze his hands.
"I could call the elders. The guys
at the branch are nice."
"Nope." He lifts my hands to his lips.
"This is just between you and me."
"And my God-guy."

We sit side by side and bend
our heads over the verses.
"Lehi's boys couldn't figure the dream
out, either. The naughty ones sat around
and complained. Nephi prayed and look"—
Michael's eyes follow as my fingers turn the pages—
"the Lord answered."
He picks up the book and reads.
"This is talking all about Jesus.
He wasn't in the dream."
"The Tree of Life is God's love."
I point to the verse.
"Nephi received a vision of Christ
because His mission to earth
is the greatest manifestation
of the Father's love for us."
"But aren't they the same guy?
I know that much from Gram's church."
"No." I flip to a picture of the First Vision.
"Father and Son—just like you
and your dad—with bodies like
ours, but perfected—Eternal.
Glorified."
He strokes my cheek.
"And you're His daughter?"
I kiss his fingers.
"And you're His son."

"Like President Bodden's blessing?"
"You remember that?"
His smoky gray eyes grasp mine.
"I can't forget it."

I put my arms around him and draw
him close. "Thank you—for trying my world."
I kiss him with all the love in my heart.
He hangs onto me. "Don't let go or I'll panic."
"Don't worry." I squeeze him. "I've got you."
He rests his forehead on mine.
"What if you're God doesn't speak to me?"
I shake my head in wonder that he
doesn't see what's so clear.
"He already has or we wouldn't be here."
Michael draws away. "That's my mom."
I pull him back close.
"She's on His side."

# Q&A

## MICHAEL'S DIVE LOG – VOLUME 10

**Dive Buddy:** Leesie
**Date:** 06/29
**Dive #:** --
**Location:** Grand Cayman
**Dive Site:** Aunty Jaz's
**Weather Condition:** hot
**Water Condition:** the only water I'm in is what's thick in the air
**Depth:** too deep
**Visibility:** murky
**Water Temp:** tepid
**Bottom Time:** all afternoon
**Comments:**

As I drive home from Aunty' Jaz's and all the next day while I'm diving, I keep thinking about what Leesie told me. To become a Mormon I have to believe in Jesus Christ. Not just that he was a great man who taught stuff that changed the world—for good or ill—depending on your point of view. I have to believe He's God's son—a God himself—my brother. And He came to save me. From what I'm not sure. I need to ask Leesie.

Leesie says God and Jesus aren't some indescribable divine force. Joseph Smith saw them. They have physical bodies. What about the Holy Spirit? How does He fit in?

And there's this huge hole in Leesie's logic. If God is literally the father of our spirits, don't we need a mother up there, too? Is that supposed to be Mary? But how could she be Jesus's mother on earth while she was being a mother in heaven? That's kind of a heavy load for one, young Jewish chick.

I only have to work the morning. After I unload the dive boat, I grab a sandwich and head out. When I get to Aunty Jaz's, Leesie's in the front clipping the giant bougainvilleas that overwhelm the shack.

"Ouch." She yells and drops the clippers. "These things have thorns!" She shoves her thumb in her mouth.

"Yeah. You need gloves."

She kicks at the clippers. "And better clippers."

"Want me to help?" I look at the mess she's making. "We used to have these in Phoenix."

"I don't know." She takes a few steps back and surveys her progress. "It seems hopeless."

I slide my arm around her waist. "We can do it together." I kiss her, and she squirms.

"Gross. I'm all sweaty."

I kiss her again. "I like sweaty."

She claps her hands over her ears and starts humming a tune that sounds like something they sang in church Sunday.

I laugh and release her. "I've got some questions for you."

"Really?" She slaps at a mosquito on my arm. "We need more bug spray, too."

Leesie washes up quick while I take cover from the mosquitoes with Aunty Jaz on the screened porch.

"That girl doesn't stop—does she?"

I sit beside Aunty Jaz. "Not when she gets her mind set on something."

Aunty Jaz looks back to make sure Leesie's still inside, leans over and whispers, "She's been busy at that computer late at night and early in the morning. She won't read any of it to me, though."

224 / angela morrison

"Me, neither." It's good to hear Leesie's working on her poetry. She's progressing faster than I expected. We still haven't had a chance to talk more about the accident—too busy with all this God stuff. It'll come. The right time.

"How are you doing with that Book of Mormon?"

I lower my voice. "I got stuck. Leesie's helping me. Is that allowed?"

Aunty Jaz's face splits wide with a smile. "Of course. So that's why she gave me that big kiss last night."

I give her a big kiss on the cheek, too.

Leesie catches us. "Are you trying to steal my fiancé?"

Aunty Jaz slaps my back. "I've turned his head, sweetie. I have that affect."

Leesie takes my hands and pulls me to my feet. "Mind if I try to win him back?"

"You can try." She winks at me.

Leesie winds her fingers through mine. "We'll be back in a couple hours. You'll be okay?"

"My nurse arrives shortly."

"We can stay until she comes."

Aunty Jaz shoos us with both hands. "Get along."

As soon as we're on the road driving towards Georgetown, Leesie bites her lower lip and folds her hands in her lap. "You have questions?"

"Yeah." I swallow. My thoughts are in a jumble. "First, how does the Holy—"

"—Ghost?"

"—fit in?"

"He's the third member of the Godhead."

"With God and Jesus?" I glance over at her. She nods. I look back at the road. "Why do you call him a ghost? That's weird."

"He doesn't have a physical body like Jesus and Heavenly Father so He can communicate with our spirits."

"Okay. Whatever. You know, this whole Heavenly Father

thing has a big problem. Who's the mother?"

"We don't know."

"You need a goddess up there. Think about it, babe. Maybe we should check out a goddess church next?"

"No need. We do believe there's a mother in heaven."

"I got it—Mary."

"No. She's Jesus earthly mother."

"And Joseph's his father—so how is he different than everyone else?"

"Check your Bible stories, hon. Joseph wasn't his father. Mary was a virgin, remember?"

Not really. Never read the stuff. "So it was like magic?"

"Miraculous. God's power. Not Magic. You read the scriptures about it yesterday. The spirit overshadowed Mary and then she was pregnant. Mary says 'great things' were done to her."

"You're saying she slept with God?"

"I'm saying we don't know the details. But she's called a handmaid of the Lord. In the Old Testament handmaids bore children for Abraham, Isaac, and Jacob. They became wives."

"Wives?" I frown, confused. "You think God's a polygamist? I have to believe that?"

"No. I'm guessing here. God made the rules. His relationship with Mary wasn't based on sin. All you have to believe is Jesus was His son."

"Not a fast-talking Jewish girl's bas—"

"Don't say that." She grabs my arm. "It hurts." She presses her hand to her heart.

"I'm sorry." We drive in silence a couple miles, reach the outskirts of Georgetown, and traffic slows up. We get stopped at a red light. I turn to her. "You believe all this stuff—literally?"

"Yes." She meets my searching gaze.

I shake my head. "I've never heard you pray to a *Mother* in Heaven."

"No. We pray to the Father in the Son's name."

"What does that mean?"

"Jesus takes our prayers to the Father and pleads for us."

"And what does the mother do?"

"We don't know for sure. I think she's there, part of everything—sharing like parents do."

"Are you making this up?"

Leesie's voice takes on an intense tone. "It's very sacred doctrine."

"So we were one big happy God family?" Sounds more like sci-fi than religion.

"In heaven? Before we came to earth? Very big. Mostly happy."

I lean back and shake my head. "How could perfect, all-powerful God-parents make their children live in such a horrible place? Suffer like—" Me. And her.

"We chose to come here. Fought for the privilege."

"Fought? Who?"

"Our other brother."

We're at the store, so the question I have about that gets lost in buying mega-clippers, two pairs of thick gloves, six different types of mosquito killer, and a giant bag of potato chips.

Leesie naps on the drive back to Aunty Jaz's, so we don't get back to our private discussion until late that night when Leesie kisses me goodnight and whispers, "Did I freak you earlier today with the Heavenly Mother stuff?"

"Nope." I smooth my hand over her furry head. "It's no stranger than everything else."

"It's why the temple is so important." She can see I'm not following. "The family is a divine entity. The heart of everything in heaven and earth."

"So you need to stick them together?" I stroke her cheek.

"Seal them." She presses her lips into my palm.

I hug her close. "Why isn't it automatic?" It should be. People who love each other should be together forever if they want to be.

"Nothing's automatic." She leans her face onto my hand. "God's too good of a teacher to go for that."

"He's God." I crouch down so we're eye to eye. "He could cut us some slack."

"If this is a test"—she touches her nose to mine—"he's got to make it hard enough for us to grow." She kisses me and retreats to the doorway. "Have you prayed?"

I shake my head.

She blows me a kiss. "Try."

## LEESIE'S MOST PRIVATE CHAPBOOK
## POEM #98, I CAN?

I blew it.
I blew it.
I'm sure that I blew it.
Too much, too fast,
too little, too slow.
I bungled it all
in a mixed up jumble.
He thinks it's crazy.

I wish he'd let me
call in the elders.
They could stop by
tomorrow to help
with the yard.
Service Project.
He'd see through that
and never speak to me
again.

Maybe he already won't speak
to me. Did I really bring up

Heavenly intimacy?

I pull my hide-a-bed out of the couch,
hit my knees beside it,
weary the Lord with my whining.
"He says he wants me to teach him
like he taught me,
but, but, but—"

*You can do this.*

"I'm not a missionary.
I don't know what I'm supposed
to teach him first or second.
What if I get something wrong?"

*Just open your mouth.*

"Really?"

A glorious, hopeful peace
blooms from my heart
and wafts warmth
to the panicked
doubt in my brain.

I crawl into bed,
curl under the sheet,
kick it off—get up,
readjust the fan,
sit on the edge
of my flimsy mattress,
staring at the black room
and chant,
"I think I can.

I think I can.
I can.
I can.
I can."

# REALITIES

## MICHAEL'S DIVE LOG – VOLUME 10

**Dive Buddy:** Leesie, then solo
**Date:** 06/30
**Dive #:** --
**Location:** Grand Cayman
**Dive Site:** Jaz's then the blow holes
**Weather Condition:** clear
**Water Condition:** decent breakers
**Depth:** just beneath the surface
**Visibility:** shining
**Water Temp:** refreshing
**Bottom Time:** hours with Leesie, a few minutes alone
**Comments:**

Long day. I teach pool and classroom sessions in the morning, and I'm out on the boat with the students all afternoon. I'm stuck filling bottles and fixing a reg after that while everyone else disappears.

I don't make it to Aunty Jaz's until after 9 PM. Leesie's got the front outdoor lights blazing—she's still clipping. She meets me at my car door. She's all over me before I can even get all the way out. Doesn't seem to care that she's sweaty tonight. Not that I'm complaining.

I get my lips free for a minute, wipe a streak of dirt from

her cheek. "Hey—this is sweet. What gives?"

"I waited and waited." Her arms are scratched up from her long struggle with stubborn bougainvillea vines. "I thought maybe I'd come on too strong yesterday, and you'd flown off somewhere."

"Why didn't you call?"

"I did. You didn't pick up."

"Sorry, babe. No cell service out on the ocean." We move off the dark sidewalk under the bright pool of light where she worked. "Looks like you took it out on the bougainvillea." The vines are butchered.

Her legs are scratched up, too. "Did I mess it up?"

My eyes move from the branches littering the yard to her face, and I know she's not talking about gardening. "No. No. You helped a lot." I bend down and kiss her.

She's trembling. "I thought I'd scared you off for good." She buries her face in my chest.

I hold her, stroke her head. She could tell me she believes in holy flying penguins, and I'd be back. "You can't get rid of me that easy, and look—" I hold up the Book of Mormon I shoved in the back of my jeans when Leesie attacked me. "Can you read with me? It's hard by myself."

She raises her head from hiding and takes the book. "Do you have more questions?"

I nod.

I get one more kiss, and she pulls me around the back to the screened porch. She already put Aunty Jaz to bed.

We sit, side by side, on the couch, knees, arms, ankles touching. She reads, stops, explains—paints the sacred stories of her childhood. She's beautiful in her element.

I listen and love her.

We get to the part where the father dies. The mean brothers want to kill Nephi. Leesie gets emotional. "Droop in sin," she reads. "That's what I did. I'd still be stuck there, miserable, if you hadn't forced me into President Bodden's office." She strokes the open page on her lap and presses her cheek to mine.

I put my arm around her. "I didn't know what else to do."

"You don't think that was inspiration?"

I lean my cheek on her head. "Desperation."

She keeps reading. "I will not put my trust in the arm of flesh." She chokes up—makes me continue.

I finish the Chapter—a few more verses. It's beautiful. I hold Leesie, and we share an intense moment born of all we've been through together—my grief, hers, our ups and downs, the love that battled its way through it all. If anything is divine—that is.

It's midnight when I tenderly find Leesie's lips and whisper good night.

As I drive back to the East End, I remember the feeling I had back in the temple garden in Hong Kong and the tunnel with all those BYU kids singing hymns. The power that stopped me from going into Leesie's room that first awful night we spent in Cayman wasn't my mom. I didn't sense Mom in Hong Kong and in the tunnel like I did the other times she helped me. But something was there. Something real. Something like I felt with Leesie tonight.

I pull the car off the road when I get to the blow holes and wander out on the coral rocks—close enough to the waves forcing themselves up through the coral tubes to feel the fine mist on my face—and stare out at the night ocean.

The sky overhead is heavy with stars.

I owe this to Leesie. At least once.

"Is it—I mean—are You—real?"

The ocean surges, seethes. An unusually large wave hits hard enough to drench me with spray.

I wipe my face and whisper, "Is that a yes?"

I have to admit there is a power in the night beyond me, beyond the ocean, beyond the sky, beyond the stars.

Something is out there.

Something big.

Something real.

Something I can no longer deny.

# NEW BEAT

## LEESIE HUNT / CHATSPOT LOG / 07/01 9:17 AM

**Kimbo69 says:** Hey girl! You're online for once.
**Leesie327 says:** Why are you up so early?
**Kimbo69 says:** Actually I'm up late. Mark's off on a trip with his friends. I can't sleep without him.
**Leesie327 says:** Michael leaves every night. I hate that.
**Kimbo69 says:** But good-bye's can be sweet.
**Leesie327 says:** Amen to that. The way he kissed me good night last night was beautiful—like a prayer.
**Kimbo69 says:** That's definitely not how Mark and I said good-bye.
**Leesie327 says:** I'll take what I can get.
**Kimbo69 says:** What are you guys doing for the 4th of July this weekend?
**Leesie327 says:** I don't know. Michael will have to work, but maybe there will be fireworks somewhere we can catch at night.
**Kimbo69 says:** Mark will be back. We'll have our own fireworks.
**Leesie327 says:** Are you done rubbing it in?
**Kimbo69 says:** Why is Michael always working? Isn't he loaded?
**Leesie327 says:** He wants to learn so when he starts his own dive operation he doesn't lose all his money.
**Kimbo69 says:** And he's diving. That's not really work.

**Leesie327 says:** He loves it—but it's hard work.
**Kimbo69 says:** It's not all that fair. He dives all day with beautiful girls, and you sit around with a sick old woman.
**Leesie327 says:** I don't sit around. I'm totally busy.
**Kimbo69 says:** Are you happy—like he is?
**Leesie327 says:** I'm all over the place. Happy one minute—fighting tears the next. My mom says that's normal.
**Kimbo69 says:** I'm glad you've got your mom to talk to again.
**Leesie327 says:** She makes more sense than I ever gave her credit for.
**Kimbo69 says:** What big plans have you got for today?
**Leesie327 says:** I did a massive hatchet job on some bushes. I got to clean up the mess.
**Kimbo69 says:** Sounds like a blast.
**Leesie327 says:** Good exercise.
**Kimbo69 says:** When is Michael coming over?
**Leesie327 says:** Late. He's got another long day.
**Kimbo69 says:** Is it gross—changing diapers?
**Leesie327 says:** What are you talking about?
**Kimbo69 says:** The old lady!
**Leesie327 says:** She doesn't wear diapers.
**Kimbo69 says:** That's a relief.
**Leesie327 says:** I help her in the bathroom and get her dressed. Make sure she eats. Test her blood. Give her meds.
**Kimbo69 says:** Shots?
**Leesie327 says:** She jabs herself.
**Kimbo69 says:** Is she getting better?
**Leesie327 says:** Her foot looks worse to me. I'm worried it'll get infected again.
**Kimbo69 says:** You have to take care of that?
**Leesie327 says:** Yeah. When the nurse doesn't come.
**Kimbo69 says:** Gross.
**Leesie327 says:** I almost lost it yesterday.
**Kimbo69 says:** I couldn't do it.
**Leesie327 says:** You could. You can do anything you really want

to.
**Kimbo69 says:** That's what you think.
**Leesie327 says:** Hey Kim—I gotta go—Michael just walked in.
**Kimbo69 says:** Is something wrong?
**Leesie327 says:** I don't know.
**Kimbo69 says:** You can't just leave me like this!
**Leesie327 says:** Bye.

## LEESIE'S MOST PRIVATE CHAPBOOK POEM # 99, HIS CONFESSION

My kayak paddle digs
deep into the turquoise water.
I pull the blade through,
raise it, dig deep again
in rhythm with Michael
paddling behind me.

He'd burst into Jaz's shack earlier,
bundled me and Aunty Jaz into his car
and sped to the big hospital near
my clinic. "Hurry, we're late."
Is the only clue he divulges.

By the time I manage
to get Jaz on her feet
he's back with a wheelchair
and a beautiful nurse
with a clipboard and thick,
long, long black hair.
I'm frozen by that hair.
But Aunty Jaz pipes up,
"Dear boy, you're mistaken
I don't have an appointment."

Michael ignores her, eases
her into the wheelchair
and races away.
I lock my hands behind
my back, so I don't touch
the inch and a half long
growth that covers my head
or pull a handful of the nurse's
beautiful hair off her
innocent, unsuspecting head.

I follow through double doors,
down halls, around a corner,
notice a "Dive Medicine Clinic" sign,
worry that Michael's bent again,
realize that makes no sense at all.
"Wait here." He motions me to a
waiting area as he pushes Jaz
through more glass doors and
around a corner.

I sit on a yellow waiting room couch,
wait and wait until—there he is!
I barge through the glass doors.
"They are prepping her for the chamber."
He's totally lost me.
"Aunty Jaz isn't bent."
He grins big and takes my hands.
"Oxygen therapy. Great for wounds that won't heal."
I frown, worried. "She can't afford this."
He shrugs. "I can."

We've got two hours to ourselves.
He's taken the whole day off.

So here we are paddling
out to his favorite free dive site.

He stows his paddle to signal
our arrival. I tuck mine alongside his.
Instead of bailing over the side,
he opens his arms wide.
"Come here, babe."
I maneuver into them,
snuggle my face
against his neck,
while his arms wrap me up.

He kisses his favorite spot
on my mangy skull and whispers,
"I think something answered."
I bolt up—almost tip the kayak.
"You prayed!" My lips attack
in jubilation before he can answer.
He holds me off.
"Not fancy words like you—
I just asked."
I have to kiss him one more time.
"That's all you have to do."
I sit back, so he can explain.

"I didn't hear a voice
or anything or see stuff
in my head like you do,
but I had this feeling—"
He pauses, can't speak for a moment.
He swallows and grips my hand.
"I, um, I—wasn't alone."

I hug him and good tears sting

238 / angela morrison

my eyes. His lips
rest on my forehead,
his arms squeeze me.
"Do you know what that means?"
He gazes off into the distance.
"We're not alone."

Before I can answer, he props me
up, and holds me by the arms,
gives me a shake. "I woke up this
morning with this idea for
Aunty Jaz burgeoning in my brain."
I smile, and try to say something,
but he gets there first.
"It grew and grew until
I picked up the phone and called
the chamber."

I let joyful tears slip down my face
to consecrate the moment.
He wipes them away.
"I love the way this feels."
I touch his cheek. "Me, too."
He takes my hand and
kisses my palm.
"Do you think this can happen
again or is it a one shot deal?"
I gather both of his hands in mine,
kneel on the kayak floor in front of him,
gaze forever into his smoky eyes.
"Whenever you're willing
to pay the price—it's there.
You've felt it before."

He nods. "What do we do now?"

I swallow and wipe my nose
with the back of my hand.
"We can call the missionaries."
His forehead creases concern.
"I love reading with you.
Can we keep doing that?"
That makes me start crying again.
He holds me close—our lips meet,
but it's more like our hearts
mesh than our mouths.

I rest my ear against his chest
try to hear if he beats a fresh rhythm
to match mine. The fuzzy outlines of
forever with Michael become
a detailed sketch, glowing and radiant.
"Did I tell you I love you today?"
He rolls over the kayak's side
into the water, deftly bringing
me with him. "Not enough."

# Chapter 30

# LOVE

## MICHAEL'S DIVE LOG – VOLUME 10

**Dive Buddy:** solo
**Date:** 07/01
**Dive #:** --
**Location:** Grand Cayman
**Dive Site:** East End dock
**Weather Condition:** calm night
**Water Condition:** not enough water pressure in the shower
**Depth:** sprinkling down on me
**Visibility:** shining
**Water Temp:** intense warmth
**Bottom Time:** hard to know—just minutes I think
**Comments:**

I was on a total high all day today. When Leesie and I picked up Aunty J, she beamed at me and swore her foot felt better already. Wound treatment in the hyperbaric chamber takes a series of one or two hour sessions over days—maybe weeks—so it was probably her O2 high talking. Still cool. Made me feel amazing.

Amazed. Astounded. That's kind of how I've felt since last night. The high lasted all afternoon while Jaz telephoned all her friends from church with the good news and hit them up for rides to and from the hospital, and Leesie and I slowly forged ahead reading The Book of Mormon. We'd read, she'd explain, and I asked questions.

I got suspicious when she insisted on skipping a whole bunch of chapters.

"What's in it?" Maybe that's where they hide all the secret stuff about polygamy.

"Isaiah. Bible prophet. He wrote in code so the king wouldn't off with his head. I get lost. Nephi explains what it means here." She smoothed down the page.

She was intensely happy. I didn't want to question her. I'm tempted to give a thumbs up to the missionaries, so I can watch her flip out. I want to keep her happy. She hasn't been like this for so long. I always knew this was a huge deal for her, but seeing how thrilled she is that I'll finally admit there seems to be a divine power out there makes me wish I could have figured it out sooner. I was grieving, angry. An idiot.

But now as I drive through Georgetown at rush hour worrying that I won't make it back to East End in time for the night dive I swapped my morning dives for, cursing my own stupidity for not taking the northern route, I wonder what's in those mysterious chapters. Maybe I'll read them myself. No harm in looking.

Leesie wouldn't lie. Or would she? Doubt creeps into the equation. I know—it's stupid. She wouldn't lie. I don't doubt I felt a divine essence last night. I can't doubt I felt led all day. I recognize I've been led before. But who says that is the same thing as the Beings she describes? Huge leap. Gigantic leap.

I'm working hard searching for that essence in the Book of Mormon. So far I'm touched and intrigued, but who is to say I won't find the same sacredness in other holy books? Should I study those, too, and pray about them? Does the Book of Mormon being true make everything else false? Leesie believes in the Bible like other Christians, plus a bunch of stuff Joseph Smith wrote. Not stuff. Revelations.

If I were in love with a Buddhist girl or a Catholic girl or a Jewish girl, would I have these feelings about her faith? Am I imagining everything to please Leesie? To keep her?

I used to think all religion was crap—crazy stuff used to enslave people. Isn't that what most educated people think? Whether they go to church or not? But if there is something real in the concept of God, is there something real in all religion? Is some lies? Some truth? How does He feel about all the evil stuff people have done—still do—in the name of religion? Is He down with crusades, burning witches, and suicide bombers?

I can't comprehend the whole Jesus Christ dying for my sins thing. Leesie says no one does—you have to take it on faith. Feel it.

Faith. That's another thing I don't get.

I see it in Leesie. She's got too much faith—in me.

I make it to East End with no time to spare for dinner. It's okay. Leesie fed me and Jaz a giant lunch. I'll live. I bolt down to the dock and start flinging tanks into the boat, pushing myself into a frenzy so I can't think up more doubts, more questions. I work so fast the boat is ready ten minutes before anybody's going to show up.

I'm sweaty and hot. I slip off my T-shirt and stand in the dock shower a minute in my swimsuit. I close my eyes and try to recapture how I felt when Leesie and I prayed together before I left Aunty Jaz's shack.

Leesie didn't make me kneel down or do anything freaky. She took my hand and bowed her head right there where we were sitting. "Bless Michael as he learns line upon line that he will come to know and Love Thee, Thy Son, and Thy gospel."

Line upon line. Step by step.

Standing on the lonely dock with my face turned up to the refreshing cool water, I try to address Him—Leesie's God—not a vague divine being. "Dear Heavenly Father," I whisper and can't continue.

I'm engulfed in love.

Intimate.

Personal.
Overflowing.
A father's love.
A brother's love.
A love that feels like home.

# Chapter 31

## PRODIGAL

### LEESIE HUNT / CHATSPOT LOG / 07/03 2:22 PM

**Leesie327 says:** Good you're online. I so need to vent.

**Kimbo69 says:** What's he done now?

**Leesie327 says:** Michael? I'm not mad at HIM. Michael is perfection.

**Kimbo69 says:** He's hot—but the guy's got his flaws.

**Leesie327 says:** I didn't think I could love him more, but every day I do.

**Kimbo69 says:** So that study thing you're doing is going well? He's swallowing the Mormon stuff?

**Leesie327 says:** It's not like that. This is the most beautiful experience. I wish I could explain it to you.

**Kimbo69 says:** No thanks. Don't turn your religious zeal on me. We have an agreement, remember?

**Leesie327 says:** He prayed. Really prayed. And God answered him. He called me so excited.

**Kimbo69 says:** God or Michael?

**Leesie327 says:** Very funny.

**Kimbo69 says:** So you're going to live happily ever after?

**Leesie327 says:** I was going to type YES, but then I thought of Phil. That will always hurt—but Michael is trying so hard, dropping all his barriers—for me.

**Kimbo69 says:** How are you going to tell Michael that you and

Phil were fighting over him in that pickup?

**Leesie327 says:** I'm never going to. I won't tell anyone. Promise me, Kim. Never say a thing.

**Kimbo69 says:** Calm down. You know you can trust me. What interrupted perfection in paradise?

**Leesie327 says:** It was dumb. I shouldn't let stuff like that upset me. I dealt with worse every day in high school.

**Kimbo69 says:** You're making me crazy. WHAT HAPPENED?

**Leesie327 says:** Michael has to work through the 4th of July weekend, so he slept on Jaz's porch last night and took me back down to East End this morning to go diving while Aunty Jaz got her treatment. Jaz's friend picked her up and took Jaz to her house for a change of scenery. She must be having a good time. She's still not back.

**Kimbo69 says:** Did you get hurt diving?

**Leesie327 says:** Dani and Seth were on the boat with us.

**Kimbo69 says:** Did Miss Sleeze-bucket hit on your man?

**Leesie327 says:** No. She tried to save him from the clutches of the evil Mormon devil-worshippers.

**Kimbo69 says:** What?

**Leesie327 says:** She grew up in the South going to one of those churches that show anti-Mormon videos to protect their flock.

**Kimbo69 says:** Churches do that?

**Leesie327 says:** She said that if I don't turn away from my evil ways and find Christ, I'll be damned. Apparently, I'm no longer a Christian.

**Kimbo69 says:** She lectured you?

**Leesie327 says:** And I sat there in stunned silence.

**Kimbo69 says:** She's one to talk.

**Leesie327 says:** My dad always taught us "contention is of the devil." Arguing with someone who wants to fight makes everyone angry. Pointless.

**Kimbo69 says:** You let her get away with it?

**Leesie327 says:** I didn't want it to get ugly in front of Michael. Turning the other cheek is a lot harder than it sounds.

**Kimbo69 says:** So what happened?

**Leesie327 says:** Michael told her to shut up. Seth almost decked him.

**Kimbo69 says:** That sounds peaceful. You did this in front of all the paying customers?

**Leesie327 says:** No. We were up front. Michael was driving the boat.

**Kimbo69 says:** He defended you. That's romantic.

**Leesie327 says:** I brokered a truce. By the time we got out to the dive site, they were all business as usual.

**Kimbo69 says:** Flakes.

**Leesie327 says:** I don't know. Maybe Dani believes the lies about us. Lots of people do.

**Kimbo69 says:** Then they should keep it to themselves.

**Leesie327 says:** No way I can argue that. Our missionaries go all over the world NOT keeping it to themselves.

**Kimbo69 says:** What are you going to do if she starts in on you again?

**Leesie327 says:** Smile and thank her for her concern. I don't want her angry and bugging Michael. He's with these people all the time.

**Kimbo69 says:** Get God to zap her. You're tight with Him.

**Leesie327 says:** He'd say I'm supposed to love her.

**Kimbo69 says:** Hah! You are crazy.

**Leesie327 says:** Certifiable—crap—there's noise in the restaurant. Somebody's in there.

**Kimbo69 says:** Maybe Jaz came home.

**Kimbo69 says:** Leesie? Where are you?

**Kimbo69 says:** Are you okay?

**Kimbo69 says:** You're scaring the panties off me.

**Kimbo69 says:** If you don't come back and answer me, I'll never chat with you again.

**Leesie327 says:** There's a massive black guy in there scrubbing the counters down. I think it's Aunty Jaz's son.

**Kimbo69 says:** The criminal?

**Leesie327 says:** No one said he's a criminal.
**Kimbo69 says:** Get out of there now!!!!
**Leesie327 says:** What if Jaz comes home, and he hurts her?
**Kimbo69 says:** What if he hurts you?
**Leesie327 says:** I'm going to go out back and call Michael.
**Kimbo69 says:** Can't you call someone closer? Like the police?
**Leesie327 says:** Oh, yeah. I wonder if 911 works here. I could try that. President Bodden. I'll call him. Right after Michael.
**Kimbo69 says:** Go hide.
**Kimbo69 says:** Get help from the neighbors.
**Kimbo69 says:** You're gone aren't you?
**Kimbo69 says:** Crap. girl. You better phone me.
**Kimbo69 says:** What's happening? I'm sitting right here. I'm not going anywhere until you tell me you're okay.
**Kimbo69 says:** Don't do anything stupid.
**Kimbo69 says:** Geeze—now you've even got me praying.

## MICHAEL'S DIVE LOG – VOLUME 10

**Dive Buddy:** the whole gang
**Date:** 07/03
**Dive #:** --
**Location:** Grand Cayman
**Dive Site:** Jaz's shack
**Weather Condition:** late, windy
**Water Condition:** kicking up white caps
**Depth:** wish I knew
**Visibility:** zero
**Water Temp:** weird, I'm cold
**Bottom Time:** too, too long
**Comments:**

When I steer the boat close enough to shore to get cell coverage on our way back in from the afternoon trip, I pick up a text from Leesie.

*J's son in rstrnt calling Pres B*

Jaz's son? Do I know Jaz has a son? I think so. What did they say about him? Restraining order? That's it. He can't come near his mother. No one ever said why. That's why I was nervous about Leesie staying there. I forgot all about it as soon as I met Jaz. She's overpowering. Did he hurt her? Threaten her? Where has he been? Why is he there now? Freak. I think Leesie's alone.

I dial Leesie. Her phone goes straight to voicemail. She always forgets to charge it. Way to go, babe.

Or maybe the dude turned it off.

I try Jaz's land line. It's busy. Off the hook? Cut? Freak. Freak. Freak.

I push the boat into high gear.

I'm working today with Gabriel and Cooper. Alex drove Leesie back to Jaz's for me while we dove this afternoon.

Cooper yells, "What are you doing? This is a no wake zone."

"I think Leesie's in trouble." I toss him my phone and explain.

Gabriel joins us at the front, catches the gist of the situation. He examines the text. "Who's Pres B?"

I concentrate on the steering the speeding boat. "The guy from her church."

Cooper puts his hand on my shoulder. "Calm down then. He's handling it."

I shrug him off. "What if he's not? What if she didn't call? Or he didn't pick up? I gotta get over there."

Gabriel hands back my phone. "We'll go, too. You might need us."

"Are you sure?"

"Of course, dude." Cooper slaps my back and yells, "Hang on tight! We're coming in hot!"

The divers in the back sit down and grab something.

Cooper gets his phone out of his dry bag and starts dialing the guys. He gets a hold of Brock who promises to have Ethan and Seth ready to go as soon as the boat touches the dock.

Gabriel grabs hold of an overhead bar for balance as I slam the boat through the cut in the reef and speed across the flat lagoon to the dock.

Dani's there to catch the ropes and offload the divers. "Go, go! I've got this."

Gabriel, Cooper and I tear out of the boat and up to the parking lot. Ethan, Seth, Brock, and Alex wait by my car.

Gabriel greets Alex with a hug. "Don't worry, mi cielo. I'm sure we'll be fine. See you later."

Alex glares at him. "Like hell you will."

"You're not going."

"And who's going to stop me?"

Apparently not Gabriel. All the guys cram into my car, and I take off—heading North. It's a mile or two longer, but there's no traffic and the road is open so we can speed. Gabriel and Alex follow in his sleek red Porsche. I wish this bucket I'm driving had that kind of speed.

Ethan's in the front seat beside me. I chuck my phone at him. "Keep trying to call her."

The car is silent except for the sound of muted dialing and the obnoxious engine. I grow more and more tense. Grip the steering wheel so hard my knuckles turn white. My arms ache.

"Freak!" A slow car ahead blocks my progress. I pull into the oncoming lane and zoom around it. An approaching car lays on its horn and brakes hard.

"Watch it." Seth yells as I whip back into my lane and the car I passed starts to honk.

I ignore him and press down on the gas, check the rearview mirror. Gabriel aims his Porsche at the gap in the middle of the road between the slow car and second car coming the other direction. He pulls up close behind me.

I focus on the road ahead. This piece of junk I'm driving shakes too much at 90 mph, so I ease it back to 85—keep it there the whole way.

I screech up to Jaz's, bail out and sprint around back.

"Leesie?" I yell. "Are you here? Leesie!"

The porch is empty.

The living quarters, too.

I hear noise in the restaurant.

I burst through the door screaming, "Leesie!" with all the guys and Alex at my back.

Leesie and Aunty Jaz sit at a table eating fish.

I turn from them to find a massive black guy with a head full of dreds barreling down on us wielding a fish cleaver.

"No! No!" Leesie leaps up, gets between us. "It's okay." She backs hard into me and holds her hands up to ward off the guy. "Didn't you get my text?"

"That's why we're here!" I hold my arms out to keep the guys back.

The fish guy backs off.

Leesie turns around. "Why didn't you call?"

I grab her shoulders. "I did." I shake her. "A thousand times."

"Oh, no." She sticks her hand in her pocket and pulls out her cell phone. It's dead. "I didn't realize. I'm sorry."

I'm shaking I'm so upset. "I tried the landline, too." I get a hold of myself, stop shaking her.

"Jaz has been using it." She grabs my sweaty hands. "I thought you were still on the water." She peaks around me at all the guys and Alex—fists clenched, panting—ready to defend her. Her face goes crimson. "I'm so, so sorry."

"Well," Aunty Jaz pipes up from her table, "now that you're here, you can help celebrate. Junior's come back to me—and he'll make fish for you all."

Junior smiles like Aunty Jaz. "Of course. Of course. Come in. We're re-opening the shack tomorrow. You're our first customers."

I collapse at a table in the back and slump down on it. Hide my face in my hands. Leesie introduces everyone to Aunty Jaz and Junior.

A few minutes later, Leesie scoots a chair close to mine. She strokes my back. "I can't believe I put you through that."

"Freak, babe. It was hell."

She combs my hair with her fingers. "I didn't know my phone was dead."

"You could have sent another text. Or left a phone message."

"You're right. I'm so stupid." Her voice shakes.

I look up. She's gone really pale. "Are you okay?"

"I am now." She squirms close.

My arms encircle her. "Were you scared?"

Her head bobs up and down, bangs my chin. "I heard him in the kitchen, got a look—hid out back. Sent you the text. Called President Bodden. He was concerned and told me to stay put until he got here. He was fast—twenty minutes—but it seemed like forever."

"He showed up by himself?" I rest my cheek on her head. It's sweaty. Poor, babe.

"One of the members is a cop. He came, too. They told Aunty Jaz to stay put, but she got here about the same time." Leesie puts her hand on my neck.

I cover it with mine. "They confronted him?"

She shrugs. "They made me stay in the cop car until it was safe."

"Thank God, you're okay."

"They all left like five minutes ago. I should have called you, though. I wasn't thinking. Will you forgive me?"

I kiss her forehead. "Uh-huh. I would have come anyway."

"But not with the posse. I feel like a fool."

"Are you kidding? They're getting the best fish on the island. Look at them." I loosen my grip on her so she can peak over my shoulder. "They're loving it."

"Where's Dani?"

"She offloaded the boat, so we could leave right away."

Her forehead wrinkles up. "Isn't there a night dive sched-

252 / angela morrison

uled?"

"Dani can guide it. They'll find somebody to drive." I squeeze her hand. "No big deal."

She snuggles close to me. "It is a big deal. You should be really mad."

"I know." I release her hand and tip her head back so I can see her face. "I'm just glad you're safe."

She kisses me. "Thank you."

"I love you."

"I know." She kisses me again.

Junior puts a plate of steaming fried fish on the table in front of me. "You want more, Sister Leesie?" He waits beside the table.

She lets me go and sits up. "I'm stuffed. Thanks."

I bend over the plate, inhale the spices, suddenly starving. "Thanks, man."

Junior grins. "You know my mum's fish?"

I nod while I load up my fork and shove it in my mouth. I close my eyes and chew in bliss while the sweet, tender fish and crisp spicy coating party in my mouth.

Junior's off frying more fish by the time I open my eyes and start digging for another bite.

"Oh, crap!" Leesie jumps up, knocking over her chair. "Kim!" She runs through the door into Jaz's living quarters. I follow with my plate of fish.

Leesie's laptop is dead, too. I plug it in for her and watch over her shoulder. Kim's frantic. Steamed at first like I was, but calms down when the whole story comes out.

She wants to know Junior's story. I do, too. Leesie let's me eavesdrop.

The gist of it is he took his dad's death hard. I can relate. Junior got mixed up with drugs, stole from Jaz, threatened her. She turned him in. The judge imposed a restraining order. He got probation and community service—left the island, ashamed, as soon as he could. Poor, Jaz. That must have killed her. He got a job frying fish in the Bahamas, cleaned up, worked hard. Came home when he heard about Jaz's foot. He called his sister—homesick for news.

I bend over and kiss Leesie's cheek. That could have been me if it wasn't for her. I took my parent's death hard. But she was there.

Leesie signs off with Kim. We sit out on the back porch holding each other—not talking or even making out. Just being.

That's all I really want.

To just be.

With her.

# THE PLAN

## LEESIE HUNT CHATSPOT LOG / 07/06 5:30 PM

**liv2div says:** hey babe, it's me…I borrowed Alex's computer.
**Leesie327 says:** Does this mean you aren't coming over tonight?
**liv2div says:** I have to teach…last minute
**Leesie327 says:** We missed you at church yesterday.
**liv2div says:** I missed going.
**Leesie327 says:** Really?
**liv2div says:** don't get mad…I've been reading the Book of Mormon without you
**Leesie327 says:** That's amazing! Read as much as you want.
**liv2div says:** I got to the part where an angel stopped that rebellious guy and his friends and told them to change their evil ways…I feel kind of like that
**Leesie327 says:** I never said you were evil.
**liv2div says:** who says you're the angel?
**Leesie327 says:** I forgot what a snot you are when we chat.
**liv2div says:** how'd you get to church?
**Leesie327 says:** Junior has a vintage VW bus.
**liv2div says:** whoa, classy wheels
**Leesie327 says:** He got it back from a friend on Saturday. I helped him scrub it this morning, but it still smells like pot.
**liv2div says:** how do you know what pot smells like?

**Leesie327 says:** Today was an education.

**liv2div says:** So, babe, what do you want to do now that Jaz doesn't need you?

**Leesie327 says:** She still needs me—lots. I'm going to help with the fish shack, too.

**liv2div says:** how long?

**Leesie327 says:** Until you're done here, I guess.

**liv2div says:** And then I can take you home?

**Leesie327 says:** Yeah. For sure. Let's go so there's plenty of time before school starts.

**liv2div says:** time for what?

**Leesie327 says:** To see my parents and Stephie. Visit Gram, and um

**liv2div says:** spill it…what else?

**Leesie327 says:** Maybe enough time to have a quiet wedding in the backyard?

**liv2div says:** What if I got baptized? Would there be time for a wedding in the temple?

**Leesie327 says:** Excuse me. My heart stopped beating. Did you really say that?

**liv2div says:** it doesn't seem impossible anymore

**Leesie327 says:** Listen, I'd love to have you get baptized that soon, but I don't want to rush you. Take your time. You have to be a member for a year before you can go to the temple.

**liv2div says:** A whole year? That's a new one. I thought all I had to do was get baptized.

**Leesie327 says:** Baptism is a huge step. Don't do it until you're totally ready. But marry me before we move down to Provo.

**liv2div says:** is there anything you want to tell me before we get married? maybe about the accident?

**Leesie327 says:** No. You know everything.

**liv2div says:** are you sure?

**Leesie327 says:** You're not getting out of marrying me. You promised.

**liv2div says:** what if I decide not to get baptized?

**Leesie327 says:** It won't make me love you less. I'll respect your decision and pray you'll change your heart.

**liv2div says:** if you start praying, I won't stand a chance!

**Leesie327 says:** So I can tell my mom to start planning a wedding?

**liv2div says:** no…don't do that

**Leesie327 says:** Please, Michael. I've got your diamond on my finger. End of the summer. You promised.

**liv2div says:** in the backyard? even if I'm not a Mormon?

**Leesie327 says:** If we're married, we can have our own apartment, no more saying good-bye every night, and we can— 24/7, remember?

**liv2div says:** I know

**Leesie327 says:** Don't you want that?

**liv2div says:** I forgot how sex-crazed you get when we chat

**Leesie327 says:** It's easier to bring it up when you're not breathing down my neck.

**liv2div says:** I make you nervous?

**Leesie327 says:** Duh. Always have. We gotta get married.

**liv2div says:** let me think about it

**Leesie327 says:** You're not getting out of it.

**liv2div says:** what am I supposed to do in Provo?

**Leesie327 says:** That's your problem.

**liv2div says:** maybe I want to come back to Cayman and work or go somewhere else

**Leesie327 says:** You need to go to college. You could go to the U or UVU.

**liv2div says:** and study what?

**Leesie327 says:** I don't care. Our kids need an educated father.

**liv2div says:** KIDS!

**Leesie327 says:** Uh-huh. Three girls and two boys.

**liv2div says:** FIVE?

**Leesie327 says:** Don't you want kids?

**liv2div says:** Yeah. I do.

**Leesie327 says:** I'm starting young. We can have lots.

**liv2div says:** We're just 19.

**Leesie327 says:** I'm almost twenty.

**liv2div says:** not…maybe we should wait that year

**Leesie327 says:** No. No way. You'll take off. Leave me again. I'll lose you.

**liv2div says:** thanks for the vote of confidence, babe…I'll stay in Provo…I won't let you out of my sight

**Leesie327 says:** But that puts all kinds of pressure on you to get baptized right away. I won't do that to you.

**liv2div says:** you aren't doing it…I am…you really want to be a mom at twenty?

**Leesie327 says:** So we'll wait a couple years on the kids. Let's still get married. The backyard will be full of flowers in August.

**liv2div says:** and what will you tell those kids of ours when they want to do that instead of hang on for the temple?

**Leesie327 says:** That their father drove me crazy every time he walked into a room, and we'd suffered long enough.

**liv2div says:** you just want my body?

**Leesie327 says:** Uh-huh.

**liv2div says:** aren't you the girl who taught me we came to earth to be tested?

**Leesie327 says:** That's not fair. You're too good a student.

**liv2div says:** get used to it, babe

**Leesie327 says:** So we wait? Crap. What do we do next?

**liv2div says:** I guess we better call the missionaries…if I'm going to do this, let's do it

## LEESIE'S MOST PRIVATE CHAPBOOK
## POEM #100, DISCUSSIONS

The next time
Michael pulls up
in front of Jaz's hopping fish shack
and I flurry out to meet him,

I'm shy—
to touch his hand,
to kiss his lips,
to tell him the requested
missionaries, sufficiently stuffed
with fish soaked in buttermilk,
breaded with Jaz's secret recipe
and fried to perfection by Junior,
wait on the porch.

Michael's different—strange to me—
I no longer lead, guide, walk beside.
He's taken control of his destiny
and mine. I worry he'll bring up
the accident again like he did online.
He kisses me instead.

His lips taste familiar
as we linger at the roadside
reconnecting after five days apart.
"Are we going to do this?" His
whisper stirs my hair.
I nod—find his lips again.
"What was that for?"
"In case you never kiss me again."
My face gets hot. "Remember?"
A phantom from his last
missionary encounter rises
menacing between us.
He wafts it away with a wave
of his hand, strong and tan,
that cups my chin.
"That's not going to happen—
Those guys were right.
I didn't have ears."

He holds my hand
and pulls me along the path
to meet the two smiling elders
who know him from church.
Guys his age—humble, excited to teach.
Michael reflects their energy,
listens, nods, accepts, believes.
At the end, he says the prayer
when they ask.
"Dear Heavenly Father"—
his voice tender, full of love—
"Thank you—thee—for opening
my eyes and giving me
Leesie to fill my heart."

I join his "amen," in the name
of Jesus Christ, and offer my own
silent thank you, in awe of the man
beside me who shakes
the missionaries hands, makes
the next appointment, sees them off,
then reaches for my hand
and brings it to his lips,
kissing, one by one, the nail prints
he left so long ago when he showed
me his wounds and I tried to anoint them
with the only balm I knew.

He pulls me into his arms,
kisses me like I'm
a daughter of God.
And my brimming
heart knows
he's ready to be
a son.

# Chapter 33

## COMMITTAL

### MICHAEL'S DIVE LOG – VOLUME 10

**Dive Buddy:** Leesie and the elders
**Date:** 07/26
**Dive #:** --
**Location:** Grand Cayman
**Dive Site:** Jaz's porch
**Weather Condition:** muggy
**Water Condition:** it's so hot I wish I was in it
**Depth:** high and dry
**Visibility:** into the future and it looks good
**Water Temp:** it's probably pushing 90
**Bottom Time:** forever
**Comments:**

"So, Brother Walden, would you like to set a date for your baptism?" Elder Kitchen is from northern Arizona.

He was stoked when I told him I'm from Phoenix. "My I-don't-know-how-many-great grandparents pioneered in Mesa." They went south from Salt Lake when Leesie's dad's ancestors went north to Idaho. Elder Kitchen punched my arm and said, "Cool. I come all the way to Grand Cayman to teach a bro from Phoenix." He grew up in Snowflake—tiny place, mostly Mormons, up on the UT/AZ border. They have winter there. Not sure why you'd want to live in Arizona where there's winter, but Elder

Kitchen loves it—misses the place like crazy.

I look from him to his companion, Elder Quincy from Ohio, to Leesie. She's holding her breath, turning blue at the edges.

"Breathe, babe." I reach for her hand. "You think I'm ready?"

Elder Quincy, who has only been a member for a couple years—and one of those was spent on his mission—rolls his eyes. "Dude, you're a lot more ready than I was." His family cut him off when he got baptized, but his ward—that's a full size Mormon congregation—back in Ohio is paying for his mission.

Leesie sets our hands on her knee and places her left hand on top. Her ring catches the sun that streams in behind us. "The question is—do you think you're ready?"

After the fourth of July holidayers left, business slacked off out at East End. It's not as dead as it will be in August when hurricane season starts to heat up, but I've only been working one dive a day—sometimes not even that. Gabriel can instruct, too. He's been taking all the students—training Alex. They want to buy a place, maybe over on Cayman Brac, and go into business together.

I'm the only guy the elders are teaching. They'd much rather teach me and eat free fish than pound on doors or try to talk to people on buses or the streets. Beach missionary work is against the rules. We've spent hours every day this month, except Mondays when they get a day to do laundry, write emails home, and play basketball and on Tuesday morning when they volunteer at a shelter, running the fans full blast on Aunty Jaz's back porch, trying not to melt without A/C, and talking about Joseph Smith, Jesus Christ, Heavenly Father and what He's got planned for me.

I close my eyes and look inside. Am I ready? Can I ever be ready? My eyes drift open. "I'm not done reading the Book of Mormon."

Leesie pats my hand. "You're close."

Elder Kitchen leans forward with his hands clasped, his

262 / angela morrison

eyes serious. "Have you prayed about it?"

I nod.

Elder Quincy mirrors Kitchen's pose and speaks with a solemn voice. "And you know it's true."

I swallow and look at Leesie. Her eyes are on my face. I whisper, "Yes. I do." Those three words bring a powerful surge of warmth, a feeling I've come to crave.

A grin grows on both elders' faces. Elder Kitchen sits up. "Then let's set a date. When are you leaving?"

Leesie and I are lost in each other. Elder K's question doesn't register. Happiness makes Leesie glow. Joyful. That's what she is. I know it sounds corny, but joy fills me up, too.

Elder Quincy clears his throat. "Are we in the way here?"

Leesie gets pink and turns to them. "We're leaving the tenth of August."

It was going to be sooner, but Gabriel and Alex are going to Cayman Brac to assess a dive operation that might be up for sale soon and convinced us to go along. Gabriel and I are staying with a friend of his who works on the Brac. The resort is comp'ing Alex and Leesie a room. Leesie made Alex promise Gabriel would not be allowed in that room before she agreed to go.

Leesie's parents were disappointed at the delay, but they were cool about it. Her dad has been cool about everything.

I put my right hand on top of Leesie's to complete the stack on her knee. "Could Leesie's dad baptize me?"

Leesie leans her head on my shoulder. "He'd love, too. Call him."

Elder Quincy's face falls. "Oh, man. We wanted to dunk you."

Elder Kitchen elbows him. "It's okay, Elder. We'll survive."

I realize what they're saying. If I wait until we go home, these guys who I've come to love like brothers, can't be there. "I could fly them all here. Leesie's family and Gram. I want Gram to be at the baptism—to feel this." I put my hand on my heart.

Leesie lifts her head. "It's getting close to harvest." Her

voice wobbles. "Dad can't leave the farm." I can tell she's thinking that he'll be doing it alone this year. No Phil to help. She
turns to me. "I'd like to drive truck for him while we're there."

"Whatever you want, babe."

Elder Quincy stands up and puts his hands on his hips.
"You call him then and set the date. We're not leaving until you
do."

Elder Kitchen stands, too. "We want a wedding invitation,
okay?"

Leesie releases my left hand, pulls her phone out of her
pocket, taps "home" on her favorites. "Hey, mom. Is dad around?
Michael wants to ask him something important." She listens to
her mom's reply and hands me the phone.

I walk over to the far side of the porch, wait for Leesie's
dad to pick up, keep my back to Leesie and the elders. What am
I doing? A voice that's been gnawing at me for a week takes over
my brain. I'm not religious. Never have been. Like my parents.
We believe in diving. That's it. Maybe this is all crazy Mormon
voodoo. And that accident. I've waited and waited. Leesie's
still holding back. That fight. I shudder like I do whenever I
think about it. I need to know about that fight. But I don't want
to know. If it was an innocent nothing, she would have told me
every detail.

"Hello? Michael?"

The sound of her dad's voice brings me back to my purpose. "Hello, Brother Hunt."

"What did you want to ask me?" He doesn't sound happy.
There's strain and sadness in his voice. Grief. How long did I
sound like that? I still do sometimes. Maybe I always will. He
probably thinks I'm calling to ask if I can marry Leesie. Does
that make him sadder?

I close my eyes and rest my forehead against the porch
post. "Would you baptize me?" My throat is dry. I croak the
words.

"What?"

"When Leesie and I are back in August—will you baptize me?"

His reply shuts that gnawing voice up. "I'd be honored, son. Of course, I will."

# *Chapter 34*

## CECILIA

### LEESIE'S MOST PRIVATE CHAPBOOK
### POEM #101, THE BRAC

A tiny plane,
a bumpy landing,
a crescent shaped skiff
of sand with nothing but
bat-filled caves, half-dozen
dive operations, one dirt road
that stretches from end to end,
diving my first wreck,
MV Capt. Keith Tibbits,
a Russian relic renamed
for us tourists,
snuggling on the beach
with Michael while he,
Gabriel, and Alex toss pros and cons,
ups and downs, hows and how-nots
into the inky sky dotted with pinpricks

morphs overnight into

Rain.

Winds.
Warnings.
Boats called in.
Airport shut down.
Hotel evacuation to the island's
built-in shelter—deep caves
that won't wash away in the onslaught
that's only hours away.

The bats lining the ceiling don't seem
to mind sharing their subterranean palace
with fifty human bodies wrapped in hotel
blankets and foil-lined emergency heat sheets
that crinkle when we move
and make me sweat.

I huddle with Michael in the mass
and sip bottled water.
"Are you scared?" He shakes
his arm that's gone to sleep
holding me.
"No. You're here." I try to imagine
the last hurricane he faced. "Are you?"
He bites off a hangnail. "Terrified."
"Did you hear this one's name?"
"Cecilia." His eyebrows draw
close together.
I touch his face. "Will she
haunt us like your Isadore?"
He wraps his arms back around me.
"We're safe. Don't worry. Cecilia can't touch *us*."
I cuddle in close and hand him my water.
The sound of the wind shifts to a new key.
His arms tighten. "Here it comes."

I brace myself for storm surge waves,
sheets of rain, vicious winds
to swamp our dry hide-out,
peel back the roots and dirt
and smash the coral skeleton
that encases us in it's embrace.
Nothing happens.
The sound mounts, echoes, screams,
but we are protected—barely even soggy.
Cramped, tired, trapped,
but safe. Michael prods
me to my feet and stretches.
We wander with refugees, careful
not to step on sleepers, meet up
with Gabriel and Alex, who've
decided not to spend his trust fund here.

"Did you hear if it's hitting the big island?"
I'm worried about Jaz and Junior.
Alex shakes her head. "I don't know."
We hang out with them, laughing
and talking like this is any another night
after a long day diving.

Hours roll by. A lady from the resort
comes along with a big basket of cereal bars.
Michael turns his nose up, but takes a handful
"Guess we won't starve." He offers them to us.
I eat one, two, three. Finish off Michael's water.
When the wind dies, I'm not sure if it's day or night.
Michael and Gabriel venture to the cave's mouth,
return to report. "Definitely the eye, mi cielo."
Gabriel's arm circles Alex. "You should
sleep in the stillness." They slip away.

Michael and I find a quiet place to whisper.
I doze and wake to find him studying my face—
troubled. About our future together?
The giant stride he'll take next week
into a brand new world with a soft woosh
of water in a baptismal font in Spokane?
Waiting a whole year to get married?
I kiss his cheek. "You know,
we can get married any weekend
if waiting gets too hard."
He tries to wipe the trouble
off his face. "I'm not worried
about that. Are you?"
My face heats up, and he kisses me,
sucks ever so gently on the corner
of my lower lip.

I let him think he's distracted
me, enjoy the kiss, initiate
another, then take his face
in my hands and try to fathom his eyes
in the waning glow of two electric lanterns
that struggle to light the cave.
"What does worry you then?"
"Nothing, babe."
"Don't lie to me. I see it.
Isadore's back, isn't she?"
"No, Leese." He closes his eyes.
"It's you." He bows his head
so our foreheads touch.
"There's something I need to know."
His eyes open—I can't breathe
while I wait for him to speak.
"You have one secret, babe. I
don't want to get close to,

but I gotta know—
was it me?"

## MICHAEL'S DIVE LOG – VOLUME 10

**Dive Buddy:** Leesie and Cecilia
**Date:** 08/06
**Dive #:** --
**Location:** Cayman Brac
**Dive Site:** the caves
**Weather Condition:** Category 3
**Water Condition:** sounds wild out there
**Depth:** somebody said the storm surge crested at 20'
**Visibility:** murky
**Water Temp:** feels cold
**Bottom Time:** lost track
**Comments:**

Leesie's face, eerie in the cave's flickering light, blanches white. She hides it against my shoulder.

I bend my head and speak into her ear. "That fight you had with Phil. You never told me what it was about."

She wraps her arms around me—too tight. I feel something damp soak through my T-shirt. Her reaction makes me want to take back the question.

I rub her back and stroke her head. I don't want to know what she's so carefully hidden—don't want to stain the perfect picture we've painted—her dad baptizing me next week, a year engaged in Provo, a wedding next August at her temple in Spokane. I don't know if I can survive what she's going to say.

I want this joyful haze we've been walking around in to last forever. But as we sat here waiting out the storm, with hours to reflect, the last unanswered question cracked open. Now I feel like I'm dangling on the edge of a deep crevice hanging on by my fingertips.

She turns her head to speak, but keeps her cheek pressed

against me. "It doesn't change anything."

"Freak, Leesie, it changes everything."

She grabs a handful of my shirt. "Don't go down that road Michael." She sniffs and wipes her face. "You saw what it did to me."

I can't reply. I'm cold—inside and out. Turmoil tosses my heart against a wall, and it shatters into a million pieces.

Leesie tries to kiss me, but I pull back.

She retreats into my T-shirt. "It doesn't change how much I love you." Her arms tighten around me. "You are my soul, my forever. What happened in that pickup truck doesn't matter."

I can't breathe. I try to break her grip, get up, get away. She won't let me. I inhale and hold my breath, stop struggling.

She kisses my neck, squeezes her eyes tight a moment, then opens them up, starts to speak through her tears. "I love my brother"—she swallows hard—"but it's not your fault he's dead. It's not my fault, either. I didn't undo his seatbelt. I didn't put ice on the road. I didn't say vile things about you."

"You're blaming him now?" The wind starts to blow again outside. Cecilia's back.

"I let him get to me."

I bend my ear towards her mouth so I can hear better.

Leesie raises her voice. "He slept while I drove up through the forest and into the mountains. I tried to figure out how I felt about Jaron, and all I could think was you." She touches my face. "Surrounded by all that beauty and stillness, the Spirit got through to me. I saw I'd misjudged you. Every mile closer to home brought me back to you. I was so happy." She squeezes me again. "It was sacred. I should have kept it to myself. But I didn't." A sob stops her. She gets control and continues. "Phil drug all my sublime feelings into the gutter. I blew up. Lost control. You know the rest."

I turn my face to the wall—trying to escape her voice.

She yells so I can hear over the roaring storm. "It's Phil's fault. It's my fault. It's ice on the road."

I shake my head, struggle to get free of her arms.

She still won't let me go. "You had nothing to do with it."

I look down at her. Freak, I stole her entire life—even her brother. "If you'd left me alone—"

"Suffering like that? How could I?"

"Phil would be packing his bags for BYU and making out with Krystal." The weight of that reality smacks me hard. It unlocks the dark place where the guilt that swallowed me when I failed to save my mother when Isadore had us both in her clutches simmers and churns it into a rampage.

I break free of Leesie's hold, get to my feet. She bows her head to the ground and sobs. Part of me longs to kneel down beside her, hold her, comfort her. But the other part needs to breath. I'm suffocating in this cave.

I trip over bodies and step on fingers as I race to the entrance and stare over the sand bag wall I helped build earlier. A Cecilia fueled wave breaks against it. The spray that hits my face beckons me.

I climb over the wall and into pure wildness. Rain and waves drench. Powerful winds drive me back. I fight them with each step forward I take. There used to be a road between the path that leads up to the caves and the exposed broken coral that creates the shoreline. Now all I see is water swirling white around my ankles as the wave recedes. The wind is full of sharp shards of shell and glass, tiny sand pellets, and bits of slime that used to be palm fronds. A piece of corrugated tin torn from a roof flies by me.

Inhale. Hold it. Exhale.

Repeat. Inhale. Fill my gut, my chest, my throat, my head. Hold it. Hold it. Hold it. Isadore didn't get me. Maybe Cecilia's interested. I struggle three steps forward. Cecilia blows me back.

"Michael?"

I close my eyes. I can't Mom. I'm sorry. I tried. I can't do this without you guys. I hurt everybody I love.

"Michael! Michael! Where are you?" My mom's voice

melds with Leesie. "Michael. Come back. Don't leave me alone."

The voice advances on me. I glance over my shoulder. She's followed me. "Michael!" She screams frantic. She sees me, rushes forward. "Michael! Michael!"

Cecilia flings a mangled chunk of metal at Leesie.

"No, babe!" I scream as she goes down.

I let the storm blow me to her, grab her limp body from the swirling ebb before waves suck her out with them. A wave crashes behind us. I scramble to the cave's mouth and over the wall before a monster attacks and drags us out with it.

I kneel by the wall, panting and praying. "Please, Heavenly Father, let her be all right."

Her eyes don't open.

She doesn't touch my face and whisper, "I love you."

I bury my face against her wet head.

She's breathing.

I press my hand over her heart.

It beats.

Strangers discover us—try to take her from me.

"She hit her head." I won't let anyone touch her. "She'll be all right." I try to remember what the doctors said about her last concussion. Something ominous about further injury. "Please, save her. Please," I pray.

No one asks what the hell we were doing out there. They seem afraid of me. Do I look that freaked?

I hold her close and cry. "Come on, babe. Please." I rock her until I fall asleep.

When I wake my arms are empty.

I leap up. Cast my eyes around the cave. Where did they put her?

And there she is.

A few feet away from me.

Talking to Alex.

# Chapter 35

## DIZZY

### LEESIE'S MOST PRIVATE CHAPBOOK
### POEM #102, ONLY ONE THING

Michael drops to his knees
beside me. "Thank God!
You're all right."
My head throbs, but I
manage mustering a weak
smile. "Just dizzy."
I turn to Alex. "He always
makes me feel like that."
Alex decides she's thirsty
and tactfully disappears.
I turn back to Michael,
stare at his knees
afraid of what his face
will tell me. "Are *we*
all right?"

He pulls me onto his lap
and kisses me until
I can't breathe.
"So you'll still have me?"

I murmur when he lets
me up for air.
He kisses my forehead
and whispers, "Are you sure?"
I press my mouth on his—
relief, love, gratitude
pouring out of me
and all over him.

He wipes tears
from my face and his.
"Don't cry, babe. I'll
deal with this. If you don't
blame me—maybe I can learn not to
blame myself." He examines
the knot on my forehead.
"There's only one thing
I can't deal with." His voice
throbs with emotion.
He clutches me close.
"I know," I whisper. "Don't
scare me like that again."
He will, for sure. I can't
guarantee I won't scare him.
That'll be our life, our test.
With enough love, enough faith,
enough understanding it won't
destroy us.

He traces the scar
that snakes through
two inches of wispy hair
coating my head.
"Let's get to that temple
of yours. I want you forever."

I kiss him until *he*
can't breathe as Cecilia
screams outside.

She isn't the first storm
we've faced.
She won't be
the last. I pray
we can weather them all
clutched in each other's arms.

# Epilogue

### LEESIE'S MOST PRIVATE CHAPBOOK
### POEM # 207, THIS DAY

As I stand gowned in white
satin and lace glowing
with thousands of seed pearls,
shaking hands and hugging
a blurr of happy people
parading through the same gym
at our stake center next to the Spokane Temple
where Michael and I first danced, first fought,
 I'm not sure if this is real or one of the thousands
of dreams I've conjured of this day.

Next to me, there's Kim, maid of honor,
BYU roommie bridesmaids and Stephie
looking too grown up in her matching dress.
Mom and Dad anchor the line wearing
truly happy expressions.
My bouquet is laced with pure white gardenias
in memory of Michael's mom. I know
she's here, smiling on us.

Michael beside me—very real in a black tux
with dark green leaves and white blossoms

fragrant on his lapel.
The guys next to him—shaking hands
and looking after Gram, who presides
in a big, cushy chair—
are companions from his mission.
Yeah. His mission.

After his baptism—
intense and beautiful in it's simplicity
and purity, Michael glowing
and handsome all in white,
like he was at the temple this morning,
my dad in the water immersing
him with the same power, same hands
that gently lay eight-year-old me
backward in the font
and brought me out all new,
Gram, Stephie, Mom and me
in the front row holding hands and crying—
Michael floated four feet above the ground
until we went down to Utah
at August's end.

He bought a condo in Orem.
I moved into an apartment near BYU
with Cadence and Dayla from last year.
Sundays trying to go to his ward and mine together
were crazy until I got called as Relief Society president
and couldn't go to his at all.
He preferred his ward full of beauty school girls
and UVU students to my nerd-stocked congregation,
so he went by himself, and I hid my jealousy
until it boiled over in an ugly fit.
He took off for Cayman—stayed away three
long, lonely weeks, came back worried.

"It isn't the same here—as in Cayman."
"The gospel isn't true in Utah?"
His face gathered into a knot.
"Just feels different."
I nod—he's right. "There's nothing
like a branch." Even the one
I grew up in. "More like a family."
Is that what he searched for?
What he found? Not me? Not God?
He saw trouble storm my eyes,
kissed my hand like he always does,
and rested his cheek on my head.
"Be patient. Give me time.
There's way more to being a Mormon
than I thought."

I took the hint, backed off, let him breathe,
lost myself in classes and callings,
smiled when he took off to dive all the hottest
spots in the South Pacific, made the most
of the time we spent together,
and loved him wherever he was,
physically or spiritually.
He started classes at UVU after Christmas,
business stuff for when he and Gabriel
invest together in a dive op.

(They are here, by the way,
Gabriel and Alex, sitting
at a table with Kim's Mark,
and Jaron and his wife,
who's expecting their second,
eating chocolate dipped strawberries
and black forest cake.)

Michael liked school more than
he expected, enough to miss it
when we went home May to August,
where I worked with Dad on the farm,
helped Michael move Gram into
the local Care Center—private room
furnished with her own dresser,
chair, living room flowered rug,
and that picture of Michael
with his mom and dad in a giant hug—
bit my tongue every time Mom
lectured me like I was fourteen again,
and hung out with Stephie
who'd grown solemn and sad
over the past year.

Michael got ordained an elder
in August, and we made
wedding plans for Thanksgiving
if the temple was open.
At our first meeting with President McCoombs
about going to the temple,
he shook Michael's hand
and said, "I'm impressed, Brother Walden,
to call you on a mission."
"We're getting married," I reminded
him, sure he'd lost his mind.
He held up his hands, pleading
innocence. "I'm merely the messenger,
Sister Hunt. The Lord wants him to serve."
Michael got this look on his face
like he'd just seen the First Vision.
"You're not going to say yes?"
He jumped at my voice like he'd
forgot I exist. "Yeah. I am. It's perfect.

Maybe I can get close to what you deserve."
"Two more years?"
His face went pale. "That won't be easy."
He turned back to President McCoombs.
"Can she go, too?"
"Not with you."
"I know—I'm not that green.
She's twenty-one in December.
Does your inspiration inbox
have a call for her, too?"

So he went to Brazil, and I spent
eighteen months in the parts
of the Geneva mission that are in France,
caught in a visa war between the church
and the Swiss government.
My French is good.
His Portuguese is better.
When Jaron came through the line
earlier, he, Michael and groom's men
companions, all got jabbering—hope it wasn't
about me.

We shake the last hand, hug
the last hug, eat cake and throw
flowers. I avoid Kim who will give
me advice about my wedding night
that I don't want.
My mom helps me change into an
ivory suit for travelling, cries
as she undoes twenty satin-covered buttons
down my back. I hug her, cry, too,
sense she's missing Phil.
"I wish he could have been here."
She closes her eyes and lifts her face

towards heaven. "He was. Don't worry.
He was."

I run through a shower of birdseed
to Gram's old car that Michael doesn't
have the heart to sell.
It's covered in Oreo's and
whip cream "Just Marrieds."
I hug Stephie and Dad,
Michael tucks me in the front seat,
shuts my door, shake's Dad's hand,
who pulls him into a hug.
"Take care of our girl, son."
"I will, sir."
"Dad."
Michael hugs him again.
"Sure, Dad."
We zoom away.

At the end of the lane
that leads from the temple and church
to Highway 27, Michael hands me
an airplane eyeshade.
"What's this?"
"Humor me."
Our honeymoon is a huge
secret surprise.
I play, put it on.
"Thanks, babe." He kisses me,
slips into an intensity
we've always held back,
has a hard time getting
free of my blindfolded clutches.
"We're not going far tonight are we?"
"Hush." He pulls out onto the highway.

Turns right. I think.
I slide over next to him—
gotta love that old bench seat—
chew on his ear while he drives.
He pushes me away.
"Get over there and buckle
your seatbelt, or we'll end up
in the back seat of this old clunker
after all."
That sounds like a great idea, but
I obey—don't want to ruin
all he's crafted for our first time.

Where ever we're going,
whatever it looks like,
whenever we get there,
whether he's chartered a boat
or rented an island, whether
it's his condo in the Keys,
Cayman, or Thailand or
somewhere brand new,
it'll be the perfect
consummation
of the forever
we pledged
to our Lord
and each other
in His holy house
this day.

## MICHAEL'S DIVE LOG – VOLUME 14

**Dive Buddy:** Leesie
**Date:** three years from Cayman
**Dive #:** 1

**Location:** secret
**Dive Site:** secret
**Weather Condition:** nice night
**Water Condition:** a little bumpy
**Depth:** not saying
**Visibility:** forever and ever
**Water Temp:** no comment
**Bottom Time:** no comment
**Comments:**

As we drive away from the reception, man and wife, alone for the first time since we vowed to love each other eternally, I try to stay calm, cool, but my heart—that I used to be able to slow at will free diving—beats so hard it pulses in my fingertips. My palms sweat. I grip the steering wheel way too hard. Good thing Leesie's blindfolded. If she saw what a wreck I am, she might want to trade me back in.

She's sniffing the air like a bloodhound, trying to figure out where we're going. I cut through a subdivision to disorient her.

"Can I let my hair down?" She wore it up all day. It's long again. She grew it out the whole time I was serving in Brazil learning to be the man of God she deserves. I don't know if I'll ever truly be there, but serving the Lord taught me so much. I've got my own cylinder of consecrated olive oil swinging from my key chain and know how to use it. I felt like I'd stepped through a time warp when Leesie met me at the plane with her hair long and gorgeous, catching the sun like the first time I surprised her staring at me in physics.

I pat her knee. "If you promise not to peak."

"That's big of you. The hairpins kill." She holds the blindfold to her eyes with one hand, slips the elastic loose with the other—pulls pins out and throws them at me.

"Ow! Are you peaking?"

She shakes her freed hair, combs her fingers through it, finding more pins, and shakes her head again. The car fills with the smell of hairspray and a tiny hint of her sweet banana mango shampoo.

"Do you know what you're doing to me?"

"Who me?" She slips the blindfold elastic back around her head and folds her hands in her lap.

We stop at a red light. "Get over here, then."

She's in my lap in a second. We make out until the car behind us blares its horn. I keep her close, drive the rest of the way with one hand and my arm around her, worrying she'll recognize the highway we're on, but she chews on my fingers instead of playing bloodhound.

I turn off the highway onto a gravel road, relieved we're almost there. When I slow way down and turn right onto a bumpy dirt road, she sits up straight. "This isn't the airport." She elbows my ribs. "Roll down your window."

I obey. Pines lining each side of the road invade the car with their sharp, clean scent.

She sniffs. Sniffs again. "This is our lake road—at Windy Bay."

I hold my breath.

"It's washed out. Dad said—" She hits my thigh. "You got my dad to lie?"

I move my hand from her shoulders to the steering wheel. Even in good condition this road is dicey. I've got my hands full managing it.

"We're going to our lake?"

Yeah, babe. Don't you remember our first date here?

"We're camping"—her voice rises in pitch—"*tonight*?"

I wish for a video camera and bite my cheeks to keep from losing it.

"Did you rent a swank RV?" She fiddles with her blindfold. "Buy a cool sail boat?"

I keep silent.

"Not a tent, Michael. Please."

As soon as the car stops, she rips off the blindfold and climbs out over me. She stops dead in her tracks when she sees the lights. She spins around. "You did this?"

My eyes move from her to the cabin and back to her astonished face. "I wanted to do something for your family—to make up for—you know." A pre-fab log cabin on their empty water front lake lot won't bring back their son, but it makes me feel less guilty for stealing their daughter.

Leesie bows her head and wipes her eyes.

I close the distance between us in a stride and scoop her up like I did when she was hurt. I haven't picked her up like this since then. I sense she's awash in the same memories that course through me.

"I love you." She snuggles her face against my neck.

I inhale her hair and carry her towards the lit cabin.

"Wait."

"What?"

"I need my shoulder bag from the back seat."

"Why?"

"I have a surprise, too."

I carry her back to the car, get the bag, slide the strap on my shoulder—all without putting her down.

I carry her into the cabin. "Do you want a tour now?"

"No." She chews on my neck.

I head upstairs.

"Was that Gram's couch in the living room?"

"I couldn't pitch her stuff. Your dad stored it at the farm when we rented out Gram's house."

Her lips press against my cheek. "I like that."

I open the door to the master, our honeymoon suite. The big window and king-size four-poster bed are draped with white gauzy stuff. The bed's made up with a six-inch thick down comforter and piled with cushy pillows.

"This is beautiful." Leesie squirms out of my arms, takes her bag, and disappears into the bathroom. Shuts the door. A high-pitched, muffled, "Look at that tub," comes from inside.

I sit down on an armchair by the window, take off my

tie, slip off my polished black dress shoes, stare at the closed bathroom door, grip the arms of the chair to keep myself from breaking it down. The sound of my heartbeat echoes in my ears. I'm sweating. I close my eyes, inhale deep. Hold it. Exhale. My eyes fly open at the sound of a turning door knob.

Leesie hesitates in the doorway. She wears the long silk skirt I bought for her in a Thailand market and a bra-top made of turquoise shells and beads that I've never seen. The Cayman-colored shell necklace I gave her hangs around her neck. My diamond on her finger flashes in the bright light coming from the bathroom.

Her cheeks flush rosy. "I packed for our island."

"I love it." I cross the room—take her hands—kiss her fingertips, her fingers, each palm—turn her left hand over and find those faint scars that fit my fingernails, kiss them one by one.

We sink to our knees. She bows her head onto my shoulder. I bury my hands in her thick, fragrant hair and offer our first married prayer, whispered thanks that she's mine.

I gather her into my arms and carry her to the bed. "Are you scared?"

Her eyes are big, but she whispers, "No." She reaches for my lips. "Are you?"

My eyebrows rise. "Terrified."

Her lips find mine, and our embrace yields to the passion we've held back for years. "Don't worry"—she's breathless as I lay her on the bed—"I'll let you up for good behavior."

She pulls me down beside her, and I'm enveloped in silk, beads, long hair, and Leesie.

*The End*

# AUTHOR'S NOTE

CAYMAN SUMMER is the third novel in Michael and Leesie's romance that began with TAKEN BY STORM. When my editor left Razorbill and her boss rejected UNBROKEN CONNEC-TION (Book #2), my readers rallied around me—giving me the guts to release it independently. I decided I had to have all those readers with me every step as I wrote CAYMAN SUMMER.

I launched http://caymansummer.blogspot.com and shared my messy rough drafts, half-baked poems, revised scenes, and finally a polished revision. My fantastic followers input and encourage-ment proved invaluable. They kept me going, kept me writing, kept my chin up. Michael and Leesie's final journey became a joyful collaboration. All my readers didn't always agree with all of my choices. We had some lively debates that gave me renewed creative energy. I loved the experience. This book is not mine alone. It's ours!

All my love,

Angela

# THANK YOU . . .

All of my blog readers and followers who loved Michael and Leesie enough to read and comment every day—first and foremost this book is for you.

The YA bloggers all over the world who've embraced me and my novels. Thank you for your energy and support.

Andy for beautifying my blog, http://caymansummer.blogspot.com. Rob for designing the striking cover and the book's interior. Rachel for letting me share her gorgeous Cayman Island photos. Shante for feeding me and reading each post along the way. Will for turning out so well despite my neglect. Jack for letting me squish him on occasion. And my wonderful, patient husband, Allen, for continuing to subsidize my alter ego.

Kathi Baron (*Shattered*), one of Michael and Leesie's original champions, who critiqued the last draft for me in record time. Plus all of my classmates, friends, and advisors at Vermont College of Fine Arts where Michael and Leesie were born.

To my agent, Erzsi, at Hen and Ink Literary, who signed me in the midst of this project and waits patiently for me to write something she can sell. Stay tuned at www.angela-morrison.com or http://caymansummer.blogspot.com for updates on new books. If you want to see what I'm working on, click on WIP in the website's top, right-hand corner.

Again, I'm in your debt. I don't think I can ever get out. Love and thanks to you all.

# ABOUT THE AUTHOR

Angela Morrison is the author of *Taken by Storm* (Books 1-3) and *Sing me to Sleep,* a 2010 Goodreads Choice Nominee for YA Fiction. She graduated from Brigham Young University and holds an MFA in Writing for Children and Young Adults from Vermont College of Fine Arts. She grew up in Eastern Washington on the wheat farm where *Taken By Storm* is set. After over a decade abroad in Canada, Switzerland and Singapore, she and her family are happily settled in Mesa, Arizona. Angela enjoys speaking to writers and readers of all ages about her craft. She has four children—mostly grown up—and the most remarkable grandson in the universe.

Find out more at www.angela-morrison.com and follow her blog, http://caymansummer.blogspot.com.

CPSIA information can be obtained at www.ICGtesting.com
Printed in the USA
238367LV00001B/174/P